ALSO BY THE AUTHOR

Ground Up: A Novel

Made in Russia: Unsung Icons of Soviet Design (editor)

Dressed Up for a Riot: Misadventures in Putin's Moscow

THE
COLLABORATORS

A Novel

Michael Idov

SCRIBNER

NEW YORK   LONDON   TORONTO   SYDNEY   NEW DELHI

Scribner
An Imprint of Simon & Schuster, LLC
1230 Avenue of the Americas
New York, NY 10020

Copyright © 2024 by More Or Less Entertainment West, Inc.

First Scribner hardcover edition November 2024

SCRIBNER and design are registered trademarks of Simon & Schuster, LLC

Simon & Schuster: Celebrating 100 Years of Publishing Since 1924

For information about special discounts for bulk purchases, please contact Simon & Schuster Special Sales at 1-866-506-1949 or business@simonandschuster.com.

The Simon & Schuster Speakers Bureau can bring authors to your live event. For more information or to book an event, contact the Simon & Schuster Speakers Bureau at 1-866-248-3049 or visit our website at www.simonspeakers.com.

Interior design by Kathryn A. Kenney-Peterson

Manufactured in the United States of America

10   9   8   7   6   5   4   3   2   1

Library of Congress Cataloging-in-Publication Data
Names: Idov, Michael, 1976– author.
Title: The collaborators : a novel / Michael Idov.
Description: First Scribner hardcover edition. | New York : Scribner, 2024.
Identifiers: LCCN 2024019348 (print) | LCCN 2024019349 (ebook) |
ISBN 9781668055571 (hardcover) | ISBN 9781668055595 (ebook)
Subjects: LCGFT: Thrillers (Fiction) | Spy fiction | Novels.
Classification: LCC PS3609.D68 C65 2024 (print) | LCC PS3609.D68 (ebook) |
DDC 813/.6–dc23/eng/20240506
LC record available at https://lccn.loc.gov/2024019348
LC ebook record available at https://lccn.loc.gov/2024019349

ISBN 978-1-6680-5557-1
ISBN 978-1-6680-5559-5 (ebook)

To Vera

THE
COLLABORATORS

CHAPTER ONE

When the MiG-29 swung into view, barely 50 yards portside, passenger Anton Basmanny in seat 12A didn't feel all that surprised.

In fact, he even knew the reason it was there. He was the reason.

From the moment he left the Istanbul safe house, things could have gone wrong in a million ways. The burner dumbphone he used to call a cab—a prepaid Nokia of the kind he didn't even know was still made, his third in as many days—could have turned out not as dumb as he hoped. The driver of the yellow *taksi* that pulled up purporting to be his ride could have had him chloroformed, cuffed, and shipped to the Russian-occupied Crimea. (He didn't, but Anton was pretty sure another car followed them all the way to the airport.) When you were the Kremlin's least favorite blogger, a lot could happen.

Not all his fears had to do with the powerful men he pissed off. The whole world was in a woozy flux. What if, in the two hours it took him to pack, get a Q-tip shoved up his nose at the Acibadem Clinic, and arrive at the airport, reality changed once more? Curfew, flight cancellation, border closure . . . and, of course, the virus itself. He might safely land in Riga, meet the guy he was there to meet, then bite it five days later in a Latvian hospital bed with a tube in his trachea. As a citizen of Russia, the only vaccine Anton was allowed to get was Sputnik V; as an enemy of Russia, he couldn't exactly swing by to get it. Plus, he'd rather chance it than let the Russians anywhere near his body with a syringe.

That's why, even when the good-looking guard with the shaped eyebrows nodded and slid his red *zagranpasport* back across the counter; even when the plane banked over the Bosphorus, the pilot promising a smooth ride in rough English; even then, Anton was unable to shake the sensation of a cold metal coil twisting in his gut. Seeing the fighter jet sidle up to the Boeing was almost a relief. The worst thing possible was finally here.

Hell, he even felt a light prick of pride. Who'd have guessed he got their goat *this* bad.

Despite the plane being in Belarusian airspace, Anton had no doubt who "they" were. Belarus was an independent state on paper only. In reality, it was more of a testing lab for the Russian government to see how much terror against its own people it could get away with. The local dictator, having just clawed out a sixth term in power with what he claimed was an 80 percent landslide vote, was currently busy jailing everyone who disagreed—including, to Moscow's telltale indifference, some Russian citizens. Anton had posted some mocking videos about the man, too, but nothing to scramble the jets about. No, if his hunch was correct and he was the target, he knew exactly whose and why.

He looked out the window again. Clouds stretched below, a matted fleece. The MiG hung close to the Boeing, matching its airspeed so well they could be two cars idling at the same red light.

"Not to worry, folks," said the pilot over the intercom in a clearly worried voice, pronouncing the *l* in "folks." People on the starboard side kept getting up to get a better look; flight attendants waved them down.

Someone behind Anton let out a single sharp sob. His neighbor in 12B blissfully snored the way he'd been since before the plane took off, mask pulled over his eyes and nose but not mouth. The young woman in a baseball cap and aviators in 11A was filming the MiG on her phone, in time-lapse mode.

"Dear passengers, please stay in your seats with the belts secu—" began the purser. "Flight attendants be seated," barked the pilot, cutting in. Anton could feel the Boeing speeding up. The floor under his feet vibrated. They were only a few dozen miles away from the Lithuanian— read NATO, read EU—border, closer to Vilnius than to Minsk. *Holy shit.* They were making a break for it.

The unseen pilot, whose accent so grated on Anton just moments ago, was suddenly his favorite person in the world, a repository for his most fervent hopes. For a second, he felt an irrational surge of optimism. Perhaps he was being *too* paranoid, if there were such an option for an internationally hunted refugee. Perhaps something had happened below, and now all the flights over the area were getting a look-see from the local air force. Perhaps this wasn't the end.

The MiG fell back in what felt like incredulity, then tore forward. With its top airspeed of 1,490 miles per hour, lapping a 737 was child's play. Once the Belarusian overshot the Boeing by about a half mile— which took it less than a second—it pitched back, slashing across the jet's path in a wide performative arc, and yo-yoed into its original portside position. The message was loud and clear.

A shudder went through the plane, and through Anton. Staring out the window, he saw the aileron on the wing flip up like a white flag of surrender; the Boeing yawed and began to bank. Anton almost chuckled. *Serves me right for hoping. How un-Russian of me.*

Below, the cloud cover broke in a few spots, revealing flat yellow fields and black clumps of forest. The pilot said something short and angry in Turkish. "Ladies and gentlemen," he continued after a pause, Anton once again finding the accent unbearable. "Please prepare for landing. We are making an emergency stop."

■ ■ ■

RIGA
AUGUST 15, 2021

The name of the Pils Bar, just off the lobby of the Grand Palace Hotel, came from the cobblestone Pils Street on which it stood, not the type of beer it served. With its plush jewel-tone chairs and stag-antler chandeliers, the bar was more of a wine drinker's place, anyway, locally famous as an executive lunch spot. *Latvia's biggest deals get done here*, an investor friend of Falk's once quipped. *Sometimes even up to a million dollars.*

Yeah, yeah. Riga was small-time, but Ari Falk liked it this way. It was all a matter of proportion. A city the size of Portland, lost for most of its history on the outskirts of various empires, it was now a rare thing—a cute-as-a-button national capital. Unless, of course, one counted the EU as yet another empire.

Falk crossed the street, pausing to let a touristy horse-drawn carriage clomp past him toward the Our Lady of Sorrows Church, and walked into the hotel. It was only ten in the morning, but as soon as he entered the bar, Falk felt like a child. The Pils's breakfast crowd, equal parts Latvians and Russians in town for business, was almost all men in suits. The locals were naturally fastidious dressers, in the Scandi style; the guests wore their Brioni and Berluti with a gloomy Slavic zeal, as if to prove something to someone. Falk was wearing a hoodie over a Weezer T-shirt.

There was a method to his wardrobe choices. Clothes defined you, and Falk's job was to stay undefined or misdefined. Twelve years ago, like many young men in the employ of the National Clandestine Service, he

4

had gone through his own dandy period, blowing his entire first salary on a bespoke suit and six identical dress shirts. It took him a few weeks on the job to notice what his superiors wore: loose-fitting sack suits one wouldn't mind sleeping in, because one often did.

At Yale, from where the CIA recruited him, Ari Falk had been an Army ROTC scholarship student—a "Rotsie," as the sniffier Elis called his ilk—and a Slavic literature major: half meathead, half egghead. Add a Jewish name, desperate poverty, and tense foster-kid demeanor, and the result was so difficult to parse that most peers gave up without trying. Back then, it made him lonely. The agency taught him to turn this opaqueness into an asset.

Plus, he liked Weezer.

Falk looked at his phone. 10:03. The plane should have landed already. The airport was barely outside the city limits, so the Russian blogger could be arriving any minute.

He took out his *other* phone and checked the texts. As far as Anton knew, he had been talking to a wealthy gay fan in Tbilisi who sometimes helped him out with airline tickets; this breakfast would be the first time he'd meet Falk as Falk. The last message from Anton was, as they'd agreed, a short ping from Istanbul at wheels-up. Whether here or still in the air, the blogger was, for all intents and purposes, finally safe.

"May I help you?" a waitress asked in English, with a Latvian lilt that made a little song of every vowel. Falk asked for a coffee, which came with a glass of water, two cookies, and a brown-sugar swizzle stick.

He liked Riga. What he hated was his job here.

A case officer with the Agency's Covert Activities department under nonofficial cover as a media investor, Ari Falk *identified, interfaced with, and utilized indigenous assets with the objective of counterpropaganda dissemination.* Translated into human, it meant helping Russian opposition journalists find and run stories damaging to the Kremlin.

5

On its face, it wasn't a bad gig. Falk wasn't spreading disinfo; he was genuinely helping understaffed and underfinanced publications report the truth. He wasn't even turning anyone against their country, unless outing Duma Deputy X as a secret Dutch citizen or Religious Moralist Y as an escort aficionado rose to the level of treason. In better circumstances his front company, Sokol Media Research, could be doing the exact same thing and simply be a news agency.

Normally, this type of initiative would fall under the purview of Moscow Station, but Covert Activities—which created Falk's post in response to Russia's 2014 annexation of Crimea—ran it directly out of Langley. The reassignment to Riga was technically a huge promotion, yet it still stung a bit. Older CIA hands, susceptible to the ancient notion of Russia as America's dark double and one worthy opponent, still considered Moscow the number one posting and everything else a step down. Falk's generation of officers, which came of age in the 1990s and into the service in the 2000s, was supposed to be immune to this bullshit: there was no red colossus in the mirror, just a second-rate kleptocracy running on past glories and petty grievances. And yet. Latvia, a historic refuge for Russians fleeing the regime, was a safe and logical place to set up shop, but perhaps *too* safe and *too* logical. Falk was well aware that some assholes at his old posting privately referred to the Riga branch as "the soft unit," with all the limp-dick connotations it entailed. Ha ha, whatever. If the strategy worked, he could take a little ribbing.

The thing was, it *didn't* work. In his seven years on the job, the main thing Falk learned was that the Russians didn't give a shit about corruption in their own government. The exposés he facilitated made for good content, sure, and looked great in the *New York Times* the next day. But no matter the regime—be it the czar, the Communists, or postmodern strongmen—the unspoken compact between the Russian people and their masters has always been that each looked away while the other stole

6

whatever wasn't bolted down. The idea that the Kremlin itself would use these revelations for internecine warfare was also a bust. For all the intel about the various factions and silos jostling for the president's ear, the system just closed ranks around every new embarrassment—and brought all its wrath down on the messenger instead.

That was the worst part. Before 2014, when Russia still looked like the West's ornery but reasonable housemate, a website or magazine that dared attack a state functionary might see their advertisers scatter, or their editor replaced with a loyalist. After Crimea, however, the game changed almost overnight. One of Falk's Russian partners got a brick of hashish planted on him. Another, the smartest young woman he'd ever met, went on trial for an old tweet deemed offensive to World War Two veterans. His exfil request for her languished on Deputy Director Harlow's desk for a month and came back denied the day after her arrest. Yet another reporter, beaten within an inch of his life by three men with steel pipes, staggered toward a nearby cop only to realize the cop was the lookout; fainting, he collapsed onto his shoulder—and went to prison for assaulting an officer. Falk felt like the farmer who adopted a new shelter cat each time a coyote ate the previous one. Once you subtracted the issue of intent, he ran a coyote-feeding program.

The Agency didn't see it that way. As long as the corruption stories got the views and Western media pickup, Falk was golden. In fact, the more miserable he felt, the more praise his operation garnered, and vice versa. When he left his apartment this morning to meet Anton, no one, including his supervisor in Virginia and two Sokol employees in Riga, had any idea how close to quitting he was.

Anton Basmanny was Falk's latest triumph and his biggest headache. The brash, twenty-seven-year-old, openly gay video blogger from Yekaterinburg made a name for himself by hounding local officials with a phone on a selfie stick, shouting out absurd questions and basically

7

inviting violence against himself. His man-on-the-street live streams became wildly popular, and it was commonly assumed that he had some serious muscle behind him: no one in Russia was this fearless without a patron. The prevailing rumor placed him as the lover of a high-ranking United Russia party boss; Anton dispelled it by showing up at the man's house in a wedding dress, camera crew in tow.

Intrigued, Falk had him studied for a good half year. The results were impressive in their mundanity. Anton came from nothing and knew no one. His parents were schoolteachers. Like Russia's other great martyrs—Solzhenitsyn, Sakharov, Navalny—he simply seemed to lack the wiring for fear and compromise that, in most of his compatriots, came preinstalled. So, a month ago, when the so-called Napoleon scoop came his way, Falk had no doubts who'd be the best man for the job.

The story was irresistibly simple. Russia's deputy minister of defense, Gleb Pervushin, kept a secret villa in Côte d'Azur, owned on paper by his ex-wife. Alone, this barely merited a yawn. A drone flight over the property, however, revealed something extraordinary: a dancing fountain with an eleven-meter column at the center, a meticulous one-quarter reproduction of the Austerlitz monument at Place Vendôme. Crowning the column was a gilded statue of the deputy minister himself, in full Napoleon Bonaparte garb complete with a bicorn hat.

This time, however, Falk wasn't going to feed another cat to the coyotes. Anton was about to take on a man with direct access to the military intelligence agency GRU and too many means of murder to count. If Anton were to do this, he'd need real protection. Falk composed a long, subtly seething letter asking for relocation funds and a safe house, and, for once, got both.

After that, all he needed to do was to slip Anton the villa's coordinates. The blogger, as the kids said, understood the assignment. He crashed the grounds in the owner's absence, wearing (naturally) the

Napoleonic uniform, waving a toy saber, and screaming abuse at the staff in decent French. He then flew straight from Nice to Istanbul, where Falk's Tbilisi Guy had arranged for an apartment, and uploaded the post from there.

The video was a smash hit by any metric, clearing fifteen million YouTube views in a week. It generated Napoleon-hat memes galore and triggered thousands of the usual angry comments about the "blood-suckers" and "hypocrites" and "the court of the mad king," the best of which Falk's two staffers dutifully collared, translated, and served up to Langley as proof that, somehow, *this* one had moved the needle on the Russian public sentiment. All bullshit, of course. But at least it was funny.

A month later, the deputy minister was out of a job.

No one, from the CIA brass to the Russian propaganda outlets, had any idea how to react. Normally, Moscow would do anything to avoid the appearance of being influenced by an outside factor, least of all by grassroots mockery. The correlation between Anton's video and Pervushin's sacking, however, was so obvious that even some state news media felt emboldened enough to go with an "Elba" pun in the headline.

One thing was clear: whatever happened, Anton was in for it. A week later, a MoD-connected Telegram channel had doxxed his new Istanbul apartment. The same night, he reported two people shadowing him at the market. Determined to keep him safe, Falk filed an exfiltration request through Moscow Station. This time, Langley got on board: in their eyes, Anton Basmanny had gone from another disposable local asset to precious cargo—the only Russian dissident whose words produced tangible results. Within four days of Falk's request, they got Anton a ticket to Riga, an unobtrusive escort to the airport, and a provisional US passport now resting in the kangaroo pocket of Falk's hoodie. It was, finally, time to relax.

Falk checked the time again. 10:25. He tried reading the news but couldn't concentrate, his eyes darting up every time someone entered the bar. He opened a mobile game where you were a student at Hogwarts solving the mystery of your vanished older brother and played it for a while. In the game, he was already up to fourth year and things were getting interesting.

The message that interrupted him came from Moscow Station. Whoever sent it used Google Chat—most of their everyday comms, surprisingly, were over regular channels. As the IT guy in charge of sweeping his devices said when Falk asked him about it once, *It's a question of risk assessment. If your risk factor is the US government, then by all means use something else.* It read, simply, YOUR EXFIL??? next to a link to a live air-traffic tracker site.

Falk clicked it and stared at TQ77's flight path. It looked like a long spoke with a sharp hook at the top. On the end of the hook writhed a little yellow airplane icon, nosing toward Minsk International. He stared at it long enough that, while he did, the plane moved a few more pixels over.

■ ■ ■

The sky over Belarus was gray; the clouds they'd pierced a minute ago now hung above like a dirty ceiling. Anton braced for the landing to be rough, which it wasn't and which, he now realized, didn't even make logical sense. The plane taxied to a stop at the farthest end of the apron, beside a grass field already teeming with military, police, and civilian vehicles. The curved brutalist heap of the Minsk airport terminal stood to the left.

He glanced around. A few people were sniffling. Some just seemed relieved to be back on solid ground and without a fighter jet hovering nearby. "*Sind wir schon in Riga?*" a small kid asked, and his mother began to cry; strangers from the next seats tried consoling her in a mix of languages. The purser kept walking into and out of the cockpit, shuttling some kind of information back and forth, and every time the door opened, a snatch of intense radio chatter would burst into the main cabin. A middle-aged couple in business class sat with their hands clasped across the aisle, staring straight ahead, as if they had just taken the same poison and were now waiting for it to kick in.

A boarding stair neared the plane, closely followed by a canvas-top Ural military truck. Whatever was to happen next, Anton felt responsible for it. Before he even knew what he was doing, he was up, out of his seat, and standing in the aisle between business and economy, swiveling back and forth to address everyone.

"Hey all," he said loudly, as if starting a live stream. Several dozen people looked up, frowning. A few faces betrayed recognition; those must have been Russian.

"My name is Anton Basmanny," he continued in English, not really sure why or what he'd say next. "I just want to, uh, I just want to apologize for everything that's happening right now. I don't mean that it's my fault. I mean that someone probably diverted this flight because of me."

Several people were already filming him, including the young woman in aviators from 11A. He tried looking into every phone's camera one by one as he spoke.

"But for you, that's good news. I'm pretty sure they're going to take me off the plane and send the rest of you on your way. So please just hang tight. That's all."

"What'd you do?" someone shouted out from the back. This was turning into an actual press conference.

"I . . ." Anton paused. "It seems so corny to say this. I told the truth? Jeez. But yeah, I told the truth. At least a little of it. The little I knew. And I tried to make it funny."

A flight attendant was on her way to stop this when someone knocked hard on the front passenger door. It sounded like the butt of a gun. She turned, ran back, reached for the latch, then jerked her hand away and looked around, desperate for a command.

"So, whatever happens to me now," Anton said, switching to Russian and talking faster, "please watch, witness, document, remember, and share. If this is how they treat people for the crime of telling you just a tiny little bit of the truth, it doesn't take a lot to imagine what else they're hiding. Peace."

As he talked, the pilot came out of the cockpit, a short, balding man in a drenched shirt and loosened tie. He tapped the flight attendant on the bicep, gesturing for her to stand aside and behind him, said something that started with "Allah," and pulled the latch himself.

The door swung out. At once, Belarusian soldiers in full tactical gear and black face masks streamed in, weapons out but pointed down, filling the aisles like a uniform mass oozing through the plane. Anton instinctively stepped aside, letting them through. No one paid any special attention to him so far. Ten or twelve soldiers stayed in the business section, two dozen more quickly distributed themselves through economy. The stench of male sweat, gunmetal, and machine oil permeated the cabin. Suddenly, the 737 felt small.

A few of the people who had been filming Anton, perhaps inspired by his speech, bravely kept their phone cameras trained at the advancing soldiers; they went down first.

Seconds later, it was obvious they were taking everybody.

■ ■ ■

It took less than ten seconds for Falk to clear the six flights of stairs between the building's ornate art nouveau entrance and the modest office space

Sokol Media Research rented on the third floor. Both his employees were already there. Inga Lace, pronounced LAT-seh, a towering freckled blonde of Latvian-Canadian extraction, paced the front room with a phone to her ear, yelling at a source at Antalya Airlines; Klaus Staubermann, a fifty-year-old German club kid with a ponytail longer and lighter than Inga's, manned the monitors in the back. The only moments in his life when Falk felt truly Jewish was when he stood between the two of them.

"Fucking Moscow is freezing us out, man," Klaus said without turning around, which was fair enough. The heavy-breathing new presence in the room could only be his boss.

"Did you try Langley?"

"They're basically still asleep. At least anyone with any say is."

"Great."

Inga hung up, signing off with, "Honestly, I'm not impressed, Kardaş. I'm not impressed. Bye," and walked into the room.

"All right," she said, tapping on her phone with both thumbs. "This isn't a lot, but I got dispatcher audio from the Minsk tower. Hi, Ari."

"That's actually quite a lot," said Falk.

She finished tapping. "There. It's in your dropboxes."

Klaus opened the file, leaned over the desk, and turned on a small Bluetooth speaker. Tower chatter filled the room, same as everywhere on the planet: tired and caffeinated at once, in English yet not exactly using it as a living language, rather as a kind of psalmbook.

"*Minsk, good morning, TQ.*"

"*TQ, Minsk Control, go ahead,*" the tower answered. The pilot's voice was surprisingly calm under the circumstances. If anything, the controller sounded like the tenser one of the two.

"*Traffic in sight, unresponsive. Requesting to know the nature of contact.*"

There followed a light rustle of native conversation off-mic. Like anyone who knew Russian well enough, Falk could follow about half of what was being said in Belarusian; it was something about emails. Inga's Russian was functional, Klaus's nonexistent, so they just searched Falk's face for mood clues.

The controller came back on the mic. "*TQ, we have information you have a bomb on board.*"

"Jesus," said Falk.

"Bullshit," said Klaus. "It would have been all over our channels."

"Obviously. Shh."

"*Roger that, Minsk. Stand by,*" said the pilot. For about a minute, the speaker issued nothing but background hiss.

"Wait, why were these controllers even talking in Belarusian?" asked Inga. "The official Minsk is all Russophone, isn't it? Speaking the *mova* on record is . . . almost rebellious."

"I can think of only one reason," said Klaus.

"Oh yeah, what's that?"

"There's a Russian in the room they don't want to understand them."

The recording came back to life. "*Minsk, no escort required. Requesting alternate route to Echo Yankee Victor India.*" The pilot switched over to the plane's PA system. "*Flight attendants be seated.*"

"That's code for Vilnius. He's gunning it for the European border. Guy's got balls," said Inga.

"*TQ,*" repeated the controller, "*for security reasons we recommend that you land here.*"

"*Who is 'we'?*" barked the pilot, by now openly irked. "*Departure authorities? Arrival authorities? Company?*"

Another burst of conversation on the other end, more legible than the first. Falk caught the words "*Eto nasha rekomendacija.*"

"*This is our recommendation,*" repeated the Minsk controller in English. After a few seconds of stunned silence, the pilot loudly swore in Turkish.

"My guess is," said Falk, "the escort just buzzed them."

"*Okay. Okay! TQ77 declaring Mayday Mayday Mayday. Diverting to Minsk.*" The wormlike soundwave undulating on the computer screen came to an abrupt end.

"This is all a ton of fun," said Klaus, turning off the speaker. "But it confirms what we already know and tells us nothing about your guy." His tone betrayed slight jealousy of Inga's resourcefulness.

"Hang on," said Falk. "Go back ten seconds, please." Something about the last bit of background chatter scratched at him. Klaus sighed and turned the speaker back on. The hushed exchange played again.

"There," said Falk. "That. The languages are close, but I'm not supposed to understand *every* word."

"So?"

"So you were right. There's a man in the room, speaking accentless Russian, telling them what to say."

"Wow," said Klaus, pleased. "They're not even trying to hide anymore, are they?"

"Sometimes the brazenness is the message," said Falk.

He felt like putting his fist through drywall. Instead, he tossed Klaus the burner he'd been using in his guise as Anton's Tbilisi contact, told him to ping Anton once every minute, and staggered out onto the office balcony for air.

The balcony was grander than the office. Two female nudes framed it on the sides, holding up an arch with a screaming, hollow-eyed Valkyrie at the center. The Valkyrie looked like Falk felt. He stared at the treetops below, then to the far side of Kronvalda Park, where Old Town's medieval spires rose. Yeah, no, he wouldn't miss Riga. The job poisoned the city for him. Losing Anton to the GRU in midair was the absolute last straw.

Inga rapped on the glass from the inside. Falk turned around, angry to be jolted out of his anger.

"What?"

"They've let them go," she said. "The plane is taking off."

Falk cracked the balcony door ajar. "What's your source?"

"Instagram." She put her hand through the crack and showed him her phone. It was playing a half-second loop of a young woman in basic influencer gear—sweats, baseball cap, aviators—flashing a V-for-victory from a window seat as a plane sped up the runway. Under the loop was a dynamic caption reading *SOOO, THIS HAPPENED,* and the location pin for Minsk. The seat behind the woman was empty.

Falk looked at it for a second, then yanked the balcony door open the rest of the way and stepped inside. "Get your things. Let's go. You too, Klaus."

"Where?"

"*Lidosta,*" said Falk. "*Flughafen.* Airport. If Anton is on that flight, I'm getting him. If he's not, I'm going wherever he is."

■ ■ ■

The holding cell was clearly improvised out of an empty customs office. Besides a row of Soviet-looking chairs with ripped red vinyl cushions, all it held was a long, low metal table—probably for rifling through luggage, although Anton couldn't help imagining his own lifeless body laid out on that slab—and a painfully wholesome Belavia wall calendar for the year 2018. The August photo was a woman with red and green ribbons in her hair, running through wheat.

For the past hour, the Belarusians have been playing some kind of chaotic three-card monte with Anton, moving him from room to room, leaving him to stew for ten minutes or so, then moving him again. In some of the rooms sat other Flight TQ77 passengers, though never more than one or two and not in the last few. If Anton had to guess, this was a psyop designed to make them all feel alone, unprotected, and suspicious of one another. (Had someone already struck some kind of deal with the captors? Had the flight left with everyone but them on board?)

If so, it worked: even when left to their own devices, the people barely talked. Everyone just stared at the floor, processing their own trauma at their own speed. Even now, it took Anton a few moments to even realize there were others in the room: the middle-aged couple he vaguely recognized from business class. They sat huddled together in the farthest, dimmest corner, where one of the two fluorescent tubes in the ceiling light panel was out and the other flickered on and off.

Anton sat down and looked at the dumb wall calendar, both to give the couple some privacy and to retain his own. The room made him flash back to elementary school: the same chalky walls, the same dull dread. At twenty-seven, he was too young to have experienced the Communist rule, but it didn't matter: Russia's public schools held on to the sour Soviet spirit for decades after 1991's supposed liberation—some figuratively, some literally. The one where his parents worked and he studied kept an alabaster Lenin at the top of the main stairs, just because no clear order to remove it ever came; when Anton's mother, the fifth- and sixth-grade algebra teacher, meekly suggested it, she was told not to "rock the boat." Anton, then eight, remembered that evening very well. It was his first encounter with hypocrisy—not because Mom didn't get her way but because Dad, the history teacher, yelled at her for it: *Irisha, come on, how can you be this naive, don't you realize what kind of country we're living in.* The Lenin stared Anton down six days a week for nine more years.

The dead ceiling tube came to life with a loud metallic ping. Anton involuntarily glanced over, catching sight of the couple in its greenish light. The man was in his late forties or early fifties, trim with a full head of silver hair, and wore an odd combination of a Rolex Submariner with a dorky half-zip pullover. The woman, a striking ageless brunette in an all-black jumpsuit, was wiping her eyes. If she'd been crying, she managed to do it in complete silence. He noticed an old scar on the left side of her face, a deep demilune that started midcheekbone and arced upward toward the earlobe. She met Anton's gaze, unblinkingly held it for a second, then smiled.

"Nice speech," she said in Russian. The man glared at her and mumbled something in English. Anton felt some satisfaction in having correctly pegged him for an American.

"Thanks," he replied. "I don't even remember what I said. I think I blacked out."

"I'm sorry," the woman said, a little incongruously. The man mumbled something to her again; Anton made a note that he seemed to understand Russian—at least well enough to disapprove of their exchange.

"So, uh, where are you from?" asked Anton, directing the question at the man, because he knew this would annoy him.

"Places." It did, and he wasn't hiding it.

"I'm sorry," repeated the woman. "My husband has been a little on edge."

"Understandable," said Anton.

The door opened, letting in two armed guards. Had it been ten minutes? Anton swiveled to look and realized that these weren't the soldiers he'd already gotten used to seeing. (Amazing how fast everything becomes routine.) Both wore black uniforms with no patches, and their weapons weren't the local AK variants everyone else carried but shorter, modern-looking bullpup rifles. The room seemed to darken again with their arrival.

Anton got up, expecting to be frog-marched to the next cell, but one of the men gestured for him to sit back down and pointed at the couple. "Here we go," said the husband to the wife, smiling a strange crooked smile. The next moment, they were in each other's arms, kissing deeply. Even with the strange men in the room, it felt like a moment all their own.

There was something different in how the guards escorted them out—a nonchalance Anton couldn't describe if he tried. It wasn't the way you led a person you were afraid to hurt, or indeed trying to hurt; it wasn't the way you led a person, period. The couple were dead weight to them, a dead weight that was still able to move by some happy accident of physics that saved them some effort.

The wife sobbed once. The husband murmured "easy, easy." The door closed, the locks turned. Anton was alone. The light in the now-empty far corner buzzed and flickered off again.

The gunshots rang loud enough that he ducked. One. Two. Neat and economical. Anton couldn't tell the direction they came from—the whole room reverberated—but the source was so close that he could hear the casings hit the cement floor. There was no doubt. There *could* be no doubt.

When the men in unmarked black uniforms returned, ten seconds or a minute or three hours later—for linear time no longer existed in Anton's Soviet classroom with the 2018 calendar—they had to lift the metal table to get him.

■ ■ ■

"Goodness gracious," said Klaus. Some of his English idiom usage was about ten degrees off, in a way that was hard to pinpoint and impossible to correct. He was referring to the gaggle of TV trucks by the airport's entrance. In the twenty-five minutes it took them to get here, the story broke all over the news.

The forced landing of a Turkish plane in Belarus was an instant global scandal. No one was buying Minsk's official bomb-threat legend—an email from a never-before-heard-of Kurdish separatist group, sent around to random airport authorities—with only the Russians making a show of immediately taking it at face value, which in itself was a huge lewd wink and basically an admission of guilt. That was the way the game was played now: each side making its lies as shameless as possible and daring others to do something about it. Falk found this professionally insulting—which, too, was the point.

He did, however, have to hand it to the enemy in one respect: hanging the whole thing on the Kurds, even by this flimsy a thread, was a smart touch. It flattered the Turks' own state mythologies and would keep them from digging into the case too hard. Antalya Airlines' press release, which every outlet was quoting now, sounded neutral and mostly concerned with the customers' inconvenience. It ended with the phrase that gave Falk some hope: "After a three-hour delay, all passengers were released and the flight was allowed to continue on to the destination."

Inga stopped the car. They had bummed a ride to the airport in her mud-encrusted Lada Niva because it was the only one parked by the office; she lived on a farm out of town.

"So. What are we?" she asked, getting out.

"Let's not complicate things. We're ourselves," said Falk. "A news organization."

They walked past a CNN truck setting up for a live report. The plane was scheduled to land in ten minutes.

Inside, the airport hummed along as usual, apart from the abnormal bustle in the arrivals zone. The local cops kept the media crews outside, but, looking at the crowd of greeters, Falk could easily pick out the people who were, in one way or another, on the clock.

"Keep your eyes peeled," he said. They had found a table by a small coffee kiosk catering to drivers in need of a boost and set up camp there. "My guess is, counting us, there are between two and four spookshops operating in this airport right now."

"I always found this expression disgusting," said Inga.

"Spookshop?"

"No, 'keep your eyes peeled.' Who peels eyes?"

"Actually, there was this ancient Roman tortu—" began Klaus, then suddenly went silent. "Hang on. Inga, let's take a selfie. Now." He whipped out a phone, sidled up next to Inga with his back to the arrivals crowd, hugged her the best he could—even sitting, she was a full head taller than him—and snapped a quick series of shots.

"Lookie who we have here," he said, zooming into the background of the image and placing the phone in the middle of the table. The heavyset man crossing the frame behind Klaus's blurry right ear did, in fact, look familiar.

"You've got to be kidding me," said Falk. "Good work, Klaus."

"I'll send it in to be sure." Klaus opened Signal and forwarded the photo to a face-recognition bot he'd set up back at the office. The bot, hooked into three separate Russian and Chinese databases and one popular app that showed users what they'd look like as anime characters, processed most ID requests faster than the Agency's own channels, and with zero paperwork. The 94 percent match came back in seconds: *NIKOLAI G. KARIKH.*

Falk knew the name well. Karikh was GRU. Before its existence became public thanks to the Salisbury Novichok screwup, he was part of the now-infamous Unit 29155, which ran destabilization campaigns everywhere from France to Montenegro. Karikh's presence in Riga wasn't much of a secret. Unlike his mates, he wasn't an eye-peeler. He was a bagman, officially employed as a VP at a gray-zone Latvian "daughter" of a Russian state bank. This, according to the clandestine world's bizarro rules, marked Karikh as someone to be monitored but tolerated. In 2020, a rumor that some of the bank's money paid for bounties on US soldiers' heads in Afghanistan frayed this already-thin status quo to a thread, but it was never confirmed.

21

Enough time had passed that Falk felt it safe to turn around and track the man with his own eyes. Karikh was on an escalator, heading up to Departures. He was wearing a blue V-neck sweater and a trucker cap, a strange combo; Falk figured that the cap was a last-second addition once he got called in. Everyone was improvising today.

Inga finished her iced coffee and got up. "Right. Klaus stays to monitor the arrivals. I'm getting us the cheapest two non-Schengen tickets I find. And you better believe I'm expensing them."

Falk smiled and nodded. At least one call he'd make in his career would be the right one. Once he left—which could be next week, if all went well with Anton—Inga would make a great case officer. Klaus was going to *hate* working for her.

Seven minutes later, passengers Ari Falk and Inga Lace, traveling extremely light from Riga to Dubai, entered the airport's international zone. Gate 22A, where Anton's plane was set to arrive any minute, was the hottest spot in the terminal; clearly, they weren't the only ones to buy their way into the front row. When Flight TQ77's status on the boards changed from "landing" to "landed," an electric charge went through the hall. A few reporters outed themselves by running toward the windows, as if the generic visual of a taxiing plane would enrich their story somehow. Perhaps they thought it had taken fire over Minsk.

Falk used the chaos to move in closer to Karikh, who strode directly toward the gate, obliterating any possibility of coincidence. He was there for Anton.

"Boss," said Inga, "doesn't it seem a bit . . . much? For a blogger? Harassing the plane and then bringing in a whole GRU welcome party?"

"For a blogger that got their ministry's number two fired? No, I'd say it's about par for the course. See, the thing about the Russians that only a select few of us get is not that they're evil or cruel. They are, but so are we. It's that they're fantastically, unbelievably petty."

As Falk talked, the Boeing's ovoid nose slowly rolled into view outside. A gate agent opened the jet-bridge doors to the ground crew. The bridge telescoped out, its canopy latching onto the side of the plane like a suckerfish.

"You're right that it doesn't add up, though," said Falk. "Karikh is not a field agent. He's a money guy. I don't understand what the play is."

The gate doors opened. The air crew emerged first, greeted by light applause that started at the gate and caught on throughout the terminal. Next came a small stampede of rumpled business-class passengers: even in extreme circumstances, the hierarchies held.

Falk found himself torn between scanning the onrush of faces for Anton's and watching the GRU agent do the same. As blazers and cashmere gave way to tracksuits and backpacks, Karikh grew increasingly tense, which suggested he didn't know where Anton sat. Wary of getting made, Falk gestured for Inga to keep an eye on the bagman and concentrated on the arrivals.

The sound he heard next was extremely familiar, yet felt like something from a past life. It was a phone alert Falk had set up for every time a new video appeared on Anton's YouTube channel. Over the last year, he had developed a Pavlovian endorphin response to it—it heralded another laugh and another small victory. The last time he heard it was five weeks ago, the day the Napoleon story came out and Anton went into hiding.

The thumbnail showed Anton at a desk of laminated plywood, its veneer bubbling and sloughing off. The blogger's eyes were red, but Falk noticed no obvious injuries. The wallpaper behind him, once white, now ran beige from water damage and worn-in smoke: a Leninist liminal space, blank yet stifling like everything the USSR touched.

PLAY. On the screen, Anton inhaled and exhaled, carefully, the way people with a broken rib do. Falk unconsciously mirrored him.

"Hey, all. My name is Anton Basmanny," he started, in a cracked, hollow voice. His eyeline indicated someone seated just to the right of the camera. "And I am an American agent."

Falk almost dropped the phone. Inga took her eyes off Karikh and gave him a concerned glance. He waved her over to watch.

"Not literally, of course," Anton continued. "But I recognize now that my actions, while not intended that way, aided a concerted effort by the West to undermine Russian sovereignty." Anton's hair was a mess; he kept nervously smoothing it with his right hand.

"What do you want to say now?" a soft male voice prompted him off-screen. Falk made a note to analyze it later.

"I want to apologize."

"To whom?"

"To Comrade—uh, to Deputy Minister Pervushin and his family."

"And?"

"And to everyone whose feelings I hurt. My videos were insensitive, in bad taste, and based on false information. They were only intended to entertain, but now I know that some people viewed them as news. That's nobody's fault but mine. They were *feik nyus*"—Anton used the English term—"and I am sorry for misleading the Russian public this way."

"Do you have anything else to add?"

Anton frowned. "I don't think so."

"Are you sure?"

For several seconds, Anton silently fiddled with a strip of veneer coming off the desk.

"Yes," he said, quieter than before, looking down. "Some of my videos may also be seen as constituting propaganda of nontraditional values."

"Mother*fuckers*," said Inga through gritted teeth.

"I understand now that, despite the correct age and content warnings on my channel, some underage viewers may have been exposed to, uh, glorifying descriptions of a degenerate lifestyle. I apologize for this as well. This is going to be the last video I post here. All I ask for now is a chance to be a private citizen. Thank you."

The video ended, automatically segueing into whatever came next on the channel—which was the Napoleon blockbuster, thirty-five million views and counting. Falk hid the phone and looked up. He half expected a miracle—Anton, emerging from the tunnel right there and then. Instead, a ground crew member rolled out a refrigerator-size carrier with a Great Dane inside. The stream of arrivals was thinning. So was the crowd of greeters; most reporters had found a willing victim to interview and wandered off with them. Falk realized that anyone still loitering by the gate ran an increasing risk of showing that they were there for someone not on the flight—that is, Anton—and began to walk away. The same thought must have occurred to Karikh a second later.

"So. You think they have him?" asked Inga, catching up.

"No. I don't think so. The video was it. They got what they wanted out of him."

Falk could barely form the words. The reality of his career-long failure was hitting him all at once. Anton's humiliation was his own. Every asset he ran straight into prison or exile, every young Russian whose back he watched the Motherland break for the sin of wanting things to be a little better, all of it came down to this. Anton Basmanny, the most fearless of them all, licking the boot at gunpoint in a musty basement. *I am an American agent.*

He could easily be too optimistic in his reasoning; the blogger might already be six feet under the Belarusian loam, and this would be undeniably his, Falk's, fault. So what now? Just keep going? How does anyone win a tennis game against an opponent who kills the ball boy every time he misses a point? *Do you have anything to add?*

"Oh, and Inga. I keep meaning to tell you. I'm putting you up for promotion."

"Wow, thank you, boss. Promotion to . . . to what?"

"To *me*." In his peripheral vision, Falk saw Karikh head for the men's room. Inga opened her mouth to ask the first of what was undoubtedly a thousand valid questions, but he stopped her.

"Gimme a minute." Not entirely sure what he was doing yet, Falk followed Karikh toward the restroom. A surge of adrenaline helped keep the darker thoughts at bay, and, for the moment, that was enough. He pushed the door and walked in.

The GRU bagman was standing at the farthest urinal from the entrance, pissing and humming a basso jazz melody. They were alone in the entire room, a state of things that clearly wouldn't last. It would be optimal if he had gone into one of the stalls, but that would be too much luck for a day this awful. It was now or never.

Falk took a running start from the door and, lunging forward with his whole weight, slammed his open palm into the back of Karikh's head.

The agent crashed into the wall, his forehead shattering the plastic cover of an herbal erection-pill ad that hung at eye level over every urinal. The trucker cap flew back from the impact; Falk automatically caught it with his left hand while pressing his right into Karikh's nape to keep him from sliding down. Unconscious, the man was still urinating; Falk waited as long as he could, then hugged him under the armpits, pushed him into the handicapped stall, and dropped him onto the seat.

"Did you kill him?" he yelled in Russian.

No answer. Falk slapped Karikh upside the ear to wake him up, while pressing the hat to his bloodied face to avoid being seen. Karikh flailed and hissed.

"Is he dead?!"

"Is who dead?" slurred Karikh through the hat.

"You know who."

"No! Who? Look, I will talk, just name the guy."

"The blogger."

"Jesus. No. They sent him back to Turkey. Why?"

Falk punched Karikh one more time, sending him off the toilet.

"Grab the floor. Stay down. It's over."

He left the stall, caught a glimpse of his own crazed face in the wash-room mirrors, and walked out, holding the door for two Finnish back-packer teens walking in.

"Everything okay?" Inga was waiting for him outside. "The coast is clear. He's almost definitely working solo."

"Walk and talk," said Falk. They broke into a light trot together; an airport was one of the few places where this looked normal. "Take Klaus and go home. I'm getting on the next flight to Istanbul. I'm sorry, I have to see this thing through."

She gave Falk a once-over, without slowing down. "Uh, boss?"

"Yes?"

"You have a little blood on your clothes. And a lot of what I hope is water on your shoes."

Falk stopped, got out of his hoodie, rolled it up, and handed it to Inga. "Get rid of it, please."

"Weezer? Really?"

"Shut up."

She grew serious. "I'm guessing my promotion is being delayed."

"Fast-tracked, more like. I've just gone way off the reservation—"

"Need to know," said Inga fast. "I don't need to know what hap-pened in there. But I do know I like the post-toilet you more than the pre-toilet you. If that makes any sense."

Adrenaline still flooding his system, Falk felt a Neanderthal urge to kiss her before walking away. So he walked away first.

■ ■ ■

Anton staggered into the hammam, fully aware of being a cliché. He was Russian, drunk, and entering a second-rate bathhouse whose main attraction—being open past ten p.m.—was also its main red flag. But, as a local meme went, "there was a nuance." His nationality was, at this point, a curse; the alcohol was a way to stop his brain from replaying the fear and self-abasement of the last few hours; and the only thing he sought in the hammam was a place to sleep. Returning to the blown safe house seemed suicidal, and hotels asked for passports.

He paid with the last crumbs of cash from his crypto debit card, got his robe and slippers, waved away all treatment offers, and was going to pass out on the nearest chaise when he smelled himself taking off his clothes; he found the strength to climb into a shower first.

The vaulted stall, with its green marble panels rising into a honey-comb dome, was beautiful despite a century's worth of chips and stains. Anton put both hands on the wall. Tepid water from a nine-foot-high nozzle beat down on his head. He tried not to let his shoulders shake as he cried.

Once he had taped the apology, the agent seated across from him smiled a closed-mouth smile, took back the smartphone he had lent Anton for the task, and handed him his passport in return. "Now let's up-load," he said. "Your login, please." Minutes ticked by as the Belarusian phone network struggled with the file. "Attaboy. Wasn't so hard, was it. I smell a hit." Anton wasn't listening. He could barely remember what he'd just said in the video. The only things on his mind were the two gunshots he'd heard, and when his own turn would come.

It never did. The KGB put him on a regular Belavia flight to Istanbul.

He spent the six-odd hours in the air hallucinating MiGs outside the window and draining little vodka bottles until the flight attendant cut him off, gave him another look, sighed, and slipped him two more. "Just be quiet," she said. The message of the day, and of his life.

Anton turned off the shower and pulled on the robe without toweling off. A rotund man, his torso entirely encased in a black chain mail of fur, glared at him from another stall. Anton hurried out. The hammam had a relaxation area with a dozen cots, arrayed in spokes around a statue of a gurgling dolphin. The second-to-last thing he did before falling asleep was text the Tbilisi friend for some money to move around tomorrow. The last thing was logging into his 2.1-million-follower, 1.5-billion-view YouTube channel, from a dumbphone that couldn't even show him his own videos, and deleting the whole thing.

"I'm sorry, sir. You can't spend the night in here." Anton opened his eyes. An elderly masked attendant was crouched next to the cot, gently shaking him awake.

"How long was I out?"

"I don't know, sir. I just started. Warm towel?"

"Thank you. And sorry." Anton took the towel, daubed his face and neck, and got up. The inebriation was still there but shading into a hangover. He must have slept for at least a few hours; good enough. He shuffled toward his locker and changed back into yesterday's clothes, which held the collected stench of two flights and one kidnapping.

The moment Anton got to the empty reception area, he knew he was made again. This time it was a thin, dark-haired man on a bench by the entrance, dressed like someone playing an American college student in a movie from fifteen years ago. Despite his attempts to assume a casual pose, he looked almost as tense and tired as Anton.

The man clocked him, kept eye contact, and got up. This was new. After a millisecond's panic, Anton took a deep breath and continued toward the hammam's carved double doors. He was too exhausted to run. If death came in a Weezer T-shirt, so be it.

■ ■ ■

After all this time, finally seeing Basmanny alive and in person felt like a win in itself. Falk got up and smiled, forgetting for a split second that Anton had no idea what he looked like. To the blogger's immense credit, he flinched but kept walking straight at Falk. His mien was, for lack of a better word, gladiatorial.

Not bad for someone whose name over the last twelve hours had, in the cruel churn of social spectacle, become synonymous with cowardice. As soon as Anton's apology video appeared online, followed by the abrupt deletion of his entire channel, the Russian state media predictably had a field day. His former fans and peers in the opposition, however, got in on the action as well. To some of them, this proved the long-held theory that he was a "Kremlin project" all along, a managed distraction. Others contrasted his seeming weakness with the stoicism of other famous dissidents. Those who pointed out the obviously forced nature of the confession ended up sounding like they were making excuses for this weakness; and, in the end, the name of the game was always perception of strength, so these voices were few. Homophobic slurs and jokes, by contrast, flew unimpeded. Falk sincerely hoped Anton hadn't checked his socials yet.

Not a soul had connected the video to the diverted flight, which fizzled out as a news story after all interviewed passengers spoke of the Belarusians' largely polite demeanor and Antalya Airlines' generous vouchers.

"Hey," said Falk. Anton walked past and to the doors, pointedly ignoring him. "My name is Ari Falk. You were supposed to meet with me in Riga yesterday."

Anton stopped and turned. The switch from despair to sarcasm was almost instantaneous. "Ah. Well, sorry to stand you up. Don't know if you heard but I don't have any media for you to invest in anymore."

"I know," said Falk softly. "I'm also Merab, from Tbilisi. I sent you 2.5 Ether a few weeks ago that you've been living on since."

It took longer for Anton to digest this, but not that much longer.

"Do you book my flights, too? 'Cause I have some real complaints about the service."

Falk laughed. "No. That was Moscow Station. Can we go now?"

"Where?"

Falk took out the provisional US passport he'd been carrying for the last twenty-four hours, handed it to Anton, and watched the blogger's eyes go wide as he saw his own photo inside. Best part of the job. Perhaps the only good one.

They walked out, into an alleyway dipped in the mustard-yellow light of a sodium streetlamp. A mess of cables overhead cut the sky into a dark mosaic. Three of the Blue Mosque's six minarets shone dimly in the distance, forming from this angle a tight sharp trident. The dawn call to prayer was still half an hour away.

"I have a plane waiting for us on the other side of the Bulgarian border," said Falk. "It's a four-hour drive from here."

"What time is it now?" asked Anton suddenly, turning the passport in his hand.

"About six a.m. You officially survived the night. Smart move with the hammam."

"Was it? You still found me."

Falk reached out and flicked the outline of the phone in Anton's breast pocket. "Get rid of it, by the way. They could have cloned it in Minsk." Anton took out the Nokia with two fingers, as if Falk's words had just turned it into a toad, and dropped it into a sewer grate.

Falk's rental car stood at the end of the block, an intentionally bland Hyundai he had parked with two wheels on the curb for extra local flavor. "And here I was expecting an Aston Martin," said Anton. This was the last thing either of them said for the next hour.

The sun came up. They weaved through the city's western suburbs, drove along the Marmara Sea coast for a bit, then turned inland. The road morphed into a charmless multilane highway; they could be anywhere in the world. Anton yawned and scratched his nose.

"How are you holding up?" asked Falk, in part to stifle his own yawn.

"Fine. Sleepy."

"I mean, with the reaction to the video and everything."

Anton chuckled. "What's the expression? Ignorance is bliss."

"Good call."

"Better you tell me." Anton turned toward him. "How big is the hijacking story? I mean, Belarus has got to be on everyone's rogue-state list, right?"

"One would think so," said Falk. "But no. It's been pretty quiet."

"What? How?"

"Come on, man," said Falk, angrily overtaking a semitruck that was slowing down the center lane. "You know the media game better than I do. When no one's hurt, they lose interest."

"No one's hurt?" Anton yelled, suddenly losing it. "Two people get executed in cold blood, two foreign citizens, and that's called 'no one's hurt' now?!"

"What the fuck are you talking about?"

For a moment, Falk and Anton stared at each other. The slighted truck was now honking and flashing its brights behind them. Then, making an executive decision, Falk threw the wheel to the right and took the nearest exit.

■ ■ ■

"Okay. Again. Everything you remember." They were sitting in a road-side döner shack, two paper cups of unbearably strong tea in front of them. Anton had just finished the broad-strokes recollection of his brief time with the middle-aged couple, the soldiers in unmarked uniforms, the two gunshots.

"I think that's all of it."

"You're an observant guy. Think. Focus. Drink some tea." Falk sipped his. It tasted like creosote and heartburn.

"As I said . . . I think the man was American, but it's a guess. She was definitely Russian. Educated. Maybe St. Petersburg?"

"And they were married?"

"She said 'my husband.' But older Russian women say that about anyone they date for over a week. Especially if it's a Westerner."

Falk grinned: the broadside may have been sexist but it squared with some of his own early misadventures. He opened a mobile dropbox and pulled up scans of TQ77's two flight manifests, one filed before the Minsk stop and one after, both procured by Inga's source at the airline.

"Okay, let's see. There are fourteen people in business. None of them share a last name, but, I agree, that means nothing. None bought their tickets together. That means *some*thing. Most importantly"—he flipped over to the next document—"here's the manifest *after* Minsk. Same four-teen people. In fact, let's look at the total number, business and econ-omy. Before, 133. After, 132. The only variable is you."

Anton stared into his untouched tea, less angry than deflated. An oily film slowly rotated on the surface of the liquid. "I saw what I saw."

"And I believe you. But ask yourself this: Wouldn't the flight atten-dants remember missing two passengers? Wouldn't their neighbors?"

"Well, I wasn't on that leg of the flight," said Anton acidly. "But my

33

guess is that the reboarding wasn't exactly by the book. People must have grabbed seats wherever they could."

"True," conceded Falk. "I mean, two people hopping on a flight unlisted is not unheard of . . . in *our* trade. So they could have been working you. Certainly explains you ending up in the same room. And the gunshots were to scare you into a confession. Which, I mean, don't beat yourself up, I'd have freaked out too," he lied.

"My hand itches," said the blogger, in the petulant tone of a six-year-old. The poor guy was really fading.

"Honestly," said Falk, "I think that's what it was. Now let's go, we have quite a bit of driving to do."

"*Sekundu.*" Anton reached for his tea, lifted the cup with surprising effort, and suddenly dropped it without taking a sip. A moment later, he was doubled over, dry heaving. Falk, worried about making a scene as much as about Anton and his hangover, grabbed him and led him outside, tossing a fistful of lira and euro on the tea-splattered table.

"That's it. Get it all out. Done?" He was practically carrying Anton to the car; the guy was a featherweight. Falk laid him out on the cramped back seat, figuring he'd better stay horizontal for the rest of the trip, and closed the door. That's when the seizures began.

The blogger gasped and thrashed around. His back arched, collapsed, arched again. This was no hangover. Something was beating him up inside, and beating him to a pulp. Unsure what to do, Falk got into the front seat, turned around, and tried to use his arms and weight to still Anton's chaotic movements so he wouldn't hurt himself. It felt like a fight. Falk's mind flashed an image of Karikh on the toilet floor.

Finally, he caught the blogger's flailing right arm by the shirtsleeve and pinned it to the headliner. A purplish, blistering rash ran between his thumb and forefinger, as if he'd closed his hand around a hot poker an hour ago.

Anton loudly inhaled through his mouth, in a kind of cord-shredding reverse scream. He did this twice. The third attempt stalled halfway. His body spasmed so hard that his right foot took out the driver's-side head-rest. And then, Anton Basmanny was dead.

The weedy, unpaved lot in front of the shack stood empty, save for a minibus rusting under a blue tarp. Beyond the weeds, highway traffic hissed like an ebbing tide. For a minute, Falk sat motionless in the driver's seat of his rented Hyundai, head on the wheel, corpse in the back. Every second of mourning was a risk and a luxury. The Agency had proto-cols for this kind of thing—the Agency had protocols for every kind of thing—but he needed a moment to sit and be human before triggering them. It might, after all, be one of his last.

Then he called the exfiltration team waiting outside Burgas, told them they had an hour and a half to prepare one atropine drip and two body bags, and started the car.

CHAPTER TWO

Maya Chou Obrandt learned of her father's death while watching TV. Well, not TV—who watches TV?—but streaming a random episode of a Peacock series because she'd been up for one of the parts a year and a half before and wanted to make sure that the girl who got it instead of her was terrible and the series was shit.

The girl wasn't terrible at all. She looked like a parallel-universe Maya, same type, same hair—the producers must have been dead set on casting a half Asian for some reason—but taller and funnier and capable of crying on cue. She also played the character as a bit of a California stoner, which, Maya hated to admit, was a great choice she wouldn't have had the nerve to suggest. Of the series itself, which started out as a heist thing and then took a hard turn into a vampire thing, she couldn't make heads or tails.

When the first breaking-news alert suddenly slotted into the screen's top right corner, it had the last name Obrandt in it, so Maya mistook it for an email. She was sprawled on a couch in one of the top floor's many purposeless "guest" rooms, unsure whose account she was using—Dad's, Mom's, or a housekeeper's. Every object around her was wildly oversize,

37

a reflection of Paul Obrandt's tastes: a cocobolo desk the width of a king bed, the LCD screen that could probably show Picasso's *Guernica* in 1:1, the massive couch shrinking her to loose change in its cushions. The sensation of smallness was sort of calming.

Before she could shoo away the first notification, a second one appeared over it, pushing it down. She missed the X with the cursor and accidentally clicked through. A moment later, she was staring at a giant photograph of a yacht in a marina. The headline above it was so incomprehensible that Maya's mind forced her to concentrate on the details of the image: the type of the boat, flybridge wide beam; the name on the stern, *A Mar*; the row of cartoonishly bright pink and yellow town houses behind. Only once every part of the photo had been seared into her mind did she manage to really read the text, word by word, despite already knowing what it said.

FINANCIER DEAD IN APPARENT SUICIDE

Paul M. Obrandt, 50, Drowns in Portugal;

Ran One of Southern California's Largest Investment Funds

More notifications were now crowding the right side of the screen, news alerts, emails, texts, all saying the same ten to fifteen words in slight variations. She turned the TV off and listened to the house. No crying. No breaking glass. Outside the window, a rotating sprinkler hit a banana leaf, drummed loudly across it for a few seconds, then chittered away. As long as Maya was the only one who knew, the information still wasn't real, because she thought of herself as not entirely real to begin with. Certainly not as real as Dad, whose personality and will, hard-coded into every item surrounding her, formed the parameters of a whole world. She rolled off the giant couch and headed downstairs, as slowly as possible, delaying, delaying, delaying.

Her mother must have heard the creaking steps. Maya had no idea which wing of the house she emerged from—Emily looked equally put-together whether planning a fundraiser or making dumplings. "Oh, come on now, no pouting," she yelped energetically from the bottom of the stairwell, squinting up at the twenty-three-year-old's blank face and broken gait. "You were the one who insisted on auditioning as 'Maya Chou.' If you went in as Obrandt, you would have got it."

■ ■ ■

BERLIN
AUGUST 17, 2021

After some back and forth, Langley allowed the meeting to take place at the Natural History Museum. If DD/CA Harlow himself was flying out to debrief him in person, Falk was not going to let this be a bedside visit. The museum stood directly across the street from the hospital; even in his present underpowered state, he could walk this far. More importantly, for what he was about to tell the boss, he needed to project at least some measure of health.

Having saved three poisoned Russian dissidents in three separate cases between 2017 and 2020, Berlin's famed Charité had developed a curious subspecialty: it became the world's hospital of choice for suspected Novichok victims. It also had strict security protocols in place that allowed patients to be taken in and out in secret—owing, perhaps, to the fact that its other close neighbor besides the Natural History Museum was the headquarters of Germany's foreign intelligence service, BND. So, when Falk's Hyundai swerved onto the Bulgarian airfield, skidding to a stop inches from the plane, it took the leader of the exfil team one look at the man behind the wheel and the corpse in the back seat to file for a change of flight plan to Berlin. Falk clambered out of the car, threw up,

39

and passed out. Two and a half hours later, he opened his eyes convinced he was in Virginia until the nurse that came to change his atropine drip irritably asked him to *bleiben Sie bitte still liegen*.

It soon became clear that secondhand contact with whatever toxin had killed Anton Basmanny accounted for about 50 percent of Falk's state. The other half was a combo of exhaustion, dehydration, and a rather understandable panic attack. By next morning, the only thing stopping Falk from venturing outside was the literal lack of anything to wear: Charité incinerated it all as a security measure. In the case of sneakers splashed with Karikh's urine, this was probably for the best. He did miss the Weezer shirt.

The new clothes arrived right before the meeting, still in the Galeries Lafayette shopping bag. Falk shed the hospital gown and quickly put everything on: white briefs, black socks, white shirt, black tie, gray suit, black shoes. Whoever had sent this stuff over had his exact measurements, a decent budget, and zero interest in the task. Falk adjusted the tie in the mirror. It went pretty well with his under-eye circles.

Unlike broiling Paris or muggy London, the back half of August in Berlin felt more like a polite preview of the fall. A cool breeze worried the lindens up and down Invalidenstrasse. A yellow tram swam by, its electric whine fast replacing the racket of combustion as the city's root note. It was certainly nice to be alive, the many caveats aside. Falk found himself wishing the walk was longer than a hundred feet.

Deputy Director Rex Harlow waited for him under the Tyrannosaurus skeleton. In the time since Falk saw him last, the old man had begun using a walking cane, but it didn't make him look frail, just dignified. "Nice kid," he said, pointing the cane at the dinosaur. "Not just a namesake but a neighbor. I'm from Montana, too, y'know." A gaggle of preschoolers in tiny hi-vis jackets, out on a *kita* field trip, swarmed the T. rex, so the two men walked away toward less popular exhibits.

"You look good, Ari," said Harlow. "I mean, under the circumstances."

"Thank you, sir. So do you."

"What do you want first? Questions or answers?"

"Some answers would be nice."

"It wasn't Novichok, for once. The docs are leaning toward VX."

"I see. Like the North Korean thing a few years ago."

"Yes, but more interesting. They found traces of two separate components on your guy's neck and hands. So we're thinking binary weapon. One part is applied earlier, let's say on his clothes in the locker, one later, on a towel or some such. Then you just wait for the victim to touch their face. Safe for the assassin, safe for bystanders. Well, sort of—you seem to have gotten some on yourself during the struggle. But overall a big improvement, considering the Russian track record in this area."

Falk nodded. "What will happen with the body? Are we flying it back? Is anyone telling the Turks? The family?"

"Afraid not. Any investigation would expose you, too." Harlow looked at Falk and misinterpreted his expression, in all likelihood deliberately. "It's *fine*. People get lost in Istanbul all the time."

Falk knew what this meant. Anton's body must have already been incinerated along with his clothes, and any further questions would be a sign of going soft.

"To be honest," he said after a pause, "I'm less interested in the how than in the why. If they wanted Anton dead, they could have done it at their leisure in Minsk. Putting him on a plane to Istanbul and killing him ten hours later is not just messy, it's idiotic. *Unless.*"

"Unless what?" Harlow's expression was that of a kind parent who knows exactly what the child is going to say but is going to listen anyway.

"Unless we're the reason he's dead, sir. Let's say the original goal was just to get a taped confession out of him. The guy's fearless, so he needs a special approach. Okay, they tail him, they yank him off the flight, they intimidate him by pretending to shoot other passengers. Finally, he breaks. And, while they have him, they check all his comms."

"As one does."

"Right. So, before, they didn't actually know he was our asset. They just called him a Western agent because they call everyone that. *After* they let him go, though, they had proof. If the apology was for the folks back home, the murder was a message to us."

"Hmm. And what was the proof, may I ask?"

"He texted an alias of mine, asking for money. And, uh . . ." Falk fell silent. They had wandered into a hall of meticulously sculpted insect models: a housefly the size of a corgi, a mosquito with the wingspan of a golden eagle. Dating back to the 1930s and 1940s, all of the models were the work of a single obsessed academic, a fact that over time had transmuted them from science props into something closer to art.

"Please continue."

"Let's just say that, earlier on the same day, an unidentified person assaulted a GRU officer and obtained info on Anton's whereabouts."

"Unidentified?"

"Unidentified."

Harlow stopped and scratched his chin. "Well, shit, son. I may have a rather low opinion of our Russian partners these days, but I do believe they're capable of putting two and two together."

Falk sighed. *Here we go.* "Sir. I take full responsibility. In my opinion, Inga Lace is more than well-qualified to run the Riga project. And I may need a career change, anyway. I am afraid, when it comes to the mission, I am no longer making the best decisions."

Harlow gave a noncommittal grunt and turned to admire the nearest display: a monstrous wheat weevil, depicted atop a grain seed as big as a pumpkin. "1940!" he exclaimed, leaning in and squinting to read the accompanying plaque. "Imagine that! The war's been going on for a year. Auschwitz already operational. And here, in Berlin, a guy sits one mile from the Reichstag, painstakingly building the world's largest weevil." Harlow delivered the last phrase with such droll gusto that Falk laughed in spite of himself.

"You find it hypocritical?" he asked.

"No. What? No. I think it's noble, in a way. Think of all the other things he could've been doing. Measuring skulls and whatnot. No, no, when the world goes to shit and you can't stop the men responsible, a weevil might be the best way out."

"And if you *can*? Like you said, he was one mile from the Reichstag."

Harlow smiled, shifted the cane to his left hand and put his right arm over Falk's shoulder, leaning on him for support as they headed downstairs and out. "Exactly. You want to fuck off and go build a weevil, I won't judge you. But let me offer you something a little better than that. Let me put you full-time on untangling this. As far as the Agency's concerned, native assets may be fair game, but they came way too close to killing a case officer of mine. And *that* we don't look upon too kindly. So find me whoever did it, and we'll take the next steps together. Sound good?"

Sometimes Falk forgot whom he was dealing with. After forty-five years in the service, the deputy director saw people's real motives before they did—because, let's face it, people had only so many real motives to begin with. What Falk thought was midcareer burnout was in fact desperate rage. He had felt it when he slammed Karikh's head into the bathroom wall. He wanted revenge, so Harlow pitched him revenge. It was that simple.

"It does, sir."

They walked out onto the museum's front portico. Harlow let go of Falk's shoulder. His ride, a black Benz with red diplomatic plates, immediately pulled up to the curb below. The old man took a few steps, then turned around.

"So which thread are you thinking of pulling first? The hammam attendant?"

"A day player, I'm sure. No, I would start with the two ghosts on the Antalya Airlines flight," said Falk. "A man and a woman—late forties, early fifties. Anton described them pretty well. They weren't on the manifest, which suggests some cooperation with the Turks."

"Sounds promising," said Harlow.

"One thing, though. He kept saying the man was American."

"Well," Harlow pursed his lips. "If the dead gay Russian said it!"

Falk winced, then reminded himself he was speaking with a seventy-three-year-old career soldier.

"I'll figure it out. Thank you for letting me do this."

"Son," said the deputy director, folding into the back seat of the Benz, "you'd do this whether I let you or not."

■ ■ ■

LOS ANGELES
AUGUST 17, 2021

The press kept chewing over the same few details. Paul Obrandt arrived in Algarve, a province on the southernmost tip of Portugal, on August 14, to meet with a fish-processing conglomerate whose pension fund he had been managing. The talks must have gone well, because later the same evening he rented a yacht in Albufeira and took the company's CEO and a few staffers on a private booze cruise to Benagil Cave, a popular local Instagram spot. According to the captain, Obrandt spent most of it locked in his master cabin, which wasn't unusual for these trips. On the way back, however, he quietly emerged on the bridge and offered the captain five thousand euro to take the boat a bit farther out into the Gulf of Cadiz. Since the sea was calm and everybody else too drunk to notice (one had to read between the lines for this bit), the captain shrugged and complied.

Obrandt must have studied the nautical charts beforehand. The slight route change took the boat from shallow waters to a mile below keel. Apart from Obrandt, the only thing missing upon the boat's return was a spare length of anchor line he must have wrapped around himself.

There'd be no body, but there was a letter. In his trademark methodical fashion, Obrandt wrote it by hand, took a picture of it lying atop a copy of that day's *Diário de Notícias*, and emailed it to his lawyer in San Francisco less than an hour before ending his life. He left the original in the cabin, alongside ten 500-euro bills for the captain.

The lawyer was now one of nine faces staring at Maya from a Zoom grid; the rest were Dad's various staffers, officers at Obrandt Investment Securities, and her own mother, who had called in separately despite being in the same house as Maya. The world's most depressing tic-tac-toe board, with white men as the Xs and women as the losing Os.

"If no one minds, I'll start reading," said the lawyer, lowering his eyes toward the printout he held in his hand. "Okay. *'Em, Maya, my dearests, sorry to be doing it this way. I need to make certain that this document supersedes my existing will, hence all the bureaucratic, slash, cloak-and-dagger bullshit.'*" He took an involuntary pause before "bullshit," torn between swearing aloud and censoring a dead man. "*'Hopefully, the procedural fussiness on display here will also remove all questions of my mental capacity.'*"

A few people smiled. "He had such a beautiful command of English," said some woman in New York, sniffling. "Especially for a non-native speaker."

"Excuse me," said Maya's mother in her square. She was speaking from her husband's downstairs study, loudly enough that Maya could hear a faint double of her voice drift through the bedroom floor. Next to her stood a glass of whiskey she must have thought was out of frame. "Linda. This is not a wake. Let's save the reminiscing for a more appropriate occasion."

"I'm so sorry, Emily," said the woman.

"Please continue, Herman."

The lawyer nodded. *"In terms of OIS stewardship, the changes are quite simple and must be implemented at once. Emily Chou, my spouse and the fund's senior managing director, becomes chairwoman. The role of SMD is to be combined with that of chief compliance officer and performed by our current CCO, Linda Lohman.'"*

In normal circumstances, this was the point where people would clap. Some almost did, but each stopped when they realized they'd be first. Then everyone just vigorously nodded and mumbled "good, good, smart" instead.

"I am writing from Portugal, having just secured an enthusiastic agreement to this change from a key investment client, the Fides pension fund. I believe the rest will fall in line. Should any issues arise with—'" Maya felt her attention wander. She noticed that the lawyer in San Francisco and Linda in New York had the same novelty mug, and fixated on that for a while.

"As you may notice,'" the lawyer read, then stopped and cleared his throat nervously. Maya's focus came back. She wished it hadn't. *"'As you may notice, I am not mentioning any reasons, or offering any justifications, for what I am about to do. Nor will I. All I want to say is that I blame no one close to me, and my most fervent wish for them is not to blame themselves. I love my wife, Emily, and my daughter, Maya, very much. To Emily, I leave all of my assets liquid and fixed, to enjoy and dispose of as she sees fit. To Maya, I leave a monthly stipend and a house I have purchased here in Portugal for just this purpose. Surprise, I guess.'"*

"Herman, that's a bit insensitive," said Linda.

"That's not me," said the lawyer. "It really does say 'Surprise, I guess.'"

Maya glanced at her mother's Zoom square to see if she was crying, too, and found it empty.

A few seconds later, the door to her bedroom opened. Mother rushed toward her and hugged her from behind. Maya felt her wet face pushing into the back of her sweater. They sobbed together, in and out of sync, as Emily reached over Maya's shoulder and slammed the laptop shut.

■ ■ ■

RIGA
AUGUST 19, 2021

Even by the standards of spy parties, the party in honor of Inga's promotion was a little sad. Falk said a short toast, Klaus put on some terrible dance music, and the three of them stood on the office balcony for a bit, looking at the park and the spires and drinking Champagne out of Russian-made IKEA glasses. Both Falk's and Inga's job titles stayed the same, but she'd be taking over the Soft Unit's main counterpropaganda activities while Falk fully concentrated on the Flight TQ77 incident. Klaus was to provide technical support to both.

"Should we move this to Chomsky?" asked Falk when the bottle was empty. Named after the leftist academic, Bar Chomsky was a somewhat bohemian watering hole.

"It's not called Chomsky anymore," said Klaus, who made it a point of pride to stay on top of these things. "Now it's just Ché."

"I guess it's radicalizing," said Falk.

"Sorry, boys." Inga took her jacket from the back of a chair and began to put it on. "One of my pigs is heavily pregnant. Do continue without me."

"What a life you lead," said Klaus.

Once she was gone, a slight tension hung in the air for a second, the way it tends to when a woman leaves a space to men and whatever is said next will be unavoidably colored by that exit.

"So," said Klaus, steering right into the skid, "she's not your subordinate anymore, eh."

"Correct," said Falk dryly. "Ché?"

"How about some work?" Klaus plopped onto an ergonomic chair, pushed off from the nearest wall with both feet, and rolled into position before his monitors. Then he opened a desk drawer, pulled out a bottle of cognac, flipped it like an '80s bartender, and slammed it down next to the keyboard.

"Fuck yeah," said Falk, a little lamely.

■ ■ ■

It didn't take too long to compile basic data on the 132 passengers of Flight TQ77 who weren't Anton Basmanny or the two ghosts. Klaus had done most of this work before Falk even came back from Berlin. None showed any intelligence ties. One business-class passenger, Adil Divanoglu, had done a stint with SADAT, a Turkish mercenary outfit; this set off a few initial alarms. Twenty-four were stateless, which seemed like a lot if one weren't familiar with Latvia's exceedingly cranky naturalization policy. Klaus also created separate lists for Russian nationals—there were fifteen on board, about average for this type of flight—and for the seven passengers whose documents suggested recent name changes or some other irregularity. There was one overlap between the two: Darya Shukhova, seat 11A, who had an alias and whose age came up as twenty-nine in some documents and thirty-four in others.

"That's right in front of Anton," said Falk. "He was in 12A. Not liking this."

Klaus pulled up Shukhova's profile. Known publicly as Dasha Lemminkainen, she was a "psychologist," which could mean anything, and a semipopular Instagram personality whose channel, InStambul, had eight-odd thousand followers in Russia and Turkey—just barely enough to do this kind of thing full-time if one so desired. Falk immediately recognized her. It was her little video that tipped Inga off to the flight's safe departure from Minsk.

"Falsch alarm," said Klaus. When he drank, his English took a bit of a Ü-turn. "Not a cover. Just vanity."

"Hang on," said Falk. "Let me see her socials for the fifteenth."

Klaus shrugged, opened Lemminkainen's Instagram, and began to scroll. In the four days since the incident, she had posted fifty-three items, not counting story shares and livecasts. Interspersed with the usual mix of highly staged nightlife vignettes, fan Q&As, sponcon, and bikini shots was some dubious advice about PTSD, which she now claimed to have as a result of the incident.

On the morning of the fifteenth, Lemminkainen had posted twice from the Istanbul airport's business lounge (despite flying economy), once from the passport control zone, which was technically illegal, and once from the jet bridge. Her next post was the video he'd seen, of the plane leaving Minsk.

"Would you believe," asked Falk, "that a person who documents every minute of their day had nothing to show from the most eventful part of it?"

"Of course not," said Klaus. "The Belarusians went through everyone's phones. Otherwise we'd have hundreds of videos with that MiG."

"Right. But people like her have multiple phones with multiple backups. She could very well have our ghosts in there somewhere."

Klaus poured Falk and himself more cognac. "Ari. If you're asking me to break into her phone, that's days of work. I am not a magic man. And now I have Inga's stuff on top of yours. Write to Moscow Station. Maybe they'll lend you some resources."

Falk took a sip and stared at Lemminkainen's Instagram feed, thinking.

"What if I got you her actual, physical phone?"

"Huh?"

"Look at her most recent story."

Klaus reloaded the page and burst out laughing. "Oh, shit, she's still in Riga. Looks like we're going clubbing after all."

"*Einer von uns*, buddy. Only one of us." Falk downed the cognac, got up, and headed out.

"I'm telling Inga!" yelled Klaus through the door.

■ ■ ■

The club took up a three-story mansion and was decorated, or rather not decorated, in the style of Budapest's "ruin bars," with unfinished walls and exposed wiring. As Falk walked from room to room, looking to match the interior with the video Lemminkainen had posted from this location seventeen minutes earlier, he couldn't help comparing it to the Russian clubs of 2006: gaudy, desperate, horny. This, of course, was better. That, of course, was more fun.

Falk's first mission had taken him to Russia straight from the Intelligence Corps, where he was working off his two-year active-duty obligation before the ROTC. It was a glorified babysitting errand. An indigenous asset on the board of a state oil corporation had grown paranoid and refused to meet with his usual handler, or anyone else under established diplomatic cover. Harlow responded by promising to find him a contact who looked *least* like a spy. A week later, twenty-two-year-old Falk was off to St. Petersburg in the guise of a Fulbright scholar writing a book on Dostoyevsky. The cover was both ingenious and confusing because it hewed so close to Falk's actual passions. (That was always part of Rex Harlow's genius: he picked his people well and built upon what and who they already almost were.) Falk met with the asset twice and spent the rest of the trip in a succession of twin beds and neon-lit restrooms. Seduction was a matter of bellying up to the bar and loudly speaking English. The rest happened by itself. He wasn't proud of these conquests, which had a whiff of the pith helmet about them, but then again—after four largely chaste years at Yale—he sort of was.

Of course, none of this was relevant now. Falk reminded himself that his whirlwind 2006 experiences were actually a liability. The intelligence community was chockablock with officers who allowed their impressions in the field from ten, twenty, even thirty years ago to dictate their decisions today, overriding new expertise and hard data. Some of the older Russia hands still cracked '90s jokes about gangsters in red club jackets, a species long extinct. In reality, Falk made sure to keep in mind, Russians' incomes, tastes, style, slang, aspirations, even their national identity, shifted several times a decade. And no, you certainly couldn't impress anyone by flashing an American Express card anymore. They had Apple Pay.

The mansion's top floor was one big performance space, with a vaulted ceiling and no stage. A man and a woman sat on a Persian rug in the middle of a respectfully swaying crowd, surrounded by samplers and pedalboards. The music they made was one single, layered drone, now reaching for a wistful minor key, now collapsing in an avalanche of static. Despite being on assignment, Falk gave himself a minute to listen.

After looking for Lemminkainen in the second-floor lounge with black lights and piped-in fog, around the backyard beer garden, and on the main dance floor, he suddenly found her by the restrooms, sitting on the bottom step of a back staircase. She was on her phone, swiping back and forth between two close-ups of a filament bulb. Something about her bare knees squeezed together, her glum face in the bluish phone light, made him rethink his approach on the spot. Or maybe it was the fact that the first floor was the only part of the club that didn't charge admission, and that all her posts from this evening were from there.

"Hi," he said in Russian. "Are you Dasha Lemminkainen?"

She lifted her head. "Yes, why?"

"I follow your account," he said. "It's cool. You were on that flight, right?"

"Oh, thank you. Yeah. It was pretty chaotic."

He sat down next to her. "Look, my name is Ari Falk, I run a media company here in Riga. I know the Belarusians probably scrubbed your phones, but if you have any photos or videos from that day, I'll buy them from you."

Lemminkainen gave him a wary look, then grinned.

"Freaking amateurs," she snorted. "They just looked in my Photos folders. Didn't even check the cloud drive. I've got, like, hours of stuff. I've even got that YouTube guy, Anton what's-his-name, giving a whole speech about how it was all his fault. Hope he's okay. He wasn't there when they let us leave."

"He flew back," said Falk. "So why didn't you post any of it?"

"My brand is, no politics," said Lemminkainen brightly. "I would lose a bunch of sponsors. So! How much?"

Falk met her gaze and, as some safety switch in him toggled off, rethought the strategy once again.

"Let's start with a drink," he said. "Also, the band upstairs sounds really cool."

■ ■ ■

LOS ANGELES
AUGUST 20, 2021

There were—probably—some good ways of asking your twenty-three-year-old daughter to write and deliver a eulogy for a father who'd just killed himself. "You're the creative one" wasn't one of them. Maya stared at the laptop, seething. The anger was drowning out the sadness. She hated him for abandoning her. She hated herself for not being enough. She hated her mother for sticking her with the task.

No one expected Maya to do a recitation of Paul Obrandt's professional successes: she barely understood what the fuck he did for a living. No, this was supposed to be a loving daughter's perspective, blindered if not blinded by that love. Something about the magical times they spent together, the lessons imparted, the values instilled, the metaphor-to-be-determined she shall now carry on in his stead. The problem was, she'd have to make most of it up.

He was charming when he wanted to be, which wasn't often. He was funny, as dads went. When she was smaller and still told him things, he really listened, remembering names and details even when the subject was some middle-school rich-girl clique spat. But money was his love language: money for toys, for travel, for acting classes, for rehab. That final helpless gift of a house in Portugal, what was that? A nonverbal apology? A mad titan's version of an impulse buy? To Obrandt's credit, his generosity may have been gnomic but it wasn't conditional. He never demanded her time or affection or good behavior in return. Maybe he was being respectful, or maybe he just didn't want those things.

He did teach her Russian. He was adamant about that, for some reason. Tutors, Sunday school, bedside reading, old weird-ass Soviet cartoons on YouTube. Even at the age of five, Maya knew she could have anything she wanted, including precious intangibles like a later bedtime, provided she asked for it in grammatically correct Russian. This was especially strange because Obrandt barely used it himself: having immigrated to the US at fifteen, he didn't have a Russian-speaking social circle or keep up with the country's media. By contrast, her mother, who used her native Mandarin daily with friends and relatives, wasn't nearly as pushy about it. Maya ended up learning a bit of both, just enough to put "fluent" on her acting résumé. Should she talk about this in the eulogy? Was this all they really shared?

"Paul Obrandt was a great man," she typed. Then she tried the same sentence in transliterated Russian, but couldn't figure out the declension: Should "great man" be in the nominative case, *velikiy chelovek*, or instrumental, *velikim chelovekom*? So much for their shared secret language. She couldn't even do *this*.

Paul Obrandt was a great man. And then he fucked off out of existence, leaving behind a dumb pathetic useless daughter, the end.

A too-polite knock on the bedroom door could only be Mom. Even housekeepers were more assertive. Maya threw the cursor into the top left corner, triggering a screensaver, and kicked away the blanket so it would at least look like she was lying on the bed, not *in* it.

"Hey."

"Hey." Emily looked gaunt. She had been up more or less since the sixteenth. "Just wanted to check in on you."

"I'm getting there. It's going to be pretty short."

"I don't mean the eulogy."

"I do. So, I was thinking I'd say a few words and then segue straight to the photos, and talk over those."

"Oh, that's a good idea," said Emily. "And look what I found. It's your dad in Ladispoli."

She handed Maya a black-and-white photo. A teen with crooked teeth and Dad's eyebrows, grinning defiantly into the lens. Not yet an adult, no longer a kid, all hormones and hunger. From what she could make of the overexposed background, he was standing on a city beach. It was strange to think of her father, born in 1970, as someone with a black-and-white childhood. The photo looked beamed in from an earlier era, perhaps a still from some postwar Italian movie. As if to counter that impression, someone handwrote "5/11/1986" in the bottom white margin, in ink that was once blue but faded into lilac.

"Isn't Ladispoli near Rome? I thought the Soviets weren't allowed to travel to places like that."

"They weren't," said Emily. "It's a refugee transit camp. I think it's the only photo of your father on his way to the US. Could you have it scanned? It'll be great for the slideshow."

"Yeah. Sure." Maya took the photo.

Emily fixed her with a long look. "Are you okay? How are you holding up?"

"I'm fine."

"Do you want to call Rachel, maybe?" Rachel was the therapist, though Maya wasn't really in therapy. More like someone to dial whenever she was tempted to fall off the wagon. Normal people had AA and NA sponsors for this. She had a lady in Pacific Palisades who charged $450 an hour. Another gift from Dad.

"I said I'm fine. Mom. Please. You have lots of other things to think about."

Emily nodded a few times. "You know, I'd really be more comfortable if Rachel were here with us. Perhaps we can offer her the guesthouse for a few days."

"*Mom.* She's not a friend of mine. She's got other clients, uh, patients."

"I'm going to call her."

"Mom!!!" Maya put her palms up, an instant apology for the yelling. "Look. I've been handling shit pretty good so far. Are you . . . are you preparing me for something else? Is there *more* bad news? *Somehow?*"

"Language," said Emily automatically, not really meaning it.

"Sorry. But am I right? You know you can tell me."

Her mother lingered, then abruptly sat down next to Maya. When she spoke again, it was in a hushed, eerily neutral tone of someone barely keeping it together.

"It's the fund. I've been trying to make sense of it for the last three days."

"And?"

"And it's gone."

"What do you mean gone?"

"I don't mean bad bets or overleverage. I mean, stripped. Sell-offs and withdrawals, going back years. Dumping entire positions. He must have spent a hundred million on exit fees alone. And none of it is back with the investors. Just . . . gone."

"I'm sorry, Mom. I don't really get any of this."

"In the simplest possible terms," said Emily impatiently, "OIS is managing about six billion dollars. Maybe half of one, at any given point, is actually ours. And that's what I am seeing in the accounts now. The rest is in the wind."

"What does it mean?"

"One of two things," Emily said, and fell silent as if she wasn't going to elaborate.

"Well?"

"Someone made him hand it over."

"Or?"

"Or 'it' never really existed. Either way, your father couldn't live with this."

Maya realized she was still holding the photo. A black-and-white teen grinned at her from a faraway beach. She put it down onto the laptop lid.

"What happens when the investors find out?"

"Google the Madoffs," her mother said, wiped her eyes with the back of her wrist, and got up. "They made two movies about them."

"You're so calm about this."

"What would you have me do?"

Suddenly, Maya snapped, surprising even herself with the force of her outburst. "I don't know! Yell? Cry? Maybe *not* make me write some bullshit eulogy for this piece of shit?!"

"How *dare* you—"

"Oh, what? What? Is he *not* a piece of shit for what he did? And I don't even mean leaving you to clean up the mess," Maya yelled, fully unhinged now and feeling almost elated with rage. "Don't you realize? It's always been about the money with him. He never loved us, Mom. He—never—loved—us. The moment the money was gone, so was he. You, me, we never factored in. We never mattered. We never mattered."

Her mother leaned lightly against the doorjamb and looked down at her own crossed arms until Maya's increasingly ragged exclamations dissolved into sobbing. Then she raised her head again.

"Are you done embarrassing yourself?"

No answer.

"I believe you are. So, please, have the eulogy and the photo scans ready by tomorrow morning. We have the A/V people coming in at nine." She closed the door behind her.

When Maya was done throwing things, one of which was the laptop, she sat motionless for a few minutes. Somehow, in that interval, the room got dark.

She picked up the computer and opened it. It still worked; the screen had just developed a corner bruise in the colors of a gasoline puddle.

Maya typed in a town name she learned four days ago and stared at it in StreetView. Then she hit Directions, just for the hell of it. A straight shot down the 405 to LAX, a bouncy blue arc across half a world, and a tiny wiggle connecting Lisbon and the Algarve coast. Her passport lay in a top desk drawer.

Dad may have been a piece of shit, but she was wrong about at least one thing. This house wasn't an impulse buy or a sociopath's farewell. He was leaving her an escape route.

■ ■ ■

RIGA
AUGUST 20, 2021

As soon as Nikolai Karikh entered the bank, Nata, the receptionist, made a face—eyes wide, teeth clenched, head cocked toward the Prestizh Lounge area—that meant an important client was in the building. Karikh's mood soured at once. He had been hoping to avoid both Nata and any face-to-face meetings today. Nata, because he hit on her unsuccessfully just a week earlier (who the hell did she think she was, by the way, saying no to him like that? The queen of Riga?). And meetings, because he'd have to explain his bandaged forehead, which would require moving his fractured jaw.

Before heading over, he popped by the executive bathroom upstairs, checking corners as he entered: a brand-new tic, acquired five days earlier. Once the room was deemed intruder-free, Karikh stood in front of the mirror, peeled off the bandage, and finger-combed his colorless hair, which he thought of as blond, over the split skin. The result looked a little emo for a vice president of a financial institution, but not entirely uncool. The new, electric blue suit was a good call, too. That bitch Nata didn't know what she was missing.

The Prestizh Lounge was set aside for EiropaBank's biggest clients, nearly all of whom, owing to its peculiar status as a private European subsidiary of a Russian state company, came from the Motherland. It was thus done up in a heavy-luxe style—velvet banquettes, Murano chandeliers, a full bar—meant to make them feel more at home than the Nordic minimalism of the bank's Euro-facing side. The morning's guests, however, would look equally out of place in both. If Karikh didn't know any better, he'd think they were the real client's security detail.

And, in a way, they were.

Karikh had a good radar for colleagues. While most of his real work at the bank—moving GRU funds out of Russia—was done online these days, sometimes Moscow still sent along a courier with a good old-fashioned briefcase. Always a deposit, never a withdrawal. These two were no couriers and carried no briefcases, either. One had a hard Northern Caucasus look and a full unibrow; the other was a pink, buzz-cut farmboy type. If he had to guess, they were Spetsnaz or Eighth Directorate, more soldiers than agents, all physical training and reptilian instinct. Karikh himself was First Directorate or, in the Aquarium lingo, a *pidzhak* (suit jacket). Each branch, naturally, thought itself superior to the other.

He also immediately knew, though he wouldn't be able to articulate how, that their appearance at the bank had something to do with the Sunday incident. Once he got out of that airport bathroom, humiliated and bleeding, he went straight home and called Moscow on a clean phone line. His jaw clicked with every vowel, radiating terrible pain into ears and sinuses, yet he kept his report as thorough as ever.

The whole chain of events on that day was weird. At eight o'clock in the morning, the bank's Russian mothership had called and ordered Karikh to meet an unnamed client arriving from Istanbul. As usual, he hadn't asked any questions. A personal pickup by a vice president indicated not just a regular whale sighting but some commotion far beyond

Karikh's pay grade; doubly so when he was told to wear a specific hat so the client would recognize him. He had bought the hat and booked a Maybach from the bank's fleet just in case.

At the airport, Karikh had been waiting for a full hour when the news broke that the flight had been diverted to Minsk. He called the mothership; no one had a clue what was going on. He called the Aquarium and was told about the Basmanny operation in the broadest of strokes. It followed, then, that his own task had nothing to do with it.

Karikh knew who Anton was even before all of GRU did. He thought his early videos were hilarious. He had even shared a few of them on VKontakte and defended him in the comments—"Come on, the guy's not really a fag, it's all part of the act." Of course, once the little twerp decided he was immortal and started making fun of the Boss, Karikh had to delete every post. Why do all the funny ones turn out to be traitors?

An hour and a half later on Sunday, amid a growing media frenzy, the Istanbul flight had arrived. Karikh couldn't have felt stupider. Since he had no idea who to look for, the only thing he could do was stand around in a trucker cap. No one coming off the plane made eye contact. Was this a setup? A prank? Some kind of operational redundancy? For a second, he thought there was a tail on him, but that was just another gaggle of lib reporters jostling to get a shot. Finally, Karikh gave up. He'd been standing around for hours, so he needed to take a piss before leaving.

Whoever assaulted him was a midlevel pro with some experience: after that first blinding slam into the wall, the hits weren't terribly strong but landed in the right places. He had spoken Russian with a slight accent, but this was Riga. Everyone spoke Russian with a slight accent, even local Russians. Karikh concluded his report with educated guesses about the attacker's height and weight. The only part he kept out was his response to the beating; in this version, he had stayed stoically silent.

That last part nagged at Karikh a bit now as he appraised his two visitors. It was unlikely but not *entirely* out of the realm of possibility that they were here for him.

"The vault," finally said one of the men, producing a biometric key card. This was uncharted territory. EiropaBank did have some safe-deposit boxes, and some clients did use them, but never on the GRU side of things.

"Right this way, gentlemen," said Karikh. He led them downstairs, using his own card to open the vault's outer door, stepped aside to let them cross into the safe area, and was about to follow when Buzz Cut put his hand on his chest and softly pushed him back out into the hallway.

"Wait upstairs, please," said Unibrow, apparently responsible for the duo's verbal communication.

"But you need two cards to open—"

The second man snapped his fingers and opened his palm in one single gesture.

"Look," mumbled Karikh, "I think we're all adults here, but you guys have to understand, too. There are rules, guidelines—"

"Cornflower," said Unibrow, interrupting. It was Unit 29155's last call sign before scattering and re-forming in the wake of the Skripal fiasco. It had never made it into the media.

A live op, then. The best strategy in these cases was to get out of the way.

"Bluebottle," Karikh ruefully responded and placed his card in Buzz Cut's hand.

When the two men reemerged in the Prestizh Lounge, several minutes later, each was carrying a duffel the size of himself. Judging by their bodies' newfound rightward lean, the weight inside the bags was not paper. Buzz Cut put his down to return the key card to Karikh; it landed with a muted metallic thud.

"So, uh, gentlemen," said Karikh, in full customer-service mode, "would you require transportation? We have some very nice sedans on call."

"Thanks, we're good," said Unibrow. "It's around the corner."

■ ■ ■

On the screen, a distant MiG-29 streaked past an airplane window. "Holy shit," said a voice in Russian. The camera whipped around to show the speaker, a young woman in shades and a cap holding the phone and making an exaggerated *What?!!* face in several variations, to give herself choices during the edit.

"Great," Inga commented blandly. "Next one, please."

"Have some respect. Ari had to selflessly fuck her for this." Klaus closed the clip.

"Incorrect," said Falk. "I bought it from her first."

"That's somehow sadder," replied Inga. Falk glanced over, trying to gauge if she was even a slight bit upset. She wasn't. *Get it out of your head,* he thought. The woman was perfectly happy on her farm, with her pigs and an artist boyfriend who wasn't exactly a sculptor but ran a foundry for other sculptors.

Klaus opened the next video, and Falk flinched. Looking at him from the screen was Anton.

The metadata placed the clip at 10:41 a.m. on the fifteenth. The plane was on the tarmac in Minsk, and Anton had about twenty hours to live. At the moment, he may have feared it was even less; if he did, though, it didn't affect his poise. Standing in an aisle, he addressed other passengers as if recording a stand-up bit for one of his videos: "... *apologize for everything that's happening right now. I don't mean that it's my fault. I mean that someone probably diverted this flight because of me.*" He spoke in English, to make sure more people got the gist. "*But for you, that's good news. I'm pretty sure they're going to take me off the plane and send the rest of you on your way. So please just hang tight. That's all.*"

Someone shouted a question Falk couldn't hear. The camera reflexively panned toward them, then back to Anton midanswer. "*It seems so corny to say this. I told the truth? Jeez. But yeah, I told the truth. At least a little of it. The little I knew. And I tried to make it funny.*" He gave a little grin, directly into Lemminkainen's camera, and the video ended.

"Hang on," said Klaus, rewinding a bit. "The people in business class." Behind Anton's shoulder, a flight attendant walked toward the camera before turning around and running to the front door instead. As she did, several people in business got up from their seats. "*And I tried to make it funny,*" said Anton again.

"There," said Falk. "3C and 3D. That's our ghosts." 3C and 3D were the only two of the sixteen business-class seats listed as empty on the manifest. Yet there they were, a man and a woman, rising from both at the same time. Klaus zoomed in, looped the relevant section, and set it to play at one-third speed, so that the backs of two blurry heads kept ominously bobbing up into the shot. His hair was silver, hers jet-black.

"These two know what they're doing, too," said Inga. "There's a guy making a loud speech behind you and you're not even going to turn and look? It's because they know he's being filmed."

They watched the loop turn over in silence. A few iterations in, it became clear that, right before the video restarted, the woman's head showed a hint of leftward motion. Klaus nudged the end point; Anton's shoulder immediately got in the way. Klaus stopped the video and went frame by frame.

"Come on," mumbled Falk to a stranger's pixelated nape. "Say what you want to say to him. Say it." The woman's head turned left five, ten, fifteen degrees as her lips neared her companion's ear. Just as the tip of

63

her nose cleared the cheek line, however, the obstruction overtook the screen again.

"Is this workable?" asked Inga. "Klaus? Isn't there some AI bullshit that can reconstruct a face from this angle?"

"I am my own AI bullshit," mumbled Klaus, zooming in even farther, to the in-flight entertainment screen in front of the man in 3C—which, unlike the woman's, was not showing a flight map but was switched completely off. The moment she discreetly leaned toward her companion, half her face rose like the moon in its reflection. "There. You're welcome."

Even at this low resolution, Falk could make out large, somewhat close-set eyes and a long thin nose. A Modigliani type. "God bless twelve megapixels," said Klaus, taking a screenshot. "Now give me a minute to fuck with some blurs and masks, and we should be good to go."

"You rule," said Falk, patting Klaus's shoulder. "Really excellent work," said Inga at the same time. Klaus swiveled in his seat, grinning ear to ear.

Within half an hour, he had put the mystery woman's portrait through enough smart filters that it began to resemble a passport photo. Unable to contribute anything to this phase of the work, Falk decided that the best use of his time would be to get the team some lunch, and ordered sandwiches. Inga busied herself with her direct duties—hand-holding the director of a Russian student theater troupe who had staged a reading of political prisoners' courtroom speeches and was told to leave the country or join their ranks as a result. Falk felt a pang of gratitude toward Harlow for pulling him off this desk, even though he realized it was not charity but a rational management call.

"Okay," said Klaus, feeding the picture to his facial-recognition bot. "Moment of truth. Actually, uh, sorry, more like a few minutes of truth. The results are garbage so far." The bot spat back a dozen under-30-percent matches, which were little more than statistical noise.

The ding of the Wolt app informed Falk that the courier with their sandwiches was downstairs. Sokol Media Research's legitimate front allowed it to accept deliveries like any normal business, but Falk liked to err on the side of caution and set the address at the ice cream kiosk across the street, at the edge of the park, which had the added advantage of being clearly visible from their balcony. Plus, it sold ice cream.

"I'll go get it," he said.

"Let me," said Inga, getting up. "You paid for it."

Falk nodded, went out onto the balcony, and checked if the courier was in place. A biker in a cyan uniform pedaled up to the kiosk and dismounted. A few seconds later, Inga emerged from the building's over-decorated entrance, three stories below the balcony, and paused on the sidewalk before crossing the nearly empty street. Falk watched the top of her blond head dutifully swivel left and right.

As she stepped off the pavement and onto the cobblestone, a man carrying a large duffel bag walked up to the building behind her back, caught the still-closing front door, and went in. What made Falk tense up more than the duffel was the precision of the timing. Another man with a similar bag rounded the corner of Strēlnieku, heading toward the same entrance. Falk had seen enough.

"Klaus," he said, stepping back into the room. "Code red. Save your work. Klaus!!"

The German was hunched over his desk with noise-canceling headphones on, fine-tuning the parameters of the ghost photo. Falk simply tore them off his head and threw them into a corner while on his way to the closet.

"What the fuck?!" yelled Klaus, turning around. By the time he did, Falk had already opened the closet, typed in a short PIN to the inside safe, and was taking out the handguns: a SIG Sauer P229 and his own CZ-75. After that, Klaus needed no further instructions. He dropped the mystery woman's photo into their internal dropbox, threw a master switch that turned off all electronics in the office at once, and took the SIG Sauer. Falk, CZ in hand, was calling Inga's mobile. The creak of the building's ancient wooden elevator drifted across the wall, receding downward; someone had called it to the ground floor.

Inga picked up, annoyed. "*I know, I know*, I'll get the ice cream too."

"Stay where you are. Don't come back in. If you hear shots, run and follow protocol." Falk hung up before giving himself a chance to add anything sentimental. He was tempted to dash back to the balcony and check if she complied, but there was no time. He turned back to Klaus.

"You. Take up position on the landing half a floor up. I'm staying here."

"Nope," said Klaus. "I need to be able to fuck it." This time, his idiom usage was fully appropriate to the context. Klaus kept the hard drives to the back-office computers inside a single enclosure, equipped with a mechanical fail-safe: one push of a button at the top dropped the whole stack into a hydrochloric acid bath. Years ago, someone, most likely Klaus himself, festooned the button with a red sticker reading *fuck it*. Falk immediately knew what he meant.

"I can push a damn button," said Falk. "Go. You have ten seconds." Outside, elevator cables sang as the cabin began to rise.

"Who said I was going to let you? I *want* to push it."

"Jesus, fine." Falk lingered at the front door. "Watch the SIG, it's double-action. The first pull is very long."

"*Verpiss dich*," said Klaus and shoved him outside.

The building's stairwell was an archetypal old-Europe affair, with wide, worn steps winding around a wrought-iron elevator cage. Falk bounded up toward the fourth floor just as the elevator stopped on the third. The doors opened.

The two men had used the time to lighten their duffels considerably.

Each was now wearing a massive Kevlar vest and carrying a ShAK-12 bull-pup assault rifle. Plug-ugly, FSB-commissioned monstrosities, designed for brutal urban warfare and nothing else, they told most of the story at once.

The elevator shuddered and crept back down to the first floor. Falk held his breath, peering through the shaft's frilly art nouveau ironwork at the landing below. The men stood to the left and the right of the office door, momentarily making Falk think they were waiting for someone else to join them. He realized he was wrong only once he heard the rifles' safeties clicking off in stereo.

These fuckers were going to shoot through the walls.

The only tactical advantage Falk could possibly have against this kind of indiscriminate killing power was expiring in about a second. He wasn't good enough to line up a shot through the elevator shaft. The sound of his running steps would give the attackers enough time to turn around. This left one option.

Falk lay on his stomach atop the curved wooden railing, pushed off, and half slid down—headfirst, right foot barely tapping the stairs. The moment his sightline cleared the corner of the elevator shaft, he twisted his torso to the left and opened fire.

The blond attacker's head threw a red halo onto the wall, hitting the brass plaque with the Sokol Media Research logo. Startled, the other, dark-haired one squeezed the trigger and only then pivoted toward the action, so that his first rounds tore through the office door and the wall over his partner's collapsing body before finally fanning out in Falk's direction.

Falk rolled back behind the shaft and shot twice just to buy himself an extra second to think. His only chance for survival was to keep climbing the stairs. He scrambled to his feet. The attacker unloaded at him directly through the shaft cage, heavy subsonic rounds tearing up cast iron in a shower of sparks; thankfully, two layers of prewar metalwork were enough to screw up the trajectories. Right at that moment, the bullet-riddled door to the office flew open. The killer turned. So did Falk. The next thing they saw was Klaus stepping out onto the landing, screaming, and squeezing the trigger into the attacker's face.

As Falk had tried to warn the German, the first shot from a double-action pistol took an extra quarter second. It was the quarter second Klaus didn't have. A nearly point-blank burst lifted him off the ground and threw his body—by that moment it was already a body—back into the room.

A floor and a half up, Falk froze, but not in grief; that would come later. He realized that, if the assassin went inside the office, he might be able to dash down and grab his dead partner's rifle. The same thought seemingly occurred to the attacker. The man looked around, calculating if he could afford the luxury of walking over, reaching down, and taking the second ShAK without being sniped from upstairs. He and Falk exchanged blind shots, keeping each other away from the well. Then the elevator began to climb again.

Whoever was in there was either a civilian or the attackers' backup. Falk watched the counterweight travel downward past him, the dusty top of the cabin rise into view, hoping all the while it wouldn't stop on the third floor.

It didn't. But as it passed, the killer lifted his rifle and unloaded the rest of the magazine straight into the cabin.

When the smoke, dust, and echoes subsided, it was a miracle that the elevator kept moving at all. It creaked past Falk, half its back wall missing. The lights inside were shot out; he couldn't see the inevitable body. As if in a trance, Falk trotted up the stairs alongside the cabin—partly to keep it between himself and the attacker, partly because of the terrible premonition of what he'd find once it stopped.

The elevator came to rest on the sixth and last floor. The left door panel slid open with a repulsive slipping noise, the right spasmed in the closed position. Falk peered in, steeling himself.

The barrage of bullets had disfigured Inga's torso and head almost beyond recognition, but even in death her pose remained her own. Gawky, defiant. A bit too big a presence for any square space, not just the one that became her coffin. Both her hands were still clutching a subcompact Beretta.

Falk took it—unclenching her still-warm fingers felt painful—mumbled "goodbye" in Latvian and crept downstairs, suddenly very aware of the silence in the building. He could hear the excited exclamations on the street outside, the faint sine wave of a distant police siren getting closer. By the time he reached the fourth floor, the quiet became almost oppressive.

Then he got down to the third and saw the reason. The dark-haired assassin's body lay sprawled face up across the landing, eyes wide, a small neat hole bisecting his unibrow. Amid the wall-tearing thunder of the ShAK fire, no one, least of all the killer himself, heard the single perfect shot delivered from a moving elevator.

Falk walked into the office and said a similar goodbye to Klaus. The nose-burning acid odor, mixing in with the smells of blood and torn-up drywall, meant that the German had destroyed all drives before stepping out. "At least you got to press the *fuck it* button," muttered Falk. The sirens were louder now.

He wiped and dropped Inga's gun and switched his with Klaus's, deleting himself from future reconstructions of the shootout. Then he grabbed some things in the office and a bag to carry them, photographed the dead assassins' faces on his phone, and took the service stairs down. Among a dozen or so bicycles parked in the backyard was one he'd placed there months before, uncovetably ugly and with a food-delivery bag over the back wheel. Inside the bag was a courier's uniform. Falk put it on top of his dusty clothes, shoved the rest of his things in instead, pulled up the hood, and pedaled out onto Pulkveža Brieža Street just as four police cars converged behind him upon the corner of Elizabetes and Strēlnieku.

As a rule, people didn't pay enough attention to delivery guys to notice if one was in tears as he rode; and if they did, then he certainly wouldn't be the first.

1986:
TERRIBLE BODIES,
EXCELLENT OPTICS

Pavlik woozily slapped his neck, sat upright, and only then opened his eyes. The mosquito that woke him up was now a silvery smudge on his palm, streaked with his own blood. The ceiling crawled with its more timid brethren, all waiting for the sleeper to extend a limb from under the three blankets.

Pavlik and his parents lived—or were staying? eleven months in, the terms had blurred—on the ground floor of a crumbling beachside apartment complex. Every other story had access to the balconies that girded the building's perimeter, and the top two could claim a Tyrrhenian Sea view, but the only thing the family's one-bedroom overlooked was a concrete parking bay. Humidity coursed through the walls, making every surface perspire and giving ten degrees Celsius in Ladispoli more bite than minus twenty had back in Moscow. Two cheap heaters glowed by the bed; the landlady had said not to leave them on overnight, but it was hard to imagine anything catching on fire in a place this dank. Pavlik wiped his hand on the top blanket. It felt cold, wet, or both.

They couldn't complain, not really. The American Jewish Joint Distribution Committee, which everyone just called the Joint, paid the rent—as it did for most of the eight thousand Soviet Jews currently scattered throughout the Roman suburbs awaiting admission into the US. The Joint also ran a free school, bombarding yesterday's Young Pioneers with a curriculum of things they'd need most in the new life: English and Judaism. It was technically voluntary but, either out of obligation or to imbue refugee life with something resembling order, everyone went. Pavlik himself had started skipping classes only recently—once he discovered The Thing.

Ladispoli was a town out of time. No one who ended up here knew how long this surreal phase would take: all immigration casework was done stateside by another charity, the Hebrew Immigrant Aid Society. Some families blew in and out of town in weeks, others stuck around for years. Anyone, at any point, could give up the wait and accept immediate free repatriation to Israel, but, to the schoolteachers' chagrin, most stubbornly held out for the US.

In Pavlik's family, the Israel talk cropped up exactly once, a month or so earlier, and led to the loudest fight between his parents Pavlik ever heard. As far as his dad was concerned, getting out of the Soviet Union was the hard part, and the rest didn't matter as much. His work—as an engineer at a state research lab attached to a refrigerator factory—placed him close enough to military technologies that his application for an exit visa had been refused the first four times. Mom, a high school English teacher, lived and breathed America since her first James Fenimore Cooper novel; she spent the week in an Austrian transit camp, the first stop of their exodus, reciting Longfellow's "The Song of Hiawatha" to Pavlik from memory. They arrived in Ladispoli on December 31, aboard a train guarded by Uzi-toting soldiers Israel had lent for the occasion. The apartment came with a small black-and-white TV. An Italian New Year's special was on, with topless dancers, which seemed to then fourteen-year-old Pavlik like the most extravagantly Western thing in the world. America seemed hours, not days, away.

And now it was eleven months later, and the cold and the mosquitos were back.

It wasn't all bad. There were movie nights, and a beach with coarse black sand, and football with wild-haired Italian kids who were miraculously up for a game at any time of day or night, as if they had no homework to do or parents to yell at them to do it. There were cheap bus excursions to Venice and Rome proper, with Russian-speaking volunteer tour guides. There were even girls, for those who had the nerve to invite one out for ice cream and the lira to pay for it. And there was The Thing, the one he skipped Hebrew school for.

Pavlik got up and made his way to the door, still wearing one of the blankets like a toga. The trick was to jump from the bedroom carpet straight onto the bathroom mat, without letting your feet touch the ice-cold cement floor of the hallway. He made the jump, brushed his teeth with West German toothpaste, and did everything else a fifteen-year-old does in the shower. When he got out, Mom was in the hallway, looking alarmed if not harried.

"Dress quick," she said. "We've got a guest and he wants to see you."

Pavlik dove back into the bedroom, pulled on a pair of jeans, put his T-shirt on inside out, took it off, put it on backward, took it off. *Please, please, please, don't let it be the police or the Carabinieri.* He steadied his breath until the terror gripping him could pass for normal teenage angst. Then he put on the shirt the right way, and walked out.

The living room doubled as the parents' bedroom. For the past eleven months, Mom and Dad slept on a foldout sofa, because the bed was too small for two and they couldn't afford a new one. Most of the days, they'd just leave it out; this morning, it was folded and covered, with cushions back in place. Seated on the sofa was an unfamiliar man of about thirty-five, with a square jaw and Robert Redford hair, dressed in tan slacks and a decidedly un-Italian bomber jacket. Dad sat somewhat awkwardly across, on a kitchen chair.

Even before the man said a word, there was no doubt in Pavlik's mind that he was an American. The hunch only grew stronger once he got up, flashed a grin, and shook Pavlik's hand. When he spoke, however, it was in accented but decent Russian.

"Good morning, Pavel," he said. "Rex Harlow, US State Department. Fantastic to meet you. Your dad and I have been chatting about some things." He patted the sofa next to him.

Pavlik sat down, dizzy with relief. He knew what this was. Everyone knew. All ex-Soviets in Ladispoli who used to work in sensitive industries got these visitors once in a while: CIA men, the rumor went, feeling around for state secrets and dual-use technologies. The USSR wasn't supposed to let anyone privy to such things emigrate—hell, those places barely hired Jews for that exact reason, on top of the everyday anti-Semitism—but the smarter ones managed to slip out anyway. Pavlik may have been only fourteen when he left, but he had already absorbed the main lesson of Soviet life: everything was bullshit. Here was the workers' paradise where an engineer would grovel before a manager of a produce warehouse for a sack of black-market tangerines. Here was the multi-ethnic utopia where a kid with curly hair and a wrong last name would be brutalized daily, with teachers pretending nothing happened, until he befriended two of the school's scariest hooligans. You could always find a way out.

"I'm so sorry but that's all we've got," said Mom, lowering a heavy tray onto the coffee table. She had put together some idealized touring-company version of Russian teatime, with raspberry jam, taralli in place of *sushki*, and tea in red-and-gold china cups they had brought along for some reason. Pavlik realized, with distaste, that she was trying very hard to impress Harlow.

"Oh, that takes me back," said Harlow, picking up and admiring a cup with a painted rooster. He took a sip. "How do you even find good Assam in Italy? There's not a tea drinker on the whole damn boot."

Mom beamed. *Ugh.* "There's a grocery in town that started catering to Russians."

"It still feels so odd, saying 'Russians' like that," said Dad. "No one in *Russia* would call us Russians. We'd always be Jews to them."

"Well, you better get ready," said Harlow. "We're not a nation known for nuance. You might even get a couple of 'commies' thrown your way once you get stateside."

"If we ever do," mumbled Pavlik.

Harlow studied him for a few moments. Then he put down the tea, in a gesture that suggested the preamble was over and a real conversation was about to begin.

"Hey, son, is that an NES console I see over there?" he suddenly asked, nodding at the gray box by the TV set. *Guess we're still in the preamble,* Pavlik thought.

"Yup."

"What's your favorite game? Mario? Zelda?"

"I like Metroid."

"Don't know that one." Harlow turned to Pavlik's parents. "Did you get him that for his birthday or something?"

"Of course not," said Mom. "I barely understand what that thing does. Pavlik got it at a flea market."

"A flea market," Harlow repeated. "I see. And do you know how much that thing *costs*?"

Shit, shit, shit.

"Um . . . Five dollars? Ten?"

"One hundred and fifty," said Harlow. "Plus the games. Sounds like someone in this household has come into a little bit of cash."

Mom clamped her hand to her mouth. Dad just sat there. Pavlik stared at his feet, feeling tentacles of panic sprout from somewhere behind his solar plexus.

"You're not in trouble, son," said Harlow. "Relax." He raised his right palm, held it stiff for a moment, locking onto a target, then expertly killed a mosquito on his left wrist. "I just want you to tell your folks how you got the money."

Pavlik didn't respond. "Okay, guess I will, then. There seems to be a popular rumor among the Russians—hope you don't mind me using the term"—Harlow smiled at Dad—"that some everyday Soviet items cost a lot more in the West than they do back home. So refugees stock up on this stuff before they leave, and try to sell it here in Italy. Army watches, binoculars, cameras, shawls. Fur hats. Commemorative pins and such. Fine china"—he lifted the rooster teacup again.

"We're no peddlers," said Dad sharply, using the pejorative *torgashi*. "Those are for us."

"Oh, I can tell. Anyway, in most cases, these rumors are dead wrong. And even when they're not, schlepping to the market and back every Sunday is almost not worth the effort, right? Unless . . . unless some enterprising teen buys it off you right here in Ladispoli and takes it to Rome all at once."

"During school hours you do this?!" gasped Mom.

"But that's not all," said Harlow. "In order to make any kind of real money, one always has to know what to sell and what to skip. You see," he continued, addressing the parents in an almost professorial manner, "one of those rumors is *half* right. Soviet cameras and binoculars have terrible bodies but excellent optics. Not just excellent; *indistinguishable* from West German, ever since you guys helped yourselves to the Zeiss factory equipment in 1945. So, yes, one could go to a flea market and sell a Russian camera for, say, thirty dollars. Or one could screw out the lens and sell it to a photo *repair* shop, as Zeiss, for a hundred. And that, Mr. and Mrs. Obrandt, is what your son did—about twenty-five times, I believe."

"Pavlik, that's disgusting. You're a profiteer," said Mom. "Sir, what can we do to fix this?"

Pavlik sat silent. Ballooning in his mind was a fully formed realization that, if this turned out to be the reason the family were denied entry to the US, he would kill himself.

"Fix this?!" guffawed Harlow. "What your kid did was goddamned brilliant! He created *value*. This took smarts, initiative, research, and, from what I can tell, a decent command of Italian. If anything, both of you should be proud."

"I'm not," said Dad through gritted teeth. "I'm mortified. We didn't run away from anti-Semites so our own son could embody the worst Jewish stereotypes."

Perhaps because he had nothing to lose, perhaps because he felt that the strange American was on his side, something tore loose inside Pavlik. "Stop with this Soviet crap!" he yelled, jumping off the sofa. "You think being an engineer is so noble? They've brainwashed you, Dad! You think you're this big dissident because you don't like the Afghan war or something, but you're no less of a *sovok* than any of them! You drank up all their poison, all their bullshit! No wonder the Americans are not taking you—why do you even *want* to go? What do you think America *is*?!" Out of breath and shaking, he grabbed his head in his hands, ran the length of the short hallway to the bedroom, slammed the door, and fell into the damp blankets face-first.

"I am so, so sorry," said Mom. "He's normally not like—" She stopped herself because Harlow was laughing, a high, clear, free laugh. "You've got a great kid, Mrs. Obrandt," he said, putting his hand on her shoulder. "Hoo boy. You, too, sir. Trust me, you have nothing to worry about. So glad I stopped by. Man oh man." Still giggling, he collected his hat, zipped up his bomber jacket, and left. Four days later, a form letter from the US Embassy in Rome informed the Obrandts that the INS had processed their immigration case and invited them in for an entrance interview.

CHAPTER THREE

Like many Home Counties family men for generations before him, Alan Keegan kept a secret bedsit in London, in a stock-brick Victorian off Clapham Common. Most of those men used theirs for entertaining company; Keegan used his to code. It was also a convenient intake point for death threats, which were a regular by-product of his work and which he'd rather not have arrive in the post alongside his sons' school reports.

The enterprise that made Keegan's name and filled his days, FleaCollar, was an OSINT project. Open-source intelligence relied on two notions: one, that enough photo, video, and bureaucratic data existed out in the open to reconstruct almost any event and debunk almost any lie; and two, that thousands of people around the globe were bored or outraged enough to do this for free. The result bobbed in uncharted waters: part journalism, part activism, part counterespionage, and part online gaming. Every morning, up to half a million anonymous users logged on to Keegan's site to browse a list of mysteries to solve and official claims to fact-check. They then picked a favorite and got to work, in a kind of high-stakes egg hunt through all the world's digital noise.

To a public obsessed with deepfakes and false flags, FleaCollar offered something irrefutable. Here's the minister's statement that he never set foot at that address—and there's the CCTV image of him arriving, dashcam footage of him leaving, and his wristwatch on a disembodied arm in a photo posted from the location and captioned *our weekiversary* in the interim. Anyone who doubted the data was welcome to check for themselves.

The big mystery, as always, was the overall motive. Unlike corporate snitch apps such as Citizen, FleaCollar wasn't helping to uphold the status quo; unlike WikiLeaks, it wasn't trying to upend it. Its closest relatives were ProPublica and Bellingcat, but FleaCollar never turned its findings into pithy prose or catchy YouTube videos. So who the hell was Alan Keegan, and who did he work for?

The actual answers were "a forty-three-year-old nerd who genuinely believed in things like integrity" and "no one." The questions were fair, though. Weeks after the project's 2016 launch, Keegan was being courted by every big media company and intelligence agency in the world. The former claimed to share his goals—"just keep doing what you're doing!"—while salivating over his volunteer network; the latter, with varying degrees of finesse, attempted to remake FleaCollar into a witting or unwitting clearinghouse for their own causes. Some fed him disinfo. Others openly asked how big of a payday it would take for him to pack it in.

Keegan ignored all entreaties. Only one suitor, an evident CIA operative using the handle Catweazle, made him briefly consider replying, because his approach was cleverer than most—he reached out through an obscure music board Keegan frequented—and his message read like it was written by a live human being:

Dear Alan,

I'm not going to beat around the bush. You do 80% of what we do for 1% of the money, and better. You don't need us; we need you. The problem is, the moment we touch you, you become us, and then everyone loses. Right now I am basically the major-label A&R guy trying to sign an indie band whose whole appeal is that they're not on a label. So, in the end, this is just a fan letter. But do let me know if you ever find yourself in need of that other 20% of what we do.

—Catweazle

Keegan emerged from the Tube, tapping his AirPods to nudge down the volume now that train noise wasn't messing with the music. In his ears was one of his favorite albums, *The Oliver Twist Manifesto* by Luke Haines, which he tended to play on repeat when he was nervous about something and needed a psych-up. Later that day, FleaCollar would be publishing an investigation into a prominent Polish politician's neo-Nazi past, and some Polish hackers were already launching DDoS attacks at its servers. Keegan mentally prepared himself to spend the day fighting them off at the network perimeter, adding filter after filter or, if things got really bad, diverting all traffic through a scrubber. It wasn't his first rodeo.

It's a beautiful night for treason, Haines crooned to a trip-hop beat. Keegan crossed the high street, cut through a sliver of park, and turned right onto the oddly named The Chase, toward his lair.

The man in front of the house was dark-haired, somewhere between IC2 and IC6 in police profiling parlance, and visibly tired. He sat on the bottom step of the entrance with his knees together, which gave him a nonthreatening look that may have been a choice. Keegan took out the AirPods and slowed his steps. He'd had his share of crazies drop by.

This one didn't look like a neo-Nazi, but then again, neither did the Polish politician. His sweat-drenched T-shirt read *Yeah Yeah Yeahs*, or rather used to read that a few hundred washes ago. This, too, thought Keegan, was perhaps a piece of nonverbal I-come-in-peace communication aimed, a little too squarely, at him.

He stole a glance at the CCTV camera mounted on a lamppost across the street, wondering if it had a good view of the visitor. Perhaps the smart thing to do would be to keep walking to Wandsworth Road, turn the corner, and jump into a cab. He had almost resolved to do just that, when the intruder lifted his head and spoke up.

"Hi," he said, in a flat American accent obvious from a single syllable. "You might know me as Catweazle. And I could really use your help."

■ ■ ■

Falk was pretty sure Keegan would recognize him. The bloody attack on Sokol Media Research was leading regional news for the second day in a row. In the official version of the events, Falk was in Berlin when it happened, but he still had to put out a statement as the head of the company. He forced himself to write a few words about shutting down operations and taking some time to grieve, both of which happened to be true.

The Latvians identified the assassins as mercenaries from ChVK Orlok, a Russian private military contractor. The Agency analyzed Falk's photos of the dead men's faces and concurred. With the ID came a plausible motive: three months earlier, a news site supported by Sokol Media Research ran a story on Orlok's atrocities in Angola. The site's editors had been on the run ever since the publication. Still, the brazenness of the assault—a daytime gunfight in the center of an EU member nation's capital—was so overwhelming that even the group's leader, Andrei "Count Orlok" Druzhinin, condemned it in an unheard-of gesture and called the two men "unstable individuals" who had been let go from the company a year earlier.

Much less explicable than the attack itself was the fact that two untrained journalists fought it off well enough to send both assailants into the grave with one clean head shot each. A media dive into Klaus's biography revealed a 1980s stint in the Bundeswehr, so he was designated the gunslinger hero and Inga the tragic victim. Some people even left flowers at the entrance to the building.

On reality's clandestine flip side, things weren't that different from the approved narrative. The Soft Unit, like its hapless front Sokol Media Research, was no more. Moscow Station would be taking over its mission as well as the investigation of both the Riga attack and the Flight TQ77 incident, though the latter was quickly receding in everyone's rearview. In the meantime, Deputy Director Harlow had Falk sent to London for two weeks of mandatory R and R. After this, he was to go back to Langley and await reassignment. The Russia phase of his career was over.

Falk loved London, fully aware that the feeling was unrequited. Unlike New York, which made it a point of pride to ignore its tourists altogether, London embraced the visitor with an enthusiasm that felt like a subtler kind of contempt: *we'll sell you a decoy of everything that makes us us, and you'll only feel like more of an intruder as a result.* He saw through the scam, and still bought in. Falk loved the weight of the city, the almost geological layering of iron and brick—the accrued monumentality of a place that's never seen a real regime change. It was comforting to know he could buy an umbrella at the same store where Oscar Wilde or Kim Philby bought theirs. He loved, too, the prickly new life sprouting between the mossy stones: the music, the clothes, the Multicultural London English pushing out old Cockney. The sense of everyone play-acting just a bit, performing a class, a gender, an accent, a pedigree, a walk. It made him feel right at home with his own form of character work. To be a Brit was to be a bit of a spy, and to be a spy was to be a bit of a Brit.

Harlow had arranged a nice house in Pimlico for the duration. It came courtesy of the Cousins, a term MI6 used to call the CIA in novels until both sides adopted it in reality. As a return courtesy, Falk would sit down with one of the Cousins for a quick debrief as soon as his emotional state allowed. He scheduled this ritual on the very first night, just to get it out of the way.

The agent in charge was a very young, very well-dressed man named Stuart Akinyemi. His cobalt Ozwald Boateng suit reminded Falk of his own embarrassing dandy period, though Akinyemi was pulling it off with much more aplomb. It was during their perfectly pleasant chat, over the course of which precisely zero information of value changed hands, that the Brit casually mentioned FleaCollar ("Isn't that kind of what you were doing in Riga?").

"I've followed them a bit," said Falk, "and I'm afraid they are our polar opposite on at least three fronts. They're not a spookshop, what they do actually matters, and they're still alive." If Akinyemi was writing up his psych eval later, as Falk suspected, this quote would surely make its centerpiece.

It also gave him an idea. Next day, Falk found himself on an hour-long jog across the Vauxhall Bridge, all the way to Clapham, and choosing to rest in the vicinity of a particular house he remembered from 2016. The day after that, he did it again, and this time didn't leave until he saw the man he was there to see.

Keegan studied Falk's face, blinking fast behind a pair of wire-rimmed glasses. "I'm not sure how I can help," he finally said.

"You can make me some tea," said Falk, getting up.

Keegan glanced to the side. "Why don't we walk to the Common and talk there."

"See," Falk replied, "this is how I know you're not a spy: you picked a block with the *most* CCTV. I have, however, taken the liberty of disabling the camera you keep looking at."

"And this is supposed to make me feel safer?"

"Kind of. Lately, people I'm seen talking to tend to die."

Keegan tensed up, evidently taking this for an intimidation attempt, but the very next moment his eyes went wide with recognition. The man truly had no poker face. "Sokol Media Research? The thing in Riga, they were after you?"

"Yup."

"Jesus. All right, come in." Keegan unlocked the front door and held it open. Falk walked inside.

The house smelled like old wood and insect killer. Keegan led him to a small semibasement apartment in the back, which took up the area where a traditional English home would have the kitchen. The studio, painted clinical white, held a twin mattress in one corner, a Tiffany lamp, an electric kettle, and stacks of computer drives. A set of sliding doors opened up to a yard with a lichen-covered angel statue.

"I'm sorry about your colleagues," said Keegan, filling the kettle. He seemed to have taken the tea request literally.

"Thanks."

"This is why we never put contributors' names on our investigations. If anyone wants FleaCollar taken out, this is the house and I am the guy." He stopped himself and went deep red in the face. "This is horrible, I— I am so sorry. I didn't mean to sound hectoring."

"It's no problem," said Falk. "To be frank, I'm not convinced it was about our work. My hunch is that whoever is doing this is just eliminating witnesses."

Keegan's eyebrows flew up. "Witnesses to what?"

Falk inhaled and exhaled. What he was about to say would be the most egregious breach of protocol in his entire career, worse than beating up Karikh; worse than if he had pressed send on that drunk rambling letter to Inga that still sat in his drafts folder, having outlived its addressee. He would be reading in not just a civilian but a foreign national. And yet, at the moment, this seemed like the only way forward.

"Have you heard of Anton Basmanny?"

"Of course. Poor bloke. They disappeared him, didn't they."

"My organization," said Falk, "is of that opinion as well. He messed with the GRU; they pulled him off a flight, found out he worked with us, and decided to send us a message. So far, so logical."

Keegan nodded. The water in the kettle began to boil.

"The guys who shot up our office three days ago were ChVK Orlok, which could mean anyone in the Kremlin orbit. You want a party, they're the catering company. The public version is, they got angry about a story we did. A working one is that, after Anton, the GRU used them to *really* drive the point home."

"This seems a bit much," Keegan volunteered, "though who knows with these people."

"Exactly," said Falk. "Now, here's the same chain of events from *my* angle. I was with Anton in his last moments. Anton told me he saw two more passengers taken off the flight—an American man and a woman who weren't on the manifest. Then he was dead. I told my colleagues, who started searching for them. Then *they* were dead."

"Correlation, not causation," said Keegan.

"Absolutely. So it shouldn't bother you that here I am, telling it to you. Right?"

The kettle loudly beeped and turned off. From the way Keegan started, it must have bothered him at least a little.

"Wait," said Keegan. "Holy shit. You don't know which side is doing this."

"I, uh . . ." Falk paused. Hearing it like this made it realer than he liked. "It's worth considering every possibility."

"And I'm the only person you know who is one hundred percent opposed to working with spies. So, naturally, you're asking me to work with you."

"I thought this might combine two of your passions," said Falk. "Sifting through large amounts of data and humiliating the CIA."

"Well, fuck me," said Keegan. "Do you take yours with milk? Because I, uh, don't have any."

■ ■ ■

OLHÃO
AUGUST 23, 2021

The funk of low tide mixed with charcoal. The combination was acrid but not entirely unpleasant; Maya could easily imagine some edgy Japanese fragrance brand bottling it, under a name like Dead Sardine. She paid the driver, grabbed her bag from the hot back seat of the taxi, and stepped out onto the calçada sidewalk.

From what she'd read about Olhão on the way—mostly Wikipedia, to be honest—the town was, like herself, a case of peaking too early. Once a fishing industry hub, it was now a pretty but sleepy spot for local vacationers and British retirees. Among Maya's pre-rehab social cohort, for whom Saint-Tropez and Amalfi were too cliché, Portugal was quite on trend lately, but not this part. They'd find nothing here to pose against—by design, it seemed. Olhão's uncoolness looked almost defiant. Only the ornate houses along the main drag, which was called Avenida da República but which everyone called simply the Avenida, because it was the only one in town, held some vestiges of old glory. One of those houses was now, inexplicably, hers.

She still couldn't believe she had done what she did. Her mother would probably explain her absence at the funeral with the usual euphemisms she'd mastered during Maya's other disappearances: *exhaustion, fragile, overwhelmed.* In fairness, Maya didn't think anyone would be too scandalized. It was just that kind of funeral: no body, no coffin, no daughter. Just a blown-up photo on an easel and the widow in a black pantsuit, holding court and keeping it together almost too well. This was as much a shareholder event as anything else, meant to bolster confidence or, more precisely, to hide panic. Half the people in the room would be Obrandt's investors. Even as they offered their condolences, the question of money would hang in the air.

The hardest part, and the only one Maya felt guilty about missing, would be to see Baba Polina, Obrandt's mother, oblivious and wheeled around by a nurse. Obrandt had always kept his parents separate from his American family. As soon as he made his first million—in the mid-1990s, barely older than Maya was now—he bought them a house in Palm Springs, but what looked like a tribute turned out to be a payoff. He had barely visited ever since, even after his father died in '99. Maya spent some time at Grandma's when she was very small, but once she turned six or so, Obrandt cut off all communication between them. She didn't know why and didn't think to ask: all Baba Polina did was read her boring Russian poems about animals anyway. Maya preferred the army of aunties on the family's Taiwanese side. And then it was too late.

Is this what he did with her now? A house as a final fuck-you? Was this how he cast people aside?

The address read 12 Rua da Unpronounceable, so it must have been off the Avenida. She turned a corner and saw it—an ochre two-story cube with a white balustrade along the roof, in a style she had just learned was called Pombaline.

The housekeeper, a Romanian woman who said she used to work for the previous owner, had met her at the airport, delivering the keys and, thankfully, no condolences. Obrandt had bought the house in the name of a company he set up the same day, and the appearance in Olhão of one Maya Chou stayed unconnected to the fading news story about some rich American who drowned off the coast.

She turned the key in the tough lock, using both hands, and walked in. Most of the ground floor consisted of one large room, with a vaulted ceiling and tilework that made her think, for some reason, of a dentist's office. The seller had left behind some furniture—a busted couch, mismatched chairs, a laminate dining table. This wasn't a billionaire con man's hideaway. The space still held traces of a normal life, rudely displaced by what she imagined was a sudden, above-the-market offer.

She walked from the living room to the kitchen, idly opening and closing drawers. A lone knife in one, a take-out menu from an Indian restaurant in another. Her father may have gone through the same motions ten days ago, perhaps while holding the same key she held now. Then he signed some papers, hopped on a yacht, and stepped into the sea. Was *this* the message? Did he trick her into coming to see what he saw on his last day on earth, perhaps to feel what he felt? But how could she? She barely knew the guy. The thought came to Maya in this exact form, jarring her. "I barely knew the guy," she said out loud, her voice echoing off the bare walls.

On the second floor was a bathroom, with a chipped clawfoot tub, and two bedrooms. The housekeeper had bought a set of cheap linens and left it in the slightly larger one. Maya mechanically made the bed, though sleeping in it seemed like a weird proposition. She felt a strong urge to get out. The only still-unexplored area was the rooftop, accessible via outside stairs from a tiny back terrace; purely as due diligence, she climbed up.

Suddenly, the appeal of the house was clearer. The view, despite the modest two-story height, took Maya's breath away. The town lay before her, all whitewashed walls and red shingles, sloping toward the greenish waters of the Ria Formosa. A pterodactyl-size stork took off from the nearby church belfry and made a slow circle over the roofs. Its mate in the nest rapidly clicked its beak, producing a rat-a-tat not unlike distant gunfire, if gunfire could sound pensive. Maya found herself smiling vaguely, as she once would when an edible hit just right. She felt very alone and very calm.

Besides herself, the only object on the roof was a rusty beach chair, turned seaward where, in a few hours, the sun would set. On its sagging seat lay a large conch-shell ashtray, holding down a piece of paper whose edges flapped with every wind gust. Maya lifted the shell, barely catching the paper—it immediately tried to escape on the wind—and sat down.

One side contained a cheesy flier for a boat-charter company in Albufeira, promising *unforgettable snorkeling, onboard snacks, and welcome bubbles*. The other side made her drop the ashtray.

It was a letter, in Russian, handwritten in a spiky script she'd known all her life from Post-it notes and permission slips.

Дочка, привет.

Прости, что так. Прости, что поздно. Прости вообще за всё.

Если я достаточно хорошо тебя знаю и правильно всё рассчитал, ты приехала сюда одна, а с момента моей смерти вряд ли прошло больше пары недель. Наверное, глупо покупать целый дом в качестве конверта и марки к этому письму, но ничего умнее мне в голову не пришло. Главное, чтобы его прочитала только ты и никто другой.

В ближайшие дни ты узнаешь про меня много

нового — и ничего хорошего. Будут говорить, что весь мой бизнес был "пирамидой," что я обокрал инвесторов, а когда меня поймали, то со страху, как говорит молодёжь, выпилился. В некотором роде это действительно так. Ты у нас человек своевольный и немного contrarian, поэтому у тебя может возникнуть соблазн начать меня защищать, придумывать моим поступкам какие-то благородные причины и т.д. Не надо. Не стоит ни горевать по мне, ни преувеличивать мои достоинства задним числом. Я был хреновым мужем и отцом и так себе предпринимателем. Но знай одно. Когда я ступил на этот путь в 1995-м, мои намерения были чисты. Звучит смешно, но я думал, что смогу изменить мир к лучшему. Мы все так тогда думали. Как говорил один российский политик, имя которого тебе ничего не скажет, "хотели как лучше, а вышло как всегда." Но мне с этой виной больше не жить, да и тебе незачем. Ты умная, ты сильная, и у тебя всё ещё впереди. Не позволяй никому себя в этом разубедить. Мне жаль только, что ты и я так и не смогли — или не успели — по-настоящему подружиться.

С любовью и горечью,

Твой непутёвый папа

P.S. Я открыл тебе счёт в NovoBanco, там лежат 250т. Маме не говори.

She could read printed Russian text okay, if the sentences were short enough, but not cursive. Maya stared at the jittery lines, struggling to make out anything beyond "hi daughter" and some random words here and there, not including the sudden outcropping of the English "contrarian" and the bank name at the bottom. The words composing the first two sentences read as "forgive me, what/that, so, forgive me, what/that, late," so she got the gist. The rest was impossible. She took out her phone and tried using WordLens, Google's augmented-reality translator. It gave her some bits of the first few lines—"It's . . . stupid to buy a house . . . an envelope for this letter . . ."—but as Obrandt scribbled on and his cursive got sloppier, it gave up, too.

Maya bit her lip, her whole body spasming with self-hatred. Even now, she wasn't up to the task. Even now, she was disappointing him. She felt like throwing something from the roof—her phone or the conch. Or herself.

The invisible stork clicked its beak disapprovingly. Another answered across town, the two volleys meeting in the salt-flavored air. She wiped her eyes, still clutching the paper.

Stupid. A fall from the second story would only break her legs or something. Come on, girl, go with the new family tradition.

The phone and the flier were already in her hands. Before she fully knew what she was doing, she dialed the number.

"*Bom dia*," answered a gruff male voice.

"Hi," she said. "I would like to rent whatever boat the late Mr. Obrandt rented from you ten days ago."

"Okay," said the man, leaving the ". . . weirdo" part silent. For a few seconds, there was nothing but the rustling of paper. Then the voice came back. "Which of the two?"

■ ■ ■

Watching Keegan work was infuriating and inspiring at once—a fantasy of what clandestine services might look like if people actually liked and trusted them. In the time it took Falk to drink his tea, Keegan had created an anonymous, ad hoc task force that was now busy scouring the internet for Flight TQ77's mystery woman in seat 3D. No single volunteer knew enough to jeopardize the mission: most simply opened back doors into various databases without seeing the data being mined. Some FleaCollar collaborators even had a free run of a Russian AI engine built to identify protesters' faces at antigovernment rallies. What they didn't get from volunteers, they bought on the darkweb *probiv* market from data brokers: passenger lists, credit card charges, passport scans.

"What's my budget?" asked Keegan without looking up from the computer. "I'm assuming you're out of pocket on this one."

"What do you want to get?"

"Istanbul airport's security footage for the day. The camera over the baggage check."

"What's the price?"

"They want three Ether."

Falk checked the daily exchange rates. Crypto kept climbing up. One Ether ran to $3,326.

"Is it necessary?"

"I'm afraid so. The databases aren't giving me anything."

"How much for just two hours? Six to eight a.m., GMT+3."

"I feel like I'm at the Grand Bazaar already." Keegan dashed off a message and waited for the reply. "One Ether."

"Shit. Fine."

A minute later, Falk was three thousand dollars poorer and the footage was downloading. In spite of the moment's gravity, his thoughts involuntarily turned to his shaky finances. He could afford two, maybe three more stunts like this.

The facial-recognition program was already scrobbling through the video at ten times the speed. Blurry passengers streaked past the scanners; once in a while a guard would yank someone aside and, the way it looked at this tempo, quickly thrash them with a security wand. Keegan began to hum "Yakety Sax" as he watched. Just before Falk could tell him to cut it out, however, he abruptly stopped and leaned in.

"Here we go." The video froze, magnifying one face and highlighting its features in eerie blue. A plot graph next to it showed a 92 percent match with the reference image lifted by Klaus. Even without the computer's help, however, Falk knew. Long but elegant nose, large eyes, a fringe of jet-black hair. Oddly, a white semicircular scar seemed to run across the woman's left cheek; it didn't in Klaus's rendering.

"It's her," said Falk.

"And the scar?"

"It's a trompe."

"Trump?"

Keegan looked confused, so Falk explained. "If you can't blend in with a crowd, you add one big fake detail that will be the only thing anyone remembers. Classic tradecraft. She has got to be a spook."

Unconvinced, Keegan reopened Klaus's rendering and ran some kind of analytic protocol on it. "Ha, I see what happened," he said. "What's that proverb about everything looking like a nail when you're a hammer? The scar is not fake, you just didn't know it was there. You see, whoever made this image extrapolated her full face from the right half. *That's* why none of the databases could find her."

Humbled—and a little pissed off—Falk gave a curt nod and concentrated on checking if any of the men in the line nearby could be the woman's companion. No one seemed to match the hair and the clothes. Keegan must have had the same idea. He rewound the footage a few seconds back, let it play, then rewound again. The blue highlights followed her like a halo, or some sort of supernatural contamination, as she passed the scanner, leaned over the luggage belt, and picked up a small bag.

"Looks like she's alone," said Falk.

"Cutting it close, too," added Keegan. The time stamp on the video read 7:20 a.m., a mere twenty-five minutes before the flight to Riga was scheduled to take off. "I'm envious. Look at her, all calm. If I get to the airport less than two hours before boarding, I am a nervous wreck."

For a moment, Falk acutely missed Klaus and his workplace repartee. Then he realized what Keegan was saying.

"Wait, that's good," he said. "That's very good. Means she might be a transfer passenger. And if she flew to Istanbul alone, there's a chance she was on the *previous* flight's manifest."

"Sadly," said Keegan, "you know what that means."

Another few minutes later, Falk's savings had shrunk in half. He also had a name and a place. Olga Yevgenyevna Ostashevskaya, b. 1974, a citizen of the Russian Federation, arrived in Istanbul at 6:55 a.m. on August 15 on a Royal Air Maroc red-eye from Tangier. As far as the immigration services were concerned, she was still in Turkey.

The name was an obvious alias. Olga Ostashevskaya had no online presence, no accounts on Facebook or the Russian social networks VKontakte and Odnoklassniki, no school ties, and just enough namesakes scattered around Eastern Europe to make the search extra-painful. It didn't matter. Falk had succeeded in anchoring one of the two Flight TQ77 ghosts in reality. She now had a life outside the plane, outside one video, outside the memories of a dead man. Who was Olga Ostashevskaya? Well, she was a female between thirty-five and fifty years old, with black fringe and the means of obtaining a fake passport. She came from Tangier to Istanbul, met up with a man, hopped on a flight to Riga with him in secret, and vanished halfway. It wasn't a satisfying answer, but, for the first time since Anton's death, it was an answer.

"Congratulations," said Keegan, getting up and stretching like a big cat. "Hope it was worth it. Do you fancy some lunch? I have a long day of neo-Nazi death threats ahead of me, and you, I'm assuming, are off to Tangier."

"I wish," Falk replied. "I'm here on a two-week wellness leave. Under the tender care of your compatriots in a house with more MI5 bugs than actual bugs, and it's got some of those too. Then it's back to Virginia and, I guess, a few years of paperwork."

Keegan opened a tiny, dorm-room-style fridge, produced a Pret A Manger sandwich, and gave half to Falk.

"How long has it sat in there?" asked Falk. "You weren't here yesterday."

Keegan gave him a look. "It's cheddar and chutney. It doesn't go bad."

I see why the guy is incorruptible, Falk thought. Keegan took an energetic bite, chewed, then frowned as if he either tasted something odd or had a new thought occur to him.

"So make a side deal," he mumbled through the cheddar.

"What?"

Keegan held up an index finger, signaling for Falk to wait until he swallowed. "So make a side deal. Give the Six boys something they want, and they'll let you nip out of the house for a few days."

"Ha, yeah, I don't think I can do that."

"Why not? You just bought black-market data from what I practically *guarantee* is a Turkish MİT agent making an extra buck. You went this far. Might as well keep going."

A part of Falk's psyche, the prim Rotsie part, bristled at the sound of that. Another, wilier, foster-kid part, calmly suggested that Keegan was right. From the moment Falk followed Karikh into the Riga airport bathroom, he wasn't a CIA case officer anymore. He was out for himself, and his only loyalty was to the memory of those he had accidentally doomed. Inga knew this before she fell victim to it; Harlow knew this and used it; Falk told this much to Keegan the second they met. So when was he going to admit it to *himself*? What was the point of toeing the company line when he didn't even trust the company to know what he was doing right this second? If his own people were covering up the ghosts of Flight TQ77 (or, as he called them now in his mind, Olga and Oleg), Falk had already been deemed expendable. And if it was the GRU, well, the brass would forgive him when he brought in the proof.

"Are you having an identity crisis?" asked Keegan. "And if you are, mind if I finish this?"

Falk silently handed him his half of the sandwich.

"So you don't think I'm being immoral," he suddenly said, surprising himself.

"On the contrary. I think you're waking up, to be honest. Again, sorry if this sounds condescending, but you asked. Institutions can't be moral. *Countries* can't be moral. Only people can. And it's a rather lovely rarity, in my opinion, when moral people from one country find a way to work with their counterparts from another. Hell, one might even say it's their moral duty."

Falk had no follow-up to this. "Thank you," he said, getting up. "I'll let myself out. Please don't die."

He was almost at the door when he felt Keegan's little benediction resonate in his brain in a more immediately actionable way. "Actually," Falk said, turning around, "could the Fourth Reich wait just a few minutes longer? I have one more name to run. Stuart Akinyemi. You can lift his face from CCTV around the address I'll give you."

"Who's that?"

"A guy who's going to write me a hall pass," said Falk.

■ ■ ■

TANGIER
AUGUST 23, 2021

The ferry trip from Tarifa took about an hour in choppy Gibraltar waters. Maya spent the last twenty minutes of it standing in line to an on-board passport control booth, where a man with a wispy mustache sold instant tourist visas and checked arrival cards and vaccination status, and missed the approach. Not that she cared. As the city grew from a thin band on the horizon to a magnificent beehive, rising around the port in every direction and every architectural style, she could barely be bothered to look up.

Perhaps she was crazy for even thinking her father could still be alive and hiding out in Tangier. She'd know more if she could read his letter, but Obrandt's handwriting in the Russian cursive, which changed half the letters to cardiogram spikes, proved unconquerable. The only native speaker to whom Maya could conceivably show it was Baba Polina in Palm Springs, her mind shattered by Alzheimer's into a kaleidoscope of present and past. She wouldn't trust anyone else to translate it; she didn't even photograph it, lest the photo end up in the cloud. The original, folded in four, lay in a Ziploc bag in her pocket.

So far, after one wild-eyed visit to Albufeira Yacht Charters, this was what she knew. On the day Paul Obrandt disappeared—she had resolved to use this word from there on out—he rented two separate boats. One was *A Mar*, the luxury booze cruiser in all the news photos, which went to the Benagil Cave and from which he vanished on the way back. The other, a much smaller and cheaper yacht called *Selena*, took off toward

Tangier at the same time, ostensibly in order to pick someone up. As the befuddled manager explained to Maya, it was still there, moored at the Royal Yacht Club de Tanger with its berthing fees and the captain's salary covered for two weeks.

What the hell did this mean? She had some difficulty imagining her father, who once got seasick watching a Jason Bourne movie because the camerawork was too chaotic, diving off the deck of a boat in the middle of the night, bobbing in the inky North Atlantic until he got picked up by another vessel, and braving the Gibraltar Strait for seven more hours, all to elude a margin call. As fake suicides went, it was too fucking close to the real thing. She was almost sure that the true answer, if and when she got it, would be crushingly dull. But she also knew she wouldn't stop looking for one.

If Maya were honest with herself, she might recognize this new obsession for what it was: a life preserver thrown to her by her own psyche. As long as she was Maya Chou Obrandt, Girl Detective, she wasn't Maya Chou Obrandt the twice-relapsed twenty-three-year-old addict, or Maya Chou Obrandt the corpse. The charter company, the car rental, the four-hour drive across the Spanish border—all of it had gone by in an adrenaline haze as thick as any substance could provide. As a side effect, she kept hallucinating her father: in a crowd, in a window, hitchhiking on the side of the road. At the ferry terminal in Tarifa, she thought she saw the Romanian woman who had handed her the house keys in the morning, but that made even less sense.

Only now, as the boat docked with a dull, full-hull thud, did she feel this hormonal rush draining out of her system, revealing in its wake the blank stupor that had hidden there all along. A can of Coke, marked in block letters *For On Board Airline and Maritime Consumption Only*, shivered on the foldout table in front of her. It tasted the same as the earth-bound kind.

The mass of passengers began to pour down to the ferry's vast car deck, which was the only way off the ship. Maya got up when almost everyone else had disembarked. She was traveling lighter than light, having left her only bag at the Olhão house and wearing clothes she'd pulled for the maximum frump factor from a clearance rack at a Chinese discount store on the Avenida. Head down, hands in pockets, no bag, she must have looked a bit odd on her way down the cargo ramp, weaving alone between rows of impatiently idling cars and trucks. Not a local, not a tourist; this left "professional Spain-Morocco commuter," which suggested contraband at best.

She slipped through the customs building like a ghost, unstopped and unchecked. Off to the side, officials were busy writing up an old man in a hooded Berber robe, apparently for bringing in a case of cigarettes. In front of her was a large family toting checkered plastic storage bags— the Global South staple Balenciaga had cynically remade in leather a few years back and sold for $2,000. She maneuvered around them and stepped onto the pavement.

The afternoon sun was already softening, turning whitewashed Medina walls sherbert orange. A just-reunited couple sat kissing on a low stone barrier that separated the embankment from the street. A black cat peered up at Maya, calculating if she had food, decided she didn't, and turned imperiously away. All around her rose a swirl of car horns, seagull cries, conversations in French and Maghrebi Arabic. Her schoolgirl French was no match for the local dialect; another failure in another language. She had better luck understanding the seagulls.

She sat on the barrier at a polite distance from the lovers, took out her phone, and looked up Royal Yacht Club de Tanger. The private marina was right by the port, barely seven hundred feet away from the ferry slip; come to think of it, this possibility should have occurred to her earlier. She could see the entrance to the club—a full-blown checkpoint, with a protective wall and a guard booth—across the bay. Maya wasn't mentally prepared to get to the goal this fast. She was hoping for at least a taxi ride to prolong the thrill of the search. Behind her, the ferry lowed mournfully, pushing off and heading back to Tarifa.

The guard booth didn't faze her one bit. *I may be useless at everything else*, she thought, *but I'm good at this.* Twenty-three years of unrelieved privilege had given Maya a distinct if ineffable aura of belonging to whatever lay beyond almost any velvet rope in the world. She had it even now, in a fake Adidas top and with a 99-cent headscarf on. "*Bonsoir*," she said into the cracked window, smiling but not too much. "*Je cherche un bateau appelé* Selena."

The guard looked up from an Arabic newspaper and explained, in a combination of French, English, and gestures, that the captain of *Selena* was out (international sign for drinking) but would *revenir* later in the night to (international sign for sleeping), as he did every night. *À quelle heure?* Shrug. *May I wait for him on the boat?* She interpreted the second shrug as a permission but slipped a fifty-euro note into the window just in case.

Selena was moored at the far end of a long, half-empty dock, looking a bit like a loner kid in a high school cafeteria. Maya knew her yachts well enough to recognize the type: a workhorse Bertram fishing boat, with wood-paneled insides that looked like a 1970s Motel 6. She hopped onto the deck, feeling it list under her weight and adjust. It was still hot, she was alone, so she took off the headscarf.

For a second, Maya tried to imagine her father climbing over the railing—in a business suit? a wetsuit? a suit under a wetsuit, like James Bond?—and collapsing onto the deck. *No, no. Nonsense.* Creaky steps led her down to an unlocked stateroom. A messy bed with a stuffed toy shark for a pillow, a three-quarters empty bottle of tequila on the side table. She kept hoping for some supernatural sense of her father's past presence, a sign, another crumb in a trail. Instead, the room just smelled like a sad drunk lived in it, sweating unmetabolized ethanol into the sheets. Sometimes what you thought was a trail was just crumbs.

She suddenly realized she hadn't slept since a fitful nap on the flight from LA, over thirty hours ago. The boat was still rocking a little from her jump aboard. The tequila inside the bottle slowly slanted a degree this way and that. Maya took it by the neck with two fingers and looked at the amber liquid for a while.

Then she poured the dregs down a tiny sink lest she be tempted again, spread the cleanest-looking top sheet over the bed, lay on top of it, and pulled her knees close to her chest. The phone showed half past seven; she set an alarm for nine, or perhaps that was already part of the dream.

■ ■ ■

Falk's legs were killing him from the earlier jog, so he gave up and got on the Victoria Line. He hadn't been to London in a few years and fumbled with an expired Oyster card like a rube, only to find out you could just wave a phone at the turnstile now.

One-half of the plan had come to him in a flash at Keegan's. The other half he formulated on the Tube back to Pimlico. It wasn't very elegant, but few in this profession were. Step one was not getting off the train at Victoria Station, as he had originally planned, but continuing on to Green Park. Step two was walking into Novikov, a Russian-owned oligarch canteen in Mayfair, sitting down at the mauve-lit bar, and ordering eight vodka shots in quick succession. Step three involved a slow and unsteady walk home in the rain.

By the time Falk got to the house, the Cousin was already there, seated in the kitchen with his palms on the table. Just as he hoped, it was

Akinyemi, the same young man who had debriefed him two days earlier. He had on the same cobalt Boateng three-piece, this time with a purple shirt and burnt sienna tie.

"Good evening, Mr. Falk," he said, injecting the *evening* with a hint of disapproval. "Thought I'd drop by to see how you're getting on. Stuart Akinyemi. I've introduced myself before but, you know, just in case."

"Hello, Stuart." Falk found the nearest chair and half sat, half slid onto it. Out of the eight vodkas he had at Novikov, six went into the flower vase atop the bar; in order for the plan to work, however, he would have to keep up the pretense of being three sheets to the wind.

"It is my understanding you're an avid runner."

"Yup."

"Good for you. Do remember to look right when you cross a street, though," said Akinyemi. "Some Americans end up in casualty this way."

Falk appreciated the man's way with words. Akinyemi could have said "emergency" for the guest's sake; instead, he used the British term, but used it for its US meaning.

"My apologies," Falk said. "I should have given you a heads-up. This wasn't work. I just wanted to see an old friend of mine from the Moscow days. Anyway, he canceled at the last moment, so no harm no foul."

"I see. And the friend's name? Just for our records."

Falk held the pause for as long as he could. "I'm sorry," he said. "Please don't take it the wrong way, but I'm not sure you're cleared for this."

To Akinyemi's further credit, he didn't even blink. His expressions were as tightly controlled as Keegan's were cartoonishly transparent. Anxiety had to find an outlet, however, so for a few seconds he drummed his fingers on the table.

"Of course, Mr. Falk, we are not limiting your movements in any way. It's just that your superiors are rather adamant about your safety, and mine are trying to exceed their expectations."

He gave a thin smile. *Good framing*, thought Falk: *we're just two working stiffs, you and I, doing our best not to piss off the bosses.*

"Sorry again," Falk said. "I promise you that the next ten days will fly by without any surprises on my end. Would you, uh, like a drink? I could go for a nightcap."

"Oh, no, no. Thank you." The contempt in Akinyemi's voice was meant to be subtle but wasn't. He got up, adjusted his sleeves to show exactly half an inch of cuff—a detail Falk noted with a great deal of silent satisfaction—crisply nodded, and left.

Apart from the few details of Akinyemi's biography he had learned at Keegan's (who thought the plan was hilarious and happily wasted another hour of his life helping out), Falk's gambit was based almost entirely on the younger man's manner and dress. Having himself once been an overambitious junior agent with a raging case of impostor syndrome, Falk knew one when he saw one. Thus he was reasonably sure that, within minutes of leaving the house, Akinyemi would be at work checking Novikov's security cameras and reservation books to verify the story Falk fed him. What he'd find would be a table for two, booked in the name of a no-show named Philip Broward.

"Philip Broward," as it happened, was the cover identity of a blatantly obvious Russian spy enrolled as a graduate student at the London School of Economics. His real name was Ilya Vareinikov; who knew what mad hubris led his masters to saddle him with an English cover despite a lockjaw Ural accent. Unlike the GRU's robust influence and SIGINT operations, its Directorate Five illegals program, grandfathered in from the Soviet era, was largely a joke. The West watched these would-be masters of disguise with the mild amusement of a parent at a school play until the political climate dictated it was time for a roundup or prisoner exchange. Falk had known about Broward and a dozen more like him for years, through the normal interagency channels. He gambled on the assumption that Akinyemi did, too. The rest would depend on how territorial the Brits would feel about a visiting Yank making shameless passes at a target they'd long been cultivating for themselves.

The bell rang in less than an hour. Falk wiped a smile from his face as he shuffled to the entrance, having at the last moment remembered to resume the unsteady gait of a drunk.

Akinyemi stood under the portico, frowning. To make the situation even more awkward, Falk opened the door and held it without stepping aside to let him in. Raindrops politely tapped the parquet just beyond the threshold.

"Right," Akinyemi finally said and fell silent again.

"What's up?"

"I, I just wanted to stop by and make sure my earlier words weren't misinterpreted. We have absolutely no objection to you having *private* meetings while recuperating in our care. But—"

"Thank you for saying that," Falk interrupted. "So it would be all right for me to reschedule with my friend?"

"Would you be open to a formal debrief afterward? Just for propriety's sake. I understand if not."

"Of course. I'll report it to my bosses, and I'm sure they'll be happy to share with yours."

Akinyemi slowly nodded, not even trying to mask disappointment. *It's time*, Falk decided.

"I'm really sorry," he said. "I know it's unfair. It's your territory. But the guy sent up a flare. Wants to chat. What could we do?"

The Brit automatically glanced left and right. The conversation was getting a bit too direct for his professional sensibilities.

"At least have the courtesy of informing us beforehand," he said.

"Look, I've had a few," Falk continued. "So whatever, forget protocol. I agree. You guys deserve a piece of this. My hands are mostly tied, but here's what I'm willing to do," he said, sounding a bit like a car salesman.

"Yes?"

"Imagine, if you will, that for the last four hours and the next forty-eight, officer Ari Falk of the National Clandestine Service just stayed in, drinking himself into oblivion. At least according to your reports, which he will bashfully confirm once he gets home."

Akinyemi paused, then cracked a grin for the first time during their brief acquaintance. "I see. And while officer Falk is on this tragic binge," he said, "would he mind if someone else met with his friend in his stead?"

"If that someone is *also* a friend? Not at all." Broward né Vareinikov was such a low-value target that an overture by the Brits would probably only raise his stock back home. A win-win-win. "But that's all the time I can buy you," Falk added for gravity.

"And in return?"

"Blackout."

"I believe that's your part of the bargain," Akinyemi couldn't help quipping.

"What I mean is, I close this door and I'm Schrödinger's cat. Am I alive, am I dead—come find out in two days. Yes?"

For a few seconds, Akinyemi stood drumming his fingers on one of the pillars holding up the portico. Then he balled up his fist and lightly punched the pillar instead. "See you Wednesday," he said, turning away and walking into the rain. "And this house better stink."

■ ■ ■

"Hey," said a voice. "Hey, lady. What the hell."

Maya opened her eyes. An unshaven man towered over her, his breath a combustible blend of alcohol and tagine. As soon as he saw her stir awake, he took a step back and raised his hands to demonstrate the lack of ill intent.

"Oh shit," said Maya, propping herself up on elbows. The phone clock showed two a.m.

"I'm so sorry. I went full Goldilocks."

"Are you the passenger? I didn't think you'd show up."

"Not really. My name is Maya Obrandt." She expected a reaction and didn't get one.

"Captain Jose Alves," the man said. He was inexplicably wearing a formal suit jacket, at least three sizes too large, over a Tweety Bird T-shirt. "Nice to meet you. So what do you mean, 'not really'?"

"Shh." Maya got off the bed, feeling dizzy with jet lag and growing fear. "Let me think for a second."

Now that she was on her feet, the captain turned out to be shorter than her. He nodded, said "Of course," and stepped outside. He seemed embarrassed to be caught drunk on the job, and the drunkenness exacerbated the embarrassment. Perhaps the best approach was to be forthright. Maya glanced at herself in the wall-mounted mirror. Red eyes, tangled hair, a print of the stuffed shark's fin across a sallow cheek. Fuck it. It was now or never.

"On the way here," she said, coming out of the state room, "you picked up a man in the Gulf of Cadiz. Right?"

Yachts' rigging clanged in the breeze. The captain sat silent on the open bridge above the deck, smoking a cigarette and staring at the city. Tangier at night looked like a different planet from the one eight hours ago. The Medina glowed orange above the bay; a fast yet mournful live instrumental wafted from a nearby teahouse, mixing in with what sounded like a quarrel between three men in French.

"I don't know anything about that," he finally said. "The company paid me to come here and wait for a passenger. That's all I know."

107

Maya climbed onto the bridge. "You don't have to lie to me."

"I'm not lying. Listen, lady—"

"That man was my father. If you picked him up, I need you to tell me where you dropped him off."

The captain ashed his cigarette into the invisible waves lapping against the hull. On the other end of the port, someone revved a motorbike, the crack of the engine echoing up and down the embankment.

"I will pay you," said Maya. "Double of what he did."

There was no reaction, which was almost encouraging. Then again, Alves could be simply trying to calculate what kind of lie to say in order to get paid.

"I don't want your money," he replied and fell silent. Was this the beginning of a confession, or did he just want her off his boat?

Maya grabbed her phone, opened Photos, found a picture of herself with her father. It was three or four years old, but there weren't many to choose from. She handed the phone to the captain, shoving it at him twice for emphasis until he reluctantly took it.

"Look," she said. "Look! That's me. That's him."

Alves sighed, brought the screen almost to the end of his nose, and squinted at the picture, apparently unaware of the phone's zoom function. Cold blue light illuminated the lower half of his face. He held it like this for several seconds. She could see the stubble around his Adam's apple move as he swallowed before speaking.

"Okay, listen," he said, lowering the phone. "I don't know why he—"

Maya's mind had no capacity for processing what happened after that. One moment, the captain was sitting next to her and talking. The next, some sort of jump cut in reality had occurred, and his body was now at her feet, black liquid pooling around the head. The phone spun across the deck before sliding off and into the water. Then and only then came the gunshot—a long wet echo, like a sonic comet's tail, with a single dry *pock* at the center. For whatever reason, this was the sequence she remembered, though parts of it had clearly switched places in the process.

She jumped to her feet. The source of the shot was impossible to guess, so she thrashed around the bridge, staring at the sea and the shore, before she finally noticed a small motorbike parked on the pier's opposite end. The rider stood astride it with his helmet still on, looking, as far as she could tell from the gleam of his visor, directly at *Selena*. In his hands was either a rifle with no stock or a long pistol with a silencer.

Out of the corner of her eye, Maya saw the yacht club's guard tumble out of his booth and run toward the man, unholstering his handgun as he did. Everything was happening far too fast for her to go from shock to hope to despair; she simply watched. The rider swiveled his torso forty-five degrees and aimed. There was almost no flash as the already-familiar *pock* echoed over the water. The guard fell forward without skipping a step, like he meant to. The rider shot him once again, then finally dismounted and stepped onto the pier.

Maya jumped from the bridge to the deck, then skidded down toward the stateroom door. A bullet hit the hull somewhere above her. The whole boat juddered. She thought about coming back up and jumping into the water, but the room seemed instinctively safer; perhaps she could hide in some storage space, or the head. She dove inside.

Through a small porthole by the bed, she saw the rider, and then just his legs, as he neared the boat. His gait was unhurried, with a feline spring. She could see the gun clearly now; he held it with both hands, pointed down. A red dot from its optical sight danced down the dock ahead of him, like an evil little insect showing the way.

What had she done, locking herself in a trap like this? She should have swum for it. Maya dashed back to the door, changed her mind, ran to the head, jumped back out. Another, louder shot; she didn't know where this one landed. She just wanted this nightmare to be over, and she was not dying on a fucking dry-flush toilet. Gathering the last of her wits, Maya grabbed the empty tequila bottle and crouched by the door. This way, when the killer walked in, she'd at least have one last thing to try.

The boat groaned and listed, accommodating new weight. She heard the steps resonate through the hull. Getting closer. She clutched the bottle tight.

And then, the asshole knocked.

He *knocked*. What the hell were you supposed to do with that?

"Just come in and end me, you coward," Maya yelled.

"I'd rather not," replied, after a slight pause, an American voice on the other side of the door. "Are you armed?"

"Fuck you."

"I'm not the guy who shot at you. Please look outside."

She glanced into the porthole. The rider's body lay sprawled across the pier, not ten feet away. His helmet hung off the side like a Christmas bauble; blood had pooled under his visor, a thin stream escaping down one corner into the indifferent waves.

"Who the fuck are *you*, then?" asked Maya.

"You're welcome, by the way," replied the voice dryly. The guy didn't sound like a cop or a soldier, she thought. He sounded like someone she'd know from Stanford or her acting classes. "My name is Ari. I'm looking for a woman named Olga Ostashevskaya."

"I'm not her."

"May I ask you what you're doing on this boat, then?"

"Looking for my father," said Maya before she could stop herself.

"What's his name?"

"Paul Obrandt."

The man calling himself Ari fell silent for a while, then cleared his throat. "Look," he said, "I think you should come out."

"*I* don't."

"Okay." The voice, she noticed, was becoming a bit more coplike. "Right now, you've got three dead guys around you, one potential ally, and one free motorcycle. If you don't come out in ten seconds, it's just going to be you and the dead guys. Your choice."

"Goddamn it," Maya said, threw the bottle onto the bed, and opened the door.

CHAPTER FOUR

Falk woke up, without ever really falling asleep. More precisely, he just stopped telling his brain to shut out the hum of the Tangier night, the whir of the AC unit, and the breath of the woman next to him. As soon as he did, the noise washed over him like the abstract synthesizer drone at that Riga club a few days earlier. What was its name? Something Finnish. No, wait, that was the woman, Lemminkainen. Falk winced at the memory lapse: he had been trained to retain such things for years. Nine days of dashing across borders and time zones in a chaotic, improvised, and deeply illegal investigation were beginning to catch up with him.

Or, perhaps, he had just gotten *very* badly sidetracked.

Falk got up, in slow motion, so as not to wake up Maya. In the dark of the suite, she was mostly a silhouette, with one small bracket of moonlight on a naked shoulder. The room only came with one bathrobe and she was half wearing it, having evidently put it on sometime after he fell asleep. Falk picked up his T-shirt from the floor, smelled two distinct species of sweat, threw it back down, and walked out as he was. If this town could handle W. S. Burroughs, he thought, it should be able to handle the sight of a guy in boxers.

The cramped, lantern-lit hallway led to a little roof terrace, open only to the residents of the two suites on the hotel's top floor. Falk stepped out and sat there for a while in a damp chaise longue, feeling warm air on his skin and pointedly not thinking. He could use a cigarette, despite not being much of a smoker, but the closest thing at hand was a box of chocolate Pocky sticks in the minibar.

All right, time to face the music. Falk began by reconstructing the night's events in order, trying not to jump immediately to the one freshest in his mind.

As soon as Stuart Akinyemi, who was by all appearances a good guy and whom he genuinely regretted bamboozling, had left the house, Falk went straight to Heathrow. He landed in Tangier via Lisbon six hours later, on a generic US passport from his Sokol Media Research go bag. The passport had one glaring flaw—its serial number was consecutive to the one his office had prepared for Anton. The one that burned with the rest of Anton's contaminated things—and, likely, body—in a furnace somewhere below a hospital in Berlin. Falk was reasonably sure, however, that no one at the Agency would be obsessive enough to flag it.

The only working lead in his search for "Olga and Oleg," the ghosts of Flight TQ77, was a Tangier address to which he and Keegan had back-traced Ostashevskaya's name. By two a.m. sharp, Falk was at the building, which turned out to be a seedy short-term rental above a seedier all-night café. The selling point for both was the view: the building directly faced the twinkling lights of the marina.

Any excitement Falk may have felt at that point was gone by two oh five. The room had been cleaned and re-rented twice in the ten days since Ostashevskaya last stayed in it. The apartment's owner was away in France; Olga had contacted him from a burner email and paid by leaving cash in the café downstairs. Falk half-heartedly showed her photo to the guy behind the counter, who shook his head no before even looking.

Whoever this woman really was, it seemed that her short life as "Olga Ostashevskaya" began here, in a Moroccan house with peeling paint and faded Cinema Rif posters, arced uneventfully through Istanbul, and ended hours later in KGB captivity somewhere in the bowels of the Minsk airport. *At least she saw the world,* Falk thought to himself, feeling very tired all of a sudden. He asked for a glass of mint tea. In front of the café, three small, dangerous-looking men were arguing in loud French.

It was all three falling silent at once that made him raise his head from the counter. The echo of a silenced, flash-suppressed gunshot was still spreading over the waterfront. Best he could tell, it came from the marina.

The next part was pure instinct and adrenaline, and hardly worth re-capping. It ended with the creak of an opening cabin door. The woman who came out looked younger than her voice. Twenty-three to twenty-five; messy hair; beautiful; a phenotype that would read as Asian to most white people but was likely a mix of things; dressed in something cheap and synthetic that looked on her like a deliberately adopted costume. This was all Falk could gather from his first glance at Maya. The words she had spoken through the door just before—*I'm looking for my father, Paul Obrandt*—rang in his ears louder than the gunshots that preceded them. He may have lost the trail of Olga but here, Falk knew at once, was his Oleg.

"This is going to sound weird," Falk said once they were off the yacht and past the bodies, "but do you think you can recognize your father from just the back of his head?"

"I think so."

He took out his phone and showed a freeze frame from Lemmin-kainen's video. The speed and intensity with which Maya burst into tears jolted him.

"Oh god, I'm sorry," Falk said.

"It's fine." She gave a kind of angry harrumph, as if berating her own body for embarrassing her, and wiped her eyes. "I'm fine. Take me out of here." The breakdown was over before it began. On average, considering the circumstances, her composure was remarkable. Falk had seen this in only two types of people: fellow pros and the very rich.

"I didn't mean to give you false hope," he said. "We don't yet know if he's alive."

"It's not about that," she replied, without elaborating.

They rode the killer's motorcycle to the Old Medina, with Maya's arms clamped around him with a force just short of a Heimlich, and stopped on a sloping side street behind Falk's hotel. Falk inspected the bike, finding nothing of interest, rolled it into a weedy construction site, then suggested changing hotels just in case. "My treat," Maya announced as she picked a new one nearby. It was a boutique riad composed of several interlinked houses, much nicer and probably five times more expensive than Falk's original choice.

"Is it safe to use our names?" asked Maya sotto voce when they headed for the reception.

"Mine should be okay. Yours depends on whether that guy was after you or the captain."

"Fine. I'll just be the nameless hooker." Falk didn't exactly blush but blinked a few times.

"Welcome, Mr. Richards," said the clerk, glancing at Falk's passport.

"*Nice,*" said Maya.

Here, again, Falk's mind requested to skip a few steps. The first few awkward minutes in the room, Falk offering her a drink and her refusing a little too vehemently. His *I didn't mean to overstep* and her response, something exceedingly movielike, along the lines of *Actually, I was hoping you would*; the exact wording would forever stay up for debate, because at that point she was already kissing him.

Between his hopeless crush on Inga and the soul-deadening work at the Soft Unit, Falk hadn't been with a woman in three or four months before Lemminkainen, which barely counted for a number of reasons. He had also never had sex this soon after putting his life in danger, and certainly not after ending someone else's. Who knows which ancient pathways this proximity to death opened up in the body and soul, but he and Maya tore at each other like each was the other's punching bag and life preserver at the same time. At one point she choked him, which he never liked; he retaliated in kind and she came immediately. The suddenness of it made him think of her crying jag hours before, and he slightly panicked and withdrew. She read it in his face and sneered. "Don't get it twisted," she said, reaching out and illustrating the idiom far too literally. "I know what I'm doing."

This also sounded like something out of a movie, and only now, reliving all of it in his head, did Falk begin to suspect something extremely obvious in hindsight. He tiptoed back into the room, picked up his phone, went back out, and googled "Maya Obrandt." The very first link was to her IMDb page.

An actress. Six or seven small roles, nothing he'd seen. A CW teen soap of the kind where the teens are played by thirty-year-olds, a Netflix Christmas movie, a Tourist on the Bus in something Marvel-adjacent. A regional talk show, As Herself.

Falk ran through the main beats of their meeting again. Could it have all been a setup to drive him into her arms? Three day players sacrificed just for this? Ridiculous. It would require far too many people from far too many institutions to be in on it—Harlow, Keegan, Akinyemi—and Falk wasn't *that* paranoid yet. Plus, you don't honey trap someone you've already tried to murder in broad daylight. You just learn your lessons and get better at murdering them.

Then there was one more factor attesting to Maya's authenticity. She *was* Paul Obrandt's daughter. Even the IMDb page he was staring at mentioned this fact, in the "Trivia" section.

And Paul Obrandt was, it was now clear, the man they were both looking for.

He clicked on the name. Compared to the few disparate bytes of data to which Falk had been clinging all week, the wealth of suddenly available information made him feel like a man beamed from an ice floe into an IHOP. It was almost nauseating. The faceless ghost he'd been chasing had been a celebrity all along. There were Q&As with Obrandt in *Fortune* and *Forbes*, fawning profiles of him in Californian lifestyle magazines, anti-Semitic screeds on alt-right (and a few hard-left) message boards, Econ 101 papers written about his fund, a photo spread of his mansion in Pacific Palisades. Last but not least, dozens of still-fresh obituaries.

All told the same story. Born in Leningrad, Soviet Union, in 1970. Arrives in the US in late 1986 and hits the ground running. Off to Stanford at sixteen, having skipped the ordeals of an immigrant kid in a 1980s American high school. An oft-repeated, too-neat business origin myth about earning a $200 tip as a hotel porter and using it to register his first company. Name on a few patents, all coauthored, all satellite tech. First million by the age of twenty-four. Shares in several big telecoms. First board seat. An interesting detour in 1995—a French broadcaster taps Obrandt to expand their business into Russia. He brokers the deal, goes back to the US, cashes out, and starts an investment fund. His timing can't be better—the Russian company bites it in the 1998 default. It's the only failure on an otherwise sparkling résumé.

With all due respect, biographies like Obrandt's were a dime a dozen. More than a million Soviet Jews had settled in the US since the early 1970s, most of them losing their already flimsy "Russian" identity with the accent and dissolving into American Jewry. Conversely, thousands of Yankee adventurers came to Russia in the 1990s; those with the strongest stomach lining made a lot of money, and those with enough sense to leave at the right time even got to keep it.

None of it explained why this man would stage his death, and what happened to him after he did.

Unless, that is, in addition to all his other activities he was also a spy. To Falk's professionally skewed eye, the combo of fake suicide and real disappearance looked like an exfil gone wrong. *Let's say he's one of ours, and the Russians find out. We help him "die," ship him to Tangier, and his handler—"Olga Ostashevskaya"—takes things from there. For whatever reason, they get on a plane to Riga. And that's where things go south. The Russians force the plane down, pull him and the handler outside, and kill them.*

Or how about the same thing with the polarity reversed? *He works for the Russians. We are onto him. He makes a break for it with his SVR or GRU contact. Our guys clock them in Istanbul. So the Russians vanish him in midair.*

In either scenario, Obrandt would have had to be an *incredibly* high-value target. That was a hell of a lot of time, money, and manpower to spend on someone. The Agency's sociopathic disregard for the lives of indigenous assets like Anton was well-established—they were "fair game," as Harlow said in Berlin; it was what drove Falk into this mess to begin with. As for the Russians, they would, notoriously, sooner kill their own officers than deal with expensive extractions. So, perhaps, viewing everything through the spook optics was not a wise idea.

Falk tabbed over to Images, half hoping to see Obrandt with Ostashevskaya. No luck. Instead there were myriad iterations of one official portrait from the Obrandt Investment Securities website and lots of frozen smiles against press walls, with the wife—Emily Chou Obrandt, Taiwanese-American, full-time socialite—present more often than not. Only one photo, staged and posed, showed the whole family at home: glamorous mom, benevolent dad, and the unsmiling daughter in early teens. He put the phone down. Seeing Maya like that felt like, well, spying.

The sky over the strait was turning gray with a premonition of sunrise. The Fajr prayer call echoed from a mosque a few blocks over. Falk headed back to the room, trying to step as lightly as possible.

"Hi," said Maya from the bed, startling him. "Did you bring any breakfast?"

"It's six a.m."

She yawned, stretched, pulled the robe back into place. "Well, *you're* no rock 'n' roll fun. What's the plan?"

Falk sat next to her, frowning. She smelled like sleep. "Get dressed. We have a lot of comparing notes to do. Also, for the record, I, um, I'm sorry."

"About what?"

"I . . . I think the sex was a mistake."

"What is Things You'll Never Hear in a Bond Movie?" she said in a game-show voice.

Falk winced. "I need you to be serious. After we talk, we go our separate ways. And not the way people do in normal life. I mean *completely* separate, with no hint we ever met. For your safety and mine, and possibly your father's. There can't be any entanglements whatsoever."

Maya sat up so their faces were level with each other. When she spoke, she matched his tone with such actorly precision it almost read as mockery. "Look, don't get offended, I'm just going to say it. Last night it was either this or a drink. I'm fifty-eight days sober, and that includes the day I spent writing a fucking *eulogy*. So you're off the hook, if that's what you need to hear. It wasn't a big deal. Thank you for saving me, and thank you for distracting me. That's literally all. Now. Do you know Russian?"

The change of topic caught Falk off guard. "*Da. A chto?*"

"Right. Of course you do." She leaned over the side of the bed, picked up her track pants, reached into a pocket and took out a Ziploc with a twice-folded piece of paper inside. "Can you read this to me before you fuck off forever?"

"What is it?"

"Oh, nothing. Just my dad's suicide note."

■　■　■

Maya had been awake for hours, pretending to sleep and debating in her head whether to show Falk the letter. She felt the shifting sheets and heard the light steps as the spy crawled out of the bed and tiptoed outside, barefoot and possibly naked, then came back twenty or so minutes later for his phone. By the time he returned the second time, it was already light out, so she performed a little pantomime of awakening. In the grapefruit Tangier sunrise, the reality of the last few hours hit her all anew: the boat, the bodies, the blood trickling into the waves from a cracked helmet, the motorcycle ride, the insane ill-advised sex. She felt like scrunching herself up into a small, hard ball of pure trauma. When Falk sat down on the bed and gave his half-apologetic goodbye spiel, she snapped at him instead, trying to sound cynical and weary. But she had also finally made up her mind.

Falk took the paper and scanned it, mouthing *whoa* at one point. Then he sat down at the tiny rolltop desk by the window, found the hotel's fancy stationery and a pen, and started writing.

"What are you doing?" asked Maya.

"Honestly, it would feel a little weird for me to read it aloud," said Falk. "Especially after, well, you know. I'd rather just give you a translation."

She gulped a minibar Evian and watched him scribble. Seeing Falk in daylight for the first time, free of last night's adrenaline goggles, Maya still found him reasonably attractive. Placing his age was a bit of a challenge.

Rail-thin, with messy black hair graying at the temples and large dark eyes sandbagged by the lack of sleep, he could be a hard-ridden twenty-eight or a youthful forty. The movie industry, despite some admirable recent efforts, still absolutely crawled with guys who looked like this; she had dated a few. None of them had shot a man through a motorcycle helmet, though, at least not in front of her.

Of the sex itself, she realized with some surprise, she remembered almost nothing. This was a good sign. Oblivion was what she had been after, and oblivion she had gotten. Maya could already tell Falk was good at guessing others' needs, but strongly suspected that this, like his shy-nice-guy act, was just his CIA bedside manner. He had probably been taught it in a special course, by some gruff professor who made the class split into pairs and practice fake empathy on each other. (In her imagination, spy training was like acting school, only with more stage combat.) Still, she couldn't help feeling a little impressed.

After ten or so minutes, Falk said "done" and politely excused himself to the lobby for some ice, leaving two handwritten pages atop the desk.

Hey daughter.

Sorry it's come to this. Sorry it comes so late. Sorry about all of it.

If I know you well enough and my predictions are correct, you've come here alone, and I've been dead for two weeks or less. It's probably stupid to buy a whole house to serve as this letter's envelope, but I couldn't think of anything smarter. The most important thing is that you and <u>no one else</u> read it.

Over the next few days, you will learn a lot about me, none of it good. You will hear that my whole business was a pyramid scheme, that I defrauded my investors and then offed myself like a coward the moment I got caught. And, in a way, all of that is true. But you're a willful kid, and a tad contrarian; so you might be tempted to start defending me, to imagine some sort of noble reasons behind my acts, etc. Please don't. I'm worthy of neither your grief nor any kind of postmortem reappreciation. I was a shitty husband and father and an average entrepreneur at best. But do know this: when I first stepped onto this path in 1995, my intentions were pure. It sounds silly but I did think I could change the world for the better. We all did back then. To quote one Russian politician whose name will not tell you anything, "we wanted the best and we got the usual." But I no longer have to live with this guilt, and neither should you. You're smart, you're strong, and you've got everything ahead of you. Don't let anyone tell you otherwise. My only regret is that you and I didn't manage—or have enough time—to become real friends.

    With love and bitterness,

                Your wayward dad

P.S. I opened an account in your name in NovoBanco. There's 250K in it. Don't tell Mom.

Falk came back with a sweating ice bucket. Maya quickly wiped her eyes.

"Thank you," she said.

"No problem." She thought he was going to make a drink, which would seem a little rude minutes after someone told you they were in recovery. Instead, he grabbed a towel from the bathroom, packed it with the ice, twisted the ends, and wrapped the whole thing around his right ankle. Maya gave an involuntary snicker.

"What?" Falk glared at her. "I have a repaired Achilles tendon."

"Nothing," said Maya. "You just—you don't look like a spy. You look—"

"Jewish," Falk offered. "You can say it."

"*No.* I mean, you look like you listen to Taylor Swift when no one's around."

Falk gave her an exaggerated frown. "I prefer Tori Amos. Especially the midperiod stuff, like *From the Choirgirl Hotel.*"

"Right. The *bangers*," said Maya. She had no idea who Tori Amos was. For a minute, they sat in a somewhat unfriendly silence.

"So," said Falk. "Let's talk about the pyramid-scheme part. It wasn't in any of the obituaries, so I'm guessing it hasn't been discovered yet."

Maya stayed silent. Falk looked at her. "Are you okay discussing it?"

"I am, but now you know as much as I do."

"The investment fund. How much is missing?"

"All of it."

"When do you think people will find out?"

"A week? A month? Never? Mom's in control now and she's pretty brilliant, so who knows."

Falk took off his compress and shook the ice into the bathroom sink. "And there I am, thinking your dad was a spook. This . . . changes things. Whatever happened to him in Minsk is almost certainly about the money." He paced around the suite, sounding almost giddy. "See, all this time I've been trying to work backward from the airplane incident. Now that I know your father's identity, I can finally go forward. The obvious next step is to find out what was waiting for him in Ri—"

Falk stopped at the window, his gaze fixed on some invisible point above the medina roofs. "Fuck," he said. "Karikh."

"What's happening right now?"

"Just me being an idiot," said Falk. "It was right there all along. In my defense, you had to know about the money to put it together. There's a guy in Riga I need to see."

"Who?"

"A banker I beat up last week. I'm afraid I have to go beat him up again."

"You mean *we* have to go to Riga—wherever that is—and beat him up," said Maya.

She didn't mean to blurt it out like that, but as soon as she did, a strange prophetic calm came over her. She knew that, whatever the next words out of Falk's mouth, this was going to happen. Her father was alive and on the lam, and she and Shy Spy were going to find him together.

Falk snorted. "As much as I'd like to see that, I think I'll be taking it from here."

"Oh yeah?" Maya had nothing to lose, so she doubled down. "On what budget?"

"Excuse me?"

She got off the bed and took a few steps toward him, half-consciously performing a slinky femme fatale walk that seemed appropriate for the occasion. "I might be a civilian but I'm not an idiot. You're not on any kind of official mission."

"How do you— Why would you think that?"

"When we switched hotels, the one you picked was way cheaper than your original one. Means you're out of pocket. If you were on assignment, you'd stay in the same price range."

For a second, Falk stared at her literally agape—his mouth slightly opened as if to say something, then closed.

"Look," Maya said, "everyone has a superpower. Mine is knowing when someone's ass is broke." He didn't crack a smile. "Come *on.* You saw the letter. The quarter million euro he left. I thought this was some kind of fuck-you money. Now I think it's find-me money."

"No. No, no, out of the question. It's messy enough that you're my main witness. You can't be my . . . benefactor."

She put her hand on his bicep, not out of affection but as a power move. On a nearby roof, a PA speaker crackled to life with a call to prayer, the day's second. "Ari. There's something you need to understand. I'll keep looking for him. You can't make me stop. So these are your choices: we can go off and do this separately, until you see on the news that I'm dead in a ditch somewhere. Or we can do it together."

Falk removed her hand, but let it linger in his. "And you're not scared?" he asked.

"I've already been shot at. If a guy like you gets used to it, so can I."

"I don't just mean that. You're not afraid of what you'll discover? Your father was running away with a woman you don't know. There's a nonzero chance he doesn't want to be found—by you or anyone else. Hell, even the marina shooter might have been his own hire."

"I don't care. I need to know why he did this. *Then* I'll decide whether to hug him or hand him over to the cops. Or both."

She was pleased to see Falk look at her with something like awe.

"And there's not going to be any will-they-won't-they tension, because we already fucked," she couldn't help adding, just to ruin the moment.

■ ■ ■

RIGA
AUGUST 25, 2021

The last thing Nikolai Karikh needed was more surprises. Or, as his grandma used to say, *adventures upon your arse*. In the ten days that had passed since the Riga airport incident, his bruises healed and the click in his jaw had subsided, but he still felt unsettled and jumpy.

To be honest, it wasn't even about the beating anymore. He was no fool; he could put two and two together. When two hard-looking men saunter into the bank, use a GRU call sign, leave with two heavy duffels, and later the same day there's automatic fire and four corpses in the middle of the city, including both men's, the math is pretty clear. Not only had Moscow ordered and evidently half botched a hit, but the art deco vaults in the EiropaBank basement had been pulling double duty as an ammo depot.

Why wasn't he—a vice president of the bank and a career First Directorate GRU officer—made aware? Who knows. It's better to keep your head down. *The less you know, the better you sleep*; another of Grandma's maxims that served Karikh well over the years, lifting him through a series of increasingly cushy gigs into his current sinecure. Thus he kept cool and asked no questions, even when Andrei "Count Orlok" Druzhinin, the tattooed commander of a notorious mercenary outfit, came on the news and claimed the two dead men as former Orlok soldiers. Karikh had never heard of military intelligence agents moonlighting at a PMC, let alone vice versa, so he assumed this was the account the Aquarium had asked Druzhinin to provide. After all, if you really think about it, they all worked for the same boss anyway.

And why would that boss want a boutique Latvian media agency shot up? Who cares. Reasons. The news quoted a statement from Sokol Media Research's surviving head, an American Jew (of *course*) named Ari Falk, saying the hit had to do with their "fearless reporting" on Orlok, which meant he'd bought the legend. Seeing Falk unnerved Karikh for some reason, but not out of any sense of empathy. Something about the guy's voice was creepy. For a second, Karikh even thought he sounded like the man who assaulted him at the airport, but that was ridiculous. Anyway, fuck him, he was probably an enemy stooge like the rest of the "free media" out there.

The thing that really bothered Karikh, if he'd care to analyze his feelings a little more, was the vague, unformed sense that all of the last weeks' events—being asked to meet a mystery client at the airport, the bathroom assault, and the shootout around the corner—were somehow bits of the same story, mushrooms sprouting from a single underground mycelium. But, again, if they were, that connection wouldn't be visible unless you dug down into the dirt. And Karikh wasn't a digging type.

So he went on about his routine, glad-handing small-fry investors, shuffling millions between "white" and "gray" accounts as directed by Moscow and his own gut, and masturbating to Facebook photos of Nata the receptionist at last year's Christmas party. And, for five days, all was well with the world.

On the sixth day, another cap sprouted.

Normally, calls from the mother ship would go to Karikh's office phone or, if the matter was sensitive, his clean mobile. This one came through the front desk, as if the caller weren't sure how to reach him. "Moscow on line two," said Nata over the intercom. "The very top."

"Is it Plesen?" Irina Plesnevitskaya, the mother bank's CEO.

"*Nope.*" The sadistic lilt in her voice disoriented Karikh.

EiropaBank's structure was tricky. It was an "affiliate" of Russia's KhromBank, which meant that KhromBank owned 20 percent of it and an Armenian-British oligarch owned the remaining eighty. (The twist was that KhromBank also owned the oligarch.) It had siblings in Yerevan, Vienna, Limassol, Dubai, and London, each under a local brand and fully compliant with local regs, which allowed the whole network to survive the sanctions levied against Russian banks after the annexation of Crimea. The chief executive and public face of the group was Irina Plesnevitskaya, an unsmiling technocrat with a dyed updo and a predilection for shawls.

KhromBank itself, however, was owned by a nearly invisible public company *also* called KhromBank, to maximize confusion; its main shareholder was the Federal Agency for State Property Management, or, in other words, the Kremlin itself. The president of this seemingly redundant superstructure was a bald, trim, tan eighty-year-old named Gennady Demin—a onetime Soviet diplomat in France, as the public knew him, and a GRU general, as Karikh did. It was Demin who created the bank, in 1995, to service a telecom he had started with the French. And it was his tacit protection that let the spy agency use the bank's subsidiaries to move massive amounts of cash around the world—a task for which every "daughter" had a dedicated VP. There was an Armenian Karikh, a British Karikh, and so on. Nikolai had even met them all once, in 2017, during a boozy weekend retreat hosted by the Dubai Karikh.

Still, technically, Karikh answered to Plesnevitskaya. Ten days ago, when he got his orders to go to the airport and roll out the red carpet for a mystery client, the call had come from her.

"Nikolai?" The voice on the phone sounded raspy but energetic. "Gennady. Don't think we've met."

Karikh felt his back straighten. He almost answered *Yes, Comrade General*, before remembering they were on an open line.

"Yes, sir. It's an honor, sir."

"Relax, relax." The man coughed or laughed, it was hard to tell. "How's the health?"

"Uh, good, thank you. Can't complain."

"That's good. Health is the only thing that matters. When you're my age, you'll understand."

Karikh couldn't come up with anything pithy, so he grunted in agreement.

"Look, Kolya," the general continued, slipping into the familiar form of "Nikolai" like they were old friends or relatives, "Irina speaks very highly of you, and my guys agree. *Reliable* is one word that comes up around your name a lot. *Discreet* is another. And that's what I need right now."

"Of course. Anything."

"Good. A new client is going to come in and make a deposit. A large deposit. Large enough that the bank itself might need some restructuring to accommodate it."

"Okay."

"And there's that discretion I've been promised." Even over the phone, Karikh could hear the general smile. "I know you heard the same thing on the fifteenth, and I know about the unpleasantness that followed. Let me guarantee you there will be no surprises this time. Write down her name."

Her? Huh. Karikh reached for a souvenir pen with the bank's logo. He kept a dozen of them in a leather holder, each a 400-euro Montblanc, for the rarefied kind of client that made it all the way up to his office to sign papers.

O-b-r-a-n-d-t, M-a-y-a.

"At this point, you're asking yourself why I'm calling you in person," continued Demin as a statement of fact. "But I also think you already know the answer." Then he hung up, without a warning or a goodbye. A few seconds later, the clean mobile in Karikh's desk began to buzz.

■ ■ ■

"Okay, let's go over this one more time."

Maya rolled her eyes in mock petulance. "I remember."

"And still."

"*Fine.* I come in. I ask to talk in his office, nowhere else. I go up, I get cold feet, I ask for a glass of water, I do the thing, I get out."

"It's okay to look nervous, by the way. Don't play it too cool in the beginning."

"I can play nervous *under* the cool. You know? How the best way to play drunk is to play sober but badly?"

Falk stared at Maya, trying to determine if she was pulling his chain. "Just be yourself."

"Okay. Shh. The music's starting."

They had been in Riga for less than seven hours, arriving on the same flight Paul Obrandt, "Olga Ostashevskaya," and Anton had taken ten days earlier. (The plane's path avoided Belarus airspace, a brand new Europe-wide regulation spurred on by the MiG incident.) Maya had booked them an Airbnb in Old Town, in the refurbished attic of a cartoonishly narrow medieval house. Wooden beams ran under the ceiling, so low even she managed to bump her head against one. Falk felt an odd urge to show the city off to her, as if they were an actual couple on an actual vacation; or, perhaps, he just didn't want to linger in one room together lest they end up having sex again. Either way, he rolled with it and took her to the nearby Dome Cathedral for a noontime organ concert. As an invisible organist played Bach's "An Wasserflüssen Babylon" and Maya took furtive photos, Falk checked and rechecked the operational details in his head.

The whole plan rested on two assumptions. He went over them again and again, probing their logic for structural weaknesses.

Assumption one. The five billion missing from Paul Obrandt's investment fund were still in the wind. He had Maya call her mother in Los Angeles to make sure; Emily Chou predictably refused to discuss the matter over the phone, which in itself was a confirmation.

Assumption two. Obrandt kept at least some of the missing money squirreled away in EiropaBank and was on his way to Riga to access it. The fact that he'd risk this trip immediately after staging his own death, and that the bank's vice president was meeting him at the airport in person, suggested a massive transaction. In the age of electronic banking and cryptocurrency, only the largest transfers still had a biometric component to them—a palm print, an iris scan, sometimes even a DNA test—that would require one's physical presence.

This wasn't a lot, but enough to play a hunch. Maya would walk into the bank, safely introduce herself as herself—Paul Obrandt's daughter, in town to attend to her late father's affairs—and ask to see Karikh. She'd say she found some papers in Los Angeles that indicated her father may have had an account here. From the banker's reaction, she and Falk would suss out if the money was still there, never got there, or had moved.

More importantly, while there, she would bug Karikh's office. The Soft Unit kept a cache of surveillance equipment hidden under a dilapidated stone gazebo in Kronvalda Park, which Falk had already dashed off to retrieve.

The concert ended with a glacial Arvo Pärt piece. Falk and Maya followed a small crowd of tourists and locals out of the cathedral and onto a square ringed with outdoor cafés. September chill was already in the air; most of the cafés had rolled out heaters. They sat down next to one—a pillar of fire contained in a long glass tube—and ordered spiced tea and coffee.

"So I guess there's a serious possibility my dad's a Russian agent, huh," said Maya. She picked a pod of star anise out of her tea, broke it apart, and threw the pieces back in. "Honestly, I don't even care. It's a better explanation than him just being a lifelong asshole for no ideological reason."

"We don't know that," said Falk. "And I don't care either, to be honest. Once this kind of money gets introduced into the equation, ideology no longer applies. There are no sides left. I just need to know who's killing every witness to his escape."

"Oh, shit, I'm sorry," said Maya. "Is it hard for you to be back in Riga so soon?"

Falk gulped down his Americano. Two weeks earlier, he had beers with Klaus at the same exact café. The Pils hotel bar, where he'd waited for Anton, stood mere feet off the square. As for Inga . . . Riga was now a city of ghosts. Maya didn't need to know any of it. Inga Lace, Klaus Staubermann, Anton Basmanny, these would just be meaningless names to her. And she had her own loss to deal with.

"It's fine," he said. "That's the job."

Getting the surveillance kit out of the cache had been the hardest part, emotionally speaking. Falk had left Maya at the Airbnb and was suddenly alone on the streets again. He couldn't help walking past the former Sokol Media Research building—the entrance boarded up, the screaming Valkyrie face above the third-floor balcony now reminding him of Inga's last moments in the elevator.

The cache itself was a flat metal case, designed to look like some Soviet-era construction detritus. It was Inga's; she refused to bring any-thing work-related home, to her artist boyfriend and their pigs. Inside, couched in black foam, lay a handful of omnidirectional mics the size of a bead, several video cameras not much larger, two clean phones, and a subcompact Czech handgun. It was a tiny version of Falk's own preferred CZ-75, which almost felt like a friendly wink across time and space from Inga herself. He'd pocketed it, silently promising the dead that he'd make it all mean something.

Maya finished her tea and poked the dregs with a cinnamon stick. "Okay," she said. "So. I did a thing. Just don't get mad."

"That depends on the thing."

"You said Dad was coming here to take the money out. I realized this makes no sense."

"Oh." Falk knit his eyebrows, masking actual displeasure with a mock one.

"Why here? Why to Riga? I checked, and this bank has branches in, like, Yerevan, Dubai, London. All these places have direct flights out of Tangier. Riga doesn't."

"So?"

"So why would he risk a layover? Two flights instead of one?"

"Tradecraft. Shaking a tail. I don't know." Falk hated to admit this, but she was raising a valid point.

"Yes you do. Because he had the money *on* him, and he was meeting someone specific to hand it over."

"And how do you carry five billion dollars?"

"Back in LA, Mom said it took him years to loot the fund without anyone noticing. I'm not an expert but you'd have to create hundreds of separate accounts to do that. Maybe thousands. So I'm guessing he'd carry the master list, or some code generator that unlocks it. Now stop looking at me like I'm a talking dog."

"Sorry." Falk did, in fact, find himself staring. Maya's reasoning was a stretch, but no more of a stretch than his own. "Okay, fine, let's say you convinced me. What did you do?"

"I changed the plan a little. I called the bank and said Paul Obrandt asked me to make a deposit."

Falk almost spat out his coffee. "You mean, like you're accomplices?"

"Yup. A nice American grifter family. Believable, no? Look, if I came in asking *about* the money, they'd just stonewall me. If they think I *have* it, they'll actually talk."

"Christ." Falk rubbed his face with both hands. "Well, congratulations. The op is off. I can't let you waltz into a GRU trap." He got up, almost knocking over the gas heater, threw a few euro coins on the table, and gestured for Maya to follow him. "Come on. I'm taking you to the fucking airport. Get on the first flight out and you might—*might*—make it home alive. Jesus fuck."

"I think you may be overreacting just a tad," said Maya dryly.

"Am I? And when they realize you don't have the money? What if they decide that the next logical move is to take you hostage until Dad shows up?"

"In a bank?!"

"A GRU slush-fund bank? Yeah. Easily."

"Then you come in and shoot everyone, with the gun I can—just as a side note—totally see in your jacket."

Falk reflexively adjusted his clothes. Maya laughed. "Gotcha."

He looked at her, looked around, and sat back down. A waiter in a red vest came to clear the table, forcing a comically long pause between them. When he was finally gone, Falk's fury had subsided a little.

"Look, I know you lost people," Maya said, all playfulness gone, "and are now superinvested in protecting me. You don't have to be."

"And you're trying to get hurt," Falk replied. "You know that, right? The only thing I don't understand is if you're dissociating or desperate."

Maya fixed him with a long unblinking look that unexpectedly made his cheeks burn. It had been a while since anyone looked at him like that.

"Get yourself a girl," she said, quoting something, "who can do both."

■ ■ ■

The EiropaBank building took great pains not to look like a bank. It wasn't a building, for starters, just two bottom floors of a residential mansion; its separate Private Banking entrance didn't even have a sign out front, except for a small brass plaque on the door that made it look like an expensive dental practice. The layout inside—a long, oak-paneled hallway with a narrow staircase in the back—suggested a converted duplex apartment. The whole place had a *Rosemary's Baby* vibe, luxurious but cursed.

Maya walked in, itchy and already perspiring in her brand-new clothes. After the sweatsuit she'd worn nonstop for the last forty-eight hours—with one very nice break—she was back in heiress drag: black slacks and a crisp cream-colored top that still retained the shape of the mannequin. She was no longer sure which of these outfits was more of a costume.

"Ms. Obrandt!" An impossibly beautiful woman her age and twice her height waved from a reception desk at the far end of the hallway. She either had a raptor bird's vision or had seen Maya close up on a CCTV monitor. "We're very happy to see you here."

"Hi." Maya gave an awkward wave back. Fear and regret swirled together somewhere in her solar plexus. *What the fuck am I doing.*

"Mr. Karikh will be right down," the woman said, getting out from behind the desk and beckoning Maya to follow. The ID tag on her sharp-shouldered jacket said *Natalia*; her *h*'s had a sandpapery Slavic texture but she pronounced Maya's last name as if it were German. "Let me show you to the Prestizh Lounge."

"*Spasibo,*" Maya mumbled.

"Oh, you speak Russian?" Natalia turned around and smiled as she walked, without breaking her stride.

"My dad was, is, Russian. Have you, uh, met him?" *Nice going, moron. Smooth. You're a regular Mata Hari.*

"Here you go." Natalia touched her ID tag to a card reader, unlocked a heavy-looking door, and held it open, all without answering Maya's question. On the other side was a tackily luxe sitting room that looked like a Swarovski truck crashed into a Roche Bobois warehouse.

"I would actually prefer to see Mr. Karikh in his office."

Something passed behind Natalia's gray eyes, a shadow of distaste suggesting it was a bad idea for a woman—or, perhaps, this woman—to do that.

"He'll be right here," she repeated in English, with a facsimile of a smile, and made herself scarce.

Maya sat down on a peach-colored velvet banquette, trying to affect a careless pose. On the other side of the room stood a full bar, its counter and back wall made of angled mirrors meant to resemble a jewel. She felt extremely aware of her own heartbeat. The top's starchy collar cut into her neck. The metal taste of fear wasn't going away; mixing in with it was a different, darker flavor she suddenly identified as anger. She was angry at Falk, for making her call her mother, and angry at herself for not doing it earlier.

The surviving Obrandts hadn't talked since Maya skipped out on the funeral. She rationalized that by the need to keep things secret: who knew if their house was bugged, or their devices compromised. It would be safer if Emily Chou kept thinking of her daughter as an aimless screwup, off the reservation and probably off the wagon at this point, fumbling her way through the resort towns of south Portugal.

In truth, however, she simply couldn't bring herself to utter any of it to Mom, even across the ocean. Imagine phoning in to say *Dad may still be alive . . . or he may have died a few hours later than we thought. The only thing we know for sure is that he lied to everyone and was last seen getting off a plane with a strange woman. Anyway, how's Grandma?* So, in an odd way, having this call be a cynical subterfuge—they needed to find out more about the state of Paul Obrandt's accounts—was the only thing that made it possible.

Didn't make it any easier, though. Hours later, Maya still felt every word of their brief dialogue like a separate little cut, a discrete ache she could assess at will. Stuck in this ridiculous room, waiting for god knows whom, she was now going over it again, line by line.

"Good of you to call." Emily sounded brittle, hollow. "Where are you?"

"Europe. How did the—"

"Funeral? Fine. Everyone came. I had a technician help me with the slideshow."

"Mom, I'm so sorry."

"I know you are. Look, I can't really talk, I'm driving to Palm Springs. Baba Polina has taken a turn for the worse. I think the news hit her pretty hard. Just let me know if you're coming back soon or not."

"Oh god. I was kind of hoping Alzheimer's would actually . . . soften the blow."

"Apparently not."

"I'll be back in a couple of days, I promise." Maya steadied her breath. "I have a quick question. Do you know anything about Eiropa-Bank? Looks like Dad had an account in it, maybe that's where some of the missing funds—"

"Maya Chou Obrandt," her mother switched her voice up a tritone, the closest she ever got to yelling. "I will not be discussing these matters with you. Not now, not ever. Now, let me know when you're coming in and if you need help with the ticket. I suggest you go straight to Palm Springs when you land. There may not be much time."

"I will. I will. I promise, I will."

"Are you drinking?"

"Mom—"

"I love you," said Emily, as a direct continuation of the previous phrase, and hung up.

Maya made herself snap out of this masochistic reverie. She had to stay alert. She had a job to do.

Under her new shirt's lapel was a tiny live mic broadcasting her speech, breath, and probably even pulse to Falk, who was waiting in a rental car just outside. Rolling in her slacks' left pocket were three micro-cameras, the size and shape of googly eyes sold by the bag in toy stores. Perhaps she should plant one here, she thought, and save the other two for Karikh's office. The Prestizh Lounge seemed like a prime place for some white-collar criminal shit.

She looked up at the mirrored bar. A balding, bow-tied bartender stared back at her. Behind him, Maya could see her own tired face, mul-tiplied manifold among liquor bottles.

"Would you like a cocktail?" the bartender called out in Russian. He must have heard her talk to Natalia. Or maybe that's what all the bank's clients spoke. "Perhaps a mimosa? Aperol Spritz?" He pronounced it *shprits* like the Russian word for syringe.

She briefly considered it. She always briefly considered it.

"Just a coffee, please." Maya got up from the banquette and walked over. The best placement for the camera would be on the bar itself, look-ing out into the room. She could wedge it in one of the slits where the mirror panels met one another. On the bank's own cameras—she had discreetly scanned the lounge ceiling, per Falk's instructions, and counted at least three—the gesture would look inconspicuous enough. She'd need the bartender to turn away, though.

"Actually," she said, "how about a Macallan? Neat."

The bartender made the impressed face men make every time a woman orders something that isn't pink, sweet, or bubbly, and went to get the bottle.

"Not the 12, please. 25." The 25 stood on a high enough shelf to require a stool. The bartender climbed up with a slight involuntary groan. Maya reached into her pants pocket, as if searching for cash, and popped the microcamera under the lip of the counter the way a bad kid would dispose of chewing gum. It wouldn't be the best angle but it would do. One down, two to go. Her heart pounded.

The bartender opened the bottle. The aroma hit her from six feet away.

"Single or double?"

"Make it a double." Smiling, she dug the nails of her right hand into her left wrist. "And, uh. This is for you, actually. Seemed like you could use one. I'll have my coffee."

The bartender stopped the pour, gave Maya a puzzled scowl from under a pair of unkempt eyebrows—*Is this very young woman flirting with me?*, she inferred, though it could have been just confusion—then nodded and splashed a bit more scotch into the glass.

"Why thank you," he said. "This doesn't happen too often."

"Not many people come in here, huh?"

"Not many *nice* people come in here."

The coffee was ready. He handed the cup to her and clinked his glass against it. "Chin-chin." An Italian cheer, adopted by Russians, actually Chinese in origin.

Maya gulped down the coffee. The bittersweet burn overwhelmed her. The liquid was half alcohol—some kind of herbal liqueur.

"What the fuck," she said, in English. The empty cup clanged back onto the saucer.

"Oh yeah, I put a little something extra in it." The bartender was beaming. "Riga Balsam. Just because you're so nice."

Fifty-nine days of sobriety down the drain. She wanted to scream. Familiar, predatory warmth was already spreading in the back of her head, like the opposite of a migraine.

"Right," she said in a coarse half whisper. "Thanks."

Are you drinking? I love you.

"There she is!" The voice came from the doorway. Maya turned to see. A pudgy man in an electric blue suit was striding toward her across the lounge, right arm outstretched, fingers splayed out. "So great to meet you. Nikolai Karikh, vice president." His handshake felt too soft. "Hope Nata and Vitya took good care of you. I've been told you'd rather talk upstairs."

As they passed reception and clomped up the creaking staircase to the second floor, Maya fixated on Karikh's thousand-dollar shoes: wholecut, closed-laced oxfords, painfully narrow. There was no way in hell a man of his build would have feet this slender. She made a note of this extreme vanity for possible later use.

"Here we are." Maya stepped into the office. It was smaller than she expected. To be frank, it didn't look all that different from her father's own workspace. Obscure financial-world trophies and certificates crowded the bookshelves around a leather-top desk, behind which Karikh promptly installed himself. He waved toward a Wassily chair, inviting her to sit.

"Do you prefer Russian or English?"

"If it's all the same to you, English," said Maya. Why cede home-court advantage.

The fear should have been cresting by now, but she was strangely calm. She'd hate to think it was the alcohol's doing. Perhaps it was the fact that Karikh's office, unlike the lounge, had a large window looking out onto the street. Were she to stand up on tiptoe, Maya would see the roof of Falk's silver Kia parked on the other side. Knowing he was close by and listening in on every word made her feel like she was on set, mic'd up, performing a scene.

And, action.

"Before we begin," she said, lowering herself into the chair, "I need assurances of your discretion."

Karikh laughed. "You have my word."

"There are no recording devices in the room, are there?" Maya asked, touching the camera in her own pocket. She did this one to make Falk smile. The mental image of him cracking up in the car lifted her spirits even more.

"Of course not," said Karikh. "Our clients can count on full confidentiality. And have, for over twenty-five years."

"Good." Maya cleared her throat. "Don't know if you know this, but my father was Paul Obrandt. He died last week, and my family and I stand to inherit his considerable . . . savings."

"Condolences," interjected Karikh. "On behalf of myself and our entire institution."

"Thank you. Now, as you know, the federal estate tax in my country is absolutely brutal."

"Oh yes. Up to forty percent, isn't it?"

"Exactly. Can you imagine? For money that's already been taxed. Just so it can stay in the family. Absurd."

"It's outrageous." Karikh bit his lip and shook his head to illustrate how vexing he, too, found the US tax code. "And we have just the right experience to help you navigate these waters." His English was impeccable, Maya had to admit, though it did seem to consist mostly of prefabricated customer-service phrases. "May I ask you where it is now?"

She had trained for this question. "Mostly in Switzerland. But the moment I start the probate process, they will report everything to the IRS."

Maya had no idea what "probate" was; this was just something Falk told her to say. She was truly acting now, as was Karikh, in a way.

"Of course." The banker sighed. "The Swiss are not what they used to be. I take it there was no living trust."

"No," said Maya, just following his lead. "Which is why I'd like to move *very* fast."

Karikh nodded. "Well. This is certainly an area where we can help. Do you, or anyone in your family, have citizenship other than the US?"

This tangent they didn't prep for. Maya figured the truth wouldn't hurt, considering the information was public and easily searchable. "My mother is a citizen of Taiwan, does that help?"

"Oh yes. In fact, it makes things much, much easier. One last question before we get into the technical details. What made you choose our bank specifically?"

Here we go. "Because my father told me to, before he died," Maya said firmly, watching Karikh's face. "It was always his plan. But he also told me I need to talk to your boss."

Karikh took a long pause. "I see," he said. "Well, I'm the executive vice president. The only person above me would be Ms. Plesnevitskaya, who's not really involved in day-to-day operations."

"This isn't day-to-day," Maya replied. "And I don't mean Plesnevitskaya. I mean your *real* boss."

"I'm sure I don't know what you mean," said Karikh.

She got up from the chair, awkwardly; there was no elegant way of getting out of a Wassily. "Thank you for your time."

"Wait, wait." Karikh stood up, too. "There appears to be some kind of misunderstanding. Why don't you stay for a minute, and we'll clear it up. I saw you order a scotch downstairs, would you like another one? I'll go get it."

Maya blinked. "Sure."

Karikh hurried out of the office. Maya waited for his steps to fade, then sprang into action. The first camera went into the heating grate under the window. She fit the second into a crevice of a dusty abstract figurine whose plinth read *Bank of the Year, 2019 (Central and Eastern Europe)*. In a final bolt of inspiration, she picked the live mic off her own lapel and stuck it onto the bottom of Karikh's office phone. She was tempted to wave to Falk through the window, but he wouldn't be able to see her at this angle, so she spoke to him instead.

"Hey." Maya addressed the general direction of the trophy cam. "Hope you can see me and hear me. I'm done here. Leaving in a moment. Be ready."

Outside, a car engine revved up emphatically. He heard.

"Were you talking to someone just now?" Karikh, holding a silver tray with two glasses, opened the door with his shoulder.

"My financial adviser," said Maya. "He's recommending we take a pause."

Karikh set the tray down on the desk and handed her a scotch. "I agree. Let's not be rash. Cheers."

Maya took the glass. She'd already broken her streak, through no fault of her own, so what's one more? Sobriety restarts tomorrow.

"Cheers." She took a long pull. It felt like installing a missing puzzle piece, on a molecular level.

Karikh had one perfunctory sip and set his drink down. "Ms. Obrandt. I am trying to accommodate your unusual request as best I can. But in order to do that, I have to ask you: What did your father tell you about our bank? Perhaps he had a personal contact here that he mentioned."

The words came to her slower than she'd have liked. "Just assume that whatever my father knew, so do I."

"But, Ms. Obrandt. I checked just now, and your father has never had an account with us. I never met him."

Maya set the half-empty glass next to Karikh's. "Your boss did."

"There you go again." Unlike the Russian banker's servility, his annoyance was genuine. "I'm terribly sorry, but I am no longer sure we can help you if you insist on—"

"Fine." Maya got up and moved toward the exit. "Sorry for wasting your time and your scotch."

She pressed the handle. It wouldn't budge. She pushed harder, then kicked the door, terror flooding her brain. "Let me out!!"

"You have to pull," Karikh called from the desk.

Maya yanked the door open, almost falling backward in the process, and stumbled noisily down the stairs. By the time she got to the ground floor, both Natalia and Vitya the bartender had stepped out into the hallway to see what the commotion was.

Falk met her at the entrance, unrecognizable to CCTV in a base-ball cap and a Covid mask. He must have dashed over the moment she screamed. "I'm your driver," he whispered, taking her by the elbow. "Yell at me."

"I told you to wait in the car!" Not great improv, but it was the best she could do under the circumstances.

They got into the Kia; Maya's hands shook as she buckled up. Falk gunned it for a couple of blocks, took a hard turn into a courtyard be-tween two apartment buildings, killed the engine, and put his phone on the dashboard.

"Good job, all in all," he said. "And now we watch. And listen."

The phone's screen displayed the feeds from all three cameras planted by Maya. The lounge cam showed the banquette where she had just sat. The bar's underside blocked the top of the frame; the camera's fisheye lens bent it into a kind of visor. The grate cam was a dud. It had shifted and now stared straight up into the ceiling, showing only a sliver of win-dow. Best of all was the trophy cam, which gave a clear unobstructed view of Karikh's desk.

The banker walked into the shot, looking noticeably winded. He must have followed Maya downstairs and come back up only now. Ka-rikh plopped down in his chair and sat there for a few moments, catching his breath.

Maya put her head on Falk's shoulder. She was feeling affectionate. "Thanks for staying close," she said and kissed his clavicle. "And for run-ning in to save me." Another kiss, on the side of his neck.

Falk withdrew, gently but firmly. "I . . . think you're drunk."

"Fuck you. Go fuck yourself."

"Okay."

On the screen, Karikh reached across the desk and finished his whis-key, then, after a pause, Maya's.

"Gross," said Maya.

"He's nervous," Falk whispered. "That's promising." Karikh jabbed the air a few times, psyching himself up, then picked up the office phone.

"Give me Demin in Moscow," he said into the intercom. A few clicks followed; then, long, clear tones. "I mic'd the bottom of it," said Maya proudly. Falk squeezed her hand in approval.

"Kolya." The Russian voice on the other end of the line belonged to an older man. "Talk to me."

"It was weird, Gennady Vladimirovich. I'm not sure what to make of it."

"Just describe it."

"She is definitely his daughter. I checked. But she was, um . . . She was trying to talk to *you*."

"What?"

"I don't know if she was fishing or if he's actually read her in."

"Does she know where the money is? Does she know where *he* is?"

"That's the weirdest part, sir. She went out of her way to signal that she did. But she still thinks he's dead. It's like he fucked *her* over, too."

Maya gasped. Falk's hand was already in hers; she gripped it so hard hers went white and his went red.

"He's alive. Ari, my dad's alive." This time it was Falk who pulled her toward himself and kissed her, on the top of the head.

"I'm disappointed, Nikolai," said the man on the phone, pointedly going back from the informal *Kolya*, and hung up. Karikh threw the receiver down, sat still for a second, then banged his fist on the desk in frustration.

Falk took his phone off the dash, typed in *Gennady Vladimirovich Demin*, and started reading aloud. "President, KhromBank Group, 1997–present. President, GallTeleCom Russia, 1995–1997. Military attaché, Soviet Embassy, France, 1982—" He stopped. "Ever heard of GallTeleCom?"

"No."

"It's the French company that briefly employed your father. He helped them expand into Russia. So it looks like Demin and he worked together."

Suddenly, Maya remembered something. She could already feel the vague shape of it in her mind even before she knew what it was. "Wait, shut up. What were those dates again?"

"1995 to 1997."

"My dad's letter." She fumbled in her bag for the Ziploc; she had kept the original and Falk's handwritten translation together. "There. *When I first stepped onto this path in 1995, my intentions were pure. It sounds silly but I did think I could change the world for the better. We all did back then.*' I've been wondering what that meant. Ari? Are you listening to me?"

He wasn't. Falk was intently staring at the phone, which showed the three surveillance feeds again. Maya followed his gaze to the screen. On the previously uneventful lounge cam, Vitya the bartender knelt in front of the banquette, a phone pressed to his ear.

"Understood," he said. This time, Falk and Maya could only hear one side of the conversation. "Yes, Comrade General. Right away." He ended the call, reached under the banquette with a soft middle-age groan, and produced a Makarov handgun.

Falk glanced at Maya. "Nice camera placement."

"Had a hunch," she replied.

Vitya walked out of the shot. For several seconds, things were quiet. On the trophy cam, Karikh sat stewing behind his desk, then raised his head sharply. Someone was knocking on the door of his office.

"Aw shit," said Falk.

"Come in," Karikh yelled. "It's open."

147

Neither of the cameras covered the door, but the banker's look told everything. As soon as it creaked open, Karikh jumped to his feet and began backing toward the window. Slowly, gun first, Vitya entered the frame from the left.

This man made me coffee twenty minutes ago, thought Maya.

Karikh's back hit the windowsill. He was now visible on the grate cam, a quaking, headless tower of a man. His left oxford took up half the shot.

"Stop," he said. His teeth chattered. "I am a GRU major. I outrank you."

"Step away from the window," said the bartender, taking aim. "We can't risk breaking the glass."

"Vitya, this is a mistake." Karikh tried another tack. "A terrible misunderstanding. I *just* spoke to Comrade General."

"Yeah. So did I."

Karikh spread his arms, pressing himself against the window in a Christlike pose. "I'll jump. I'll scream and jump."

"Suit yourself," Vitya said, lowered the gun, and shot him in the left foot. The oxford exploded into the camera. Maya's hand flew up to cover her mouth, so fast she hurt her front teeth.

"Won't be taking my IRA to *this* bank," murmured Falk.

"Dude, no," said Maya through the hand. "No quips."

Karikh collapsed on the floor. On the trophy cam, Vitya calmly walked around the desk and stood astride him, pointing the gun down.

"Please!" They could no longer see the banker, but the mic on the desk phone picked up his sobbing as he writhed between Vitya's legs. "I did everything I was asked, everything. I-I-I even helped those two Spetsnaz guys who came for ammo five days ago. I—"

"Exactly," replied Vitya and fired twice at two slightly different angles. Chest, head.

1995:
CORMORANT REACH

The madness started with a cold call to the San Francisco office. The secretary picked up, listened for longer than usual, said "Wow" in her trademark flat tone that might or might not have been sarcastic, and transferred the call to Paul's line. "The guy says he's from the State Department," she yelled through the door. "That's the CIA, right?"

Paul looked at the button with the blinking light next to it, deciding whether to press it at all. It could have been some dumb prank. Having an actual office with an anteroom and a secretary and a skyline view at the age of twenty-five made Paul a bit of an odd bird within the very same group of friends that eagerly expected him to pick up every bar tab. Most of them were proud slackers who took their fashion cues from Seattle and their work ethic from a harbor seal. Success was called "selling out," a concept Paul couldn't grasp if he tried, which he didn't. Then again, being the group's resident sellout was better than the resident Russki.

"Thanks, Heather." Paul cleared his throat—in these moments, he still felt like a teen impersonating an adult—and picked up.

"Paul Obrandt speaking," he said, a fifth below his natural register, taking care to elide the persistent Russian L at the end of his own name.

"Now, this is going to be a fun memory test," said the voice on the other end. "Rex Harlow, how are ya."

"I'm sorry?"

"Doesn't ring any bells?" The man sounded more amused than disappointed. "Not even those of, say, St. Peter's Basilica?"

Paul had no idea what this was supposed to mean but a sudden discomfort gripped him nonetheless; he thought about hanging up but, for some reason, didn't.

"Oh well," the voice continued. "That's why I'm calling from downstairs. Maybe the face will jog your memory." And the line went dead.

The call had given Paul no real reason for dropping his work and riding twelve floors down to meet some potentially crazy visitor—who probably wasn't even there to begin with—except the man's chipper confidence that that was exactly what was going to happen. It was a neat trick, thought Paul as he got up from his desk. Something to try in the future.

The lobby boasted a brand-new Starbucks—the company had recently begun to install them directly in office buildings' atria. The man who stood waving in front of it was in his midforties, dressed in a Serpico leather jacket so out of fashion it was already back; in his free hand was a paper cup with two tea bag strings tucked into the sleeve, and that detail struck Paul as dimly familiar. He took an uncertain step forward.

"You know the owner?" the man asked in lieu of a greeting, gesturing at the café sign with the cup.

"Not personally. The guy's a genius, though," said Paul. "They just had their second two-for-one stock split. Now everyone wants in."

"I have no idea what you just said." The man laughed. "I just wish their tea was better. Maybe you can tell him if you two ever meet."

Right, a psycho, then. Paul was about to turn around, but it was the laugh itself—big, loud, and more youthful than expected—that made him finally place the visitor. "Oh my god. Rex Harlow. From Ladispoli."

"Bingo."

They found a table in a far corner, under a bland mural in browns and greens. Paul almost said something like *So, how have you been* but realized the inanity of it just in time. He decided to ask an actual question instead.

"We got our US entry documents right after your visit. Mom and Dad always felt you had something to do with that. Is that true?"

"Heh. What's the phrase? 'Neither confirm nor deny.'"

"Well," said Paul, "thank you, anyway. How can I help you?"

Harlow sipped his oversteeped tea. He was not in a hurry. "So, America has been good to you, eh? A millionaire by twenty-five."

"Barely. I'm putting everything back into the company."

"Great scheme, too," said Harlow. "Find fresh-off-the-boat engineering nerds, help them file US patents, then buy those patents off them."

"You're making it sound like a swindle," said Paul, mildly annoyed. "I don't buy anything off anyone. I form partnerships."

"Oh, my apologies. I'm not up on the lingo. So when you turn around and lease these patents to big telecoms, are your partners happy?"

Paul shrugged. "They make money."

"But not *millions*."

Paul could physically feel the last dregs of patience draining out of him. It happened to him often, these little rages; more often now than before.

"They all read the contracts they sign. If some people still have the commie mindset where all they want is a salary on the first of the month, it's not my job to fix it. Seriously, man, can I help you?"

Harlow let the pause hang in the air. The suit-and-tied crowd murmured around them. The café's PA system was playing a song by Suzanne Vega, a soft fingerpicked number, and it calmed Paul down a bit.

"I want you to go see someone," Harlow finally said. "In my line of work, I meet extraordinary people. Like you. Sometimes I see opportunities that I myself can't take. The government sector is capricious like that. But I do hate seeing them go to waste. There is an old man in Sea Ranch, looking to invest some hundred and fifty million into a new broadcasting company. He thinks you can be the one to build that company for him. And I agree."

For a second, Paul just sat there, digesting the number. "Where?"

"In Sea Ranch."

"No, where would I be—"

Harlow laughed again. "Look at you. Yes, there's a catch. There's always a catch. Doesn't mean it's not the luckiest break in your entire life."

"So what are you, my fairy godmother? Will you show up in another ten years next?"

"I can guarantee you I won't."

"Sorry," said Paul. "But I need way more information."

"Can you say the same thing but in Russian?" suddenly asked Harlow. Paul did. "Happy?"

"Hmm." He wasn't. "Ten years is a lifetime, isn't it, when you're fifteen on one end and twenty-five on the other. You've got a slight accent in your Russian now, did you know that? But that's fine. It'll buff out."

"Who cares?"

"Just promise me you'll see the guy." Harlow got up from his chair, slipped the sleeve off his cup, and left the cup itself on the table, a strange gesture. "Tomorrow at dinnertime. Old-folks dinnertime, that is. Don't drive, don't take a taxi. Only the bus. Talk soon. *Ciao.*"

Paul watched the visitor cross the marble lobby and vanish in the revolving doors, then realized that he never got the address. He switched his attention to the cup. Scrawled across it in a barista's felt-tip pen were the words *Cormorant Reach.*

"That's a hell of a way to misspell Rex Harlow," he said out loud.

■ ■ ■

There was no need to guess the house number. According to the map, the road called Cormorant Reach only had one.

The fact that the investor lived out here was eccentric enough in itself. Not quite a town, Sea Ranch was a utopian private development from the '60s, clinging to the oceanside cliffs a hundred miles north of San Francisco. The area was awash in aging idylls like this—experiments in communal living, eco-conscious kibbutzim, spiritual retreats. Collectivism on a capitalist's dime. Perhaps the guy owned the whole thing. Still, it was odd; the investors with whom Paul normally dealt lived in places like Berkeley and Palo Alto, not in centrally planned hamlets up the coast.

Odder still were Harlow's instructions. The first bus had gotten Paul as far as Santa Rosa. The second, to Anchor Bay, wasn't even meant to stop here but he had talked the driver into depositing him on the shoulder. He was now five excruciating hours into the trip, and still a mile away from the destination. A full workday wasted on transit. This had better be good.

The house, when he finally glimpsed it through the trees, didn't scream wealth. Like every building in Sea Ranch, it was a timber-frame box with redwood siding, silvered by time, and a sloping roof that formed a wedge against the ocean winds. If not for its carefully considered golden-ratio proportions, it would look like a barn. The narrow forest path leading to it turned into a raised catwalk in the last stretch, making Paul think of a Ray Bradbury story he liked as a kid. He had forgotten the title—he read it in a Russian translation, anyway—but it was the one where the butterfly metaphor came from. A time machine is invented and immediately put to commercial use; you can pay to see live dinosaurs as long as you keep to a special suspended walkway. A man steps off, squashes

155

a prehistoric butterfly, and when he comes back, the US has a fascist for president.

Here he was, then, stomping down the path, about to see a live dinosaur.

The woman who opened the door was sixty or so, with two long gray braids, dressed in a fleece atop a kaftan. "Sorry," she said, gesturing for Paul to come in. "The heater is on the fritz. We're making do."

Paul stepped in. It was, indeed, very cold. The inside of the house looked like something out of a 1960s whiskey ad: a sunken conversation pit whose inner walls did double duty as bookshelves, a bulbous fireplace suspended from the ceiling by its own chimney. The floor, in the few places where it was visible under an overlapping grid of Middle Eastern rugs, was slabs of polished stone.

"Paul Obrandt!" boomed a voice from the pit. The man Harlow sent him here to meet lounged in an Eames chair, feet as close to the fire as feasible without roasting the soles of his slippers. He didn't strike Paul as all that old, at least not old enough for it to become his defining characteristic: the same age as the woman, perhaps. He leaned out of the chair, with some difficulty, and patted a nearby Moroccan pouf. Paul awkwardly descended the three steps into the pit and sat down, feeling a little like a summoned lapdog.

"Jane and I are ecstatic that you're here. Ecstatic." The man extended his hand. His skin was dry and near translucent, calling to mind the vellum of an expensive invitation; Paul was afraid he'd break it if he squeezed too hard.

"I realize I need to introduce myself," said the host. "But, at this point, you must also understand that any name you'll hear me say won't be my real one. So you might as well just make one up in your mind."

How about Cormorant, thought Paul, but didn't say it out loud. There was something avian about the man, too, though he looked more like a large wading bird than sea fowl: an ibis, say, or an egret.

"Look, Paul, I'm going to ask you some heavy questions right now. Don't let them freak you out."

"Sure."

"Are humans, by and large, good or evil?"

Paul had had some run-ins with the eccentric Californian rich. One potential investor in his company wanted to see his astrological chart first; another wouldn't sign any contracts on a Wednesday because of something to do with Norse mythology. This wasn't it. This was a test whose purpose and parameters he didn't yet grasp.

"If I believed in God, I'd probably see things in Gnostic terms," he said. "We're flawed matter, but with a hidden light inside. Unfortunately, I don't."

". . . And?"

"I think most humans just want to be left alone," said Paul.

Cormorant pursed his lips. "So you're a young Libertarian. *Atlas Shrugged*, all that?"

"God no. In fact, I think Ms. Alisa Rosenbaum did more harm to capitalism than Lenin." The old man snorted. He seemed to enjoy the barb.

"I think the state has a role," Paul elaborated. "Being left alone is a luxury right now. You need a lot of infrastructure in place to make it a human right."

"National infrastructure? Or global?" The questions came faster now. It looked like Cormorant was ramping up to trick him into blurting out something he'd later regret.

"Ideally both. I like the UN, wish it had more teeth. I like the European project, the idea of uniting cultures through economic policy. It can be like a nonevil USSR."

"Are any cultures inherently superior to others?"

"Just ask me if I'm a racist. No. Nurture over nature, every time. All cultural issues are class issues."

"Huh. You're an anti-Communist Marxist! Fascinating. Is the US good?"

The offhand way Cormorant introduced this question succeeded in tripping Paul up. He cleared his throat, opened his mouth, closed it.

"Okay," he said, slowly. "I am an immigrant, as you know. So I know I'm supposed to be grateful, and I am. Is this a perfect country? No. Can it be, a hundred years from now? Maybe. It's the only one that aspires to treat humans as a species."

"What do you think about Russia?" The man just jumped to the next question, as if checking off boxes. Paul felt a surge of anger coming on.

"The short answer is, I don't," he said. "My family fought too hard to leave it behind. How many more of these have you got before we get to talk business?"

"My boy," said Cormorant. "We've been talking business for ten minutes now."

The woman, whose name was almost certainly not Jane, reappeared, carrying a tray with two coffees and weird snacks: raisins, pine nuts, a dish of candy-coated fennel seeds. It looked like a spread for an anteater.

"Thank you," Paul said, ate a pinch of pine nuts out of courtesy, and turned back to Cormorant. "Look, Harlow told me you want to start a broadcasting company, and it's pretty obvious that you want to start it in Russia. I mean, objectively it makes sense. It's a big emerging market, they have a whole telecom infrastructure to reinvent. I know a lot of people my age are heading there and making real money, at least if their cars don't blow up first. But I— If you're looking for a Russia expert, I'm not the guy. I don't have any ins there. I haven't kept up. Plus, the Communists might come back any moment."

"Exactly," said Cormorant. "Which is why I'm not offering you to go to Russia on some tawdry business errand. I'm offering you to go and save it."

Paul looked around, as if for a hidden camera. "Is this a joke?"

"Absolutely not." Cormorant sat up in the Eames and swung his legs to the side, perching on the edge and facing Paul directly. "Let's go back to those Gnostics that you so aptly mentioned. Most of the time, in most of the places, the light is under attack. On a rare occasion, however, the enlightened get to turn the tables. And that's the short moment when good things can get done—before humanity defaults back to its worst instincts."

"Okay."

"In Russia, that moment is right now. There's some actual democracy happening. The KGB—sorry, FSB, how could I—are in retreat. Some of them are betting on the Communists and some are cozying up to Boris and his free-market crew. This state of things will last for one more year if we're lucky. Next summer is the presidential election. Boris will have to win, despite being the most hated man in the country, and whatever emerges on the other end of that election won't be a democracy any-more. In fact, the only way *anything* works after that is if the FSB comes back as the glue holding it all together."

"Okay," repeated Paul.

"So imagine, for just a second, that it doesn't have to be like that. That there's another way."

"Are you asking me to run? I'm afraid Russia is not ready for a twenty-five-year-old Jewish president with a US passport."

Cormorant laughed. "Are you familiar with Konovalov?"

"Yes." Sergei Konovalov was, by all accounts, a great man. A Soviet biochemist of international renown, in 1980 he had become a vocal critic of the Afghan war. Unprepared to shove a Nobel winner into prison, the Kremlin reluctantly allowed Konovalov to emigrate—which is when he cemented his legend by refusing to do so. Five years of forced treatments in psychiatric hospitals followed. Released by Gorbachev's personal decree into a changing country, the gaunt, hollow-eyed Konovalov became Russia's closest thing to a living saint. To everyone's disappointment, he had retreated into science and took no further interest in public life, apart from issuing a periodic plague-on-both-your-houses homily.

"Imagine if someone like that ran Russia," said Cormorant. "A man of complete and utter integrity. A mix of Mandela and Sakharov."

"Yes, that would be amazing. But it's a dream. Last I checked, integrity was not on the table."

"It could be. Dreams have a way of becoming reality once you put them on TV," said Cormorant, and Paul finally understood what it was they were talking about this whole time.

"The game, right now, is *bands and frequencies*," Cormorant continued. "The USSR had a chunk of the spectrum reserved for future military use, by an army that can no longer afford a pair of warm boots. So let's imagine an international telecom that takes it off their hands and enters the Russian market with 2G phone service, FM radio, cable TV, and a federal broadcast channel of its own. Imagine all these services run at the Western level of talent and expertise. Imagine them advocating for the values we share. And, when the right time comes, for Konovalov."

"The army may be corrupt and starving," said Paul, "but would they really sell these frequencies to an American?"

"American, as in some guy named Craig who chews gum, keeps his shoes on indoors, and speaks to them through an interpreter? Probably not. To a Jewish *boychik* who wore a Young Communist League pin only ten years ago? Sure they would."

"Okay, maybe," said Paul, a little hurt by the distinction. "But it's not just the Russians you have to persuade. Washington made its choice. They're all in on Boris."

Cormorant nodded. "Rex wasn't kidding about you being smart. But we are not Washington. We are, well . . . Sea Ranch."

"Please. Are you telling me Rex is not CIA?"

"Oh, Rex is *very* much CIA," Cormorant said casually. "In fact, he is the incoming chief of Moscow Station. Which, again, is why it has to be you."

"Wait. You can't . . . you can't just say it to me like this. I haven't agreed yet."

Haven't you? Cormorant's smile seemed to say as he went on. "The venture capital financing your company will be French. In the eyes of the world, you will come to Russia supported by the sane European center and not-all-the-way-to-Stalin left, while the old US of A keeps throwing its weight behind Boris. And the best part? No one will ever suspect you of doing it for a cause, because you'll be making so much damn money."

Paul felt dizzy. He got up from the pouf and walked around the floating fireplace for a bit, trying to regain some sense of reality. Not-Jane came back and removed the coffee tray. The old man watched him from the Eames, head cocked to the side, like he had just painted him and was pretty happy with the result.

One of the bookshelves built into the pit walls was a shrine of sorts to Konovalov: Soviet academic journals from the 1960s, five or so copies of an American-published biography, a neat stack of laminated newspaper clippings. Paul picked up the book, a solemn dust-jacketed tome from Princeton University Press.

"Ah, that. Rex's work," said Cormorant.

"He *wrote* this?"

"Of course not. Just gave a little nudge to the author. There's a TV movie based on it, too."

"I was going to ask if Konovalov knew about your plans for him," said Paul, slotting the book back in the gap between two just like it. "I guess this answers my question."

"It does not," replied Cormorant with unexpected metal in his voice. "We're not installing a puppet here. He wants to run, and he will certainly be happy to have your support, but that's where it ends. You will be the only one to know this support's full extent. Understood?"

"Yes, sir," said Paul, chastened. His gaze fell on the freshest clipping, from *Corriere della Sera*. It described Konovalov's rare trip abroad for an audience with the pope. Paul could still read Italian, thanks to the year in Ladispoli, but what caught his attention was a dark-haired young woman standing a step behind Konovalov in the photo. Long aristocratic face, large eyes set just a tad close; ravishing, despite the shapeless black dress and bowed head.

"Who's that?" he asked. "Wife, daughter? Lover?"

"Executive secretary," said Cormorant. "Quite a brilliant young thing, your age. She will probably end up his campaign manager."

"You'd really let twentysomethings run this?" asked Paul, just to say something that wouldn't be a comment on her appearance.

"Who else?" thundered Harlow's voice from the entrance. "The grown-ups were the ones who blew it!"

The incoming chief of Moscow Station walked up to the edge of the pit and waved at Paul for the second time in two days. "I trust you two had a good talk."

"All I hoped for and more," said Cormorant.

"I knew it. Come on, Pavlik," said Harlow, "I'll give you a ride back into town."

Paul didn't realize it had gotten dark until they were outside. The air smelled like pine sap. A large insect kept hitting the lamp above the front door with a dull *thunk* that he could still hear even after he couldn't see the house. For a minute, they silently trod the creaky catwalk, Harlow first, Paul trailing behind. Harlow's car, a Buick of an indeterminate color, stood parked on the shoulder at the far end of the path.

"So what kind of dossier on me did you give him?" asked Paul.

Harlow stopped, turned around, leaned back on the railing, and grinned.

"Just the facts. That you hate the Soviet Union but feel very strongly about Russia. You pretend that you don't, but you do. You have no Russians in your social circle. You've never slept with a Russian girl."

"What the fuck," said Paul. "How long have you—"

Harlow just raised his voice and continued over him. ". . . You get angry when it's mentioned, yet you bring it up unbidden. You took three years of accent-reduction courses. But the thing is, ever since you were a fifteen-year-old hawking camera lenses, every good idea in your head involved Russia. And that's what I told him. That you *think* you need to leave it behind to come into your own. When what you *really* need is to come back on a white fucking horse and show them who's boss."

Paul stood in the middle of the catwalk, staring past the trees at the nearly invisible surf. He knew every word of this was right, if only from how much it hurt. Strangely, though, he wasn't angry. Pacific waves crashed and hissed in the dusk.

"And if I said no?" he asked.

"I'd still give you a ride," said Harlow, joking but perhaps not. "It would just be shorter."

CHAPTER FIVE

Falk stared out of the compartment window. Smudged Nordic scenery streamed past, birches and aspens already turning yellow. The darker it got, the clearer he could see his own tense frown in the glass. The Russian border was only a few miles out.

The train was Latvian, with modern fittings. Falk had taken a first-class compartment, which had a full-size bed, two armchairs, and an en suite shower. It was an eccentric choice for a solo traveler with no luggage, but the splurge had a strategy behind it: people in first class tended to get shorter and more perfunctory border checks. For all the centralized, digitized, post-9/11, late-pandemic security rituals adopted by every state, some aspects of travel hadn't changed since the 1800s New York Harbor—when those arriving in steerage headed for quarantine, and those in staterooms disembarked with barely a hat tip. Money was still the best form of ID.

He wistfully recalled the old Soviet cars that still ran on these tracks in 2006, during his first Russia tour. Sooty, drafty, redolent of creosote and tobacco, they had had a touch of Eastern Bloc romance to them: the communal water boiler, the rough but real linens, the glasses of tea

165

rattling in filigreed metal holders. The sensible Scandi luxury surrounding him now felt a little generic in comparison.

Ugh, Falk thought, not the corny old Russophilia rearing its head again. Something about going to Moscow always woke the dormant Slavic lit major in him.

Even, it would seem, when the trip was a likely suicide run.

As soon as he and Maya said their stilted goodbyes at the Riga airport, Falk called Keegan and asked for any and all CCTV footage from the streets around the EiropaBank branch. Sure enough, it showed the two Sokol Media Research attackers—their faces acid-etched into Falk's memory—entering the bank and exiting, with heavy duffel bags, minutes before the raid. Major Karikh hadn't been lying in his last moments.

He had also called them Spetsnaz, which in this case meant Spetsnaz GRU: an infamous unit used in paramilitary foreign missions. Its training regimen reportedly included baroque tasks designed to dehumanize both the enemy and the soldier himself—shooting a stray dog, beheading a rabbit and drinking its blood, body-searching a mutilated corpse. Those were the people who killed Inga and Klaus, and now he was going to Moscow for a chat with their master.

Normally, day-to-day movements of a high-ranking Russian military intelligence officer would take a roomful of SIGINT specialists to nail down. But Demin's modus operandi was to hide in plain sight—his civilian guise as the suave eighty-year-old head of a bank meant a public persona, public engagements, and even a publicly listed work address. After minutes of basic research, Falk knew that Demin kept a suite of offices just outside of Moscow, on the top floor of the Matryoshka building in the Skolkovo technology park. He even knew the building: a black, thirteen-story pyramid with floors arranged around a central void in the shape of a giant Russian nesting doll. It was intended as some kind of artistic statement, but ended up projecting an intensely malevolent vibe instead. That a GRU slush fund would occupy the doll's head was almost too perfect.

For all his rage, Falk was just sane enough to realize that any physical move against Demin would be not only self-sacrificial but pointless. Even if he managed to get up to the thirteenth floor of the Matryoshka, bluff or shoot his way past the doubtlessly military-trained security, end the man himself, leave no fingerprints, exit the building alive, safely escape Russia, and reinstall himself back at the Pimlico safe house without Akinyemi or Harlow being any the wiser—an extremely unlikely series of ifs!—the impact of this improbable caper on the known universe would be nil. Anton, Inga, and Klaus would still be dead. The Russians would get themselves a new Demin. Paul Obrandt, his mystery woman, and their stolen billions would remain in the wind. He, Ari Falk, would still get pulled from the field and spend the next thirty years shuffling papers at Langley—or whatever would replace papers, or Langley, by then. And Maya? Maya would go on, alone, abandoned, and traumatized for life. Ironically, that last part may have done more than any other to make him stifle his worst instincts.

What Falk had resolved to do instead hewed much closer to his actual area of expertise as a case officer. He was going to recruit someone.

The biggest piece of intel his investigation had yet produced—frankly without meaning to—was hard proof that Russian military intelligence, operating out of a bank branch on EU territory, assassinated two European citizens and came close to assassinating an American. In and of itself, this was a bigger bombshell than anything else Falk had ever worked on. At the moment, despite the sanctions against the Russian financial sector, KhromBank's international "daughter" banks were still tolerated in the West. Properly framed, Falk's and Maya's findings would give both

Washington and Brussels the long-needed leverage to sanction the whole company and arrest its funds abroad.

Now, *that* would have an impact. Obrandt's loot was chump change compared to all of KhromBank's foreign holdings. If Demin's superiors in the Kremlin found out that he'd jeopardized their entire setup while chasing after a measly five *yards*—slang for billion—they'd do to him everything Falk would have liked to, and likely more. The only reason Demin wouldn't be facing an unfortunate fall out of his Matryoshka office window is that the building was a pyramid. He'd just slide down.

That's what a grown-up's revenge looked like. Falk already had the evidence of conspiracy in the video and audio of Karikh's last moments. All he needed now was an insider willing to show him how, exactly, the money moved within the KhromBank system. And he was going to Moscow to find one.

Zilupe, the last station on the Latvian side, whipped by the windows. Falk checked the time. In another hour, Maya would be changing planes in Munich. Twelve more hours later, she was scheduled to touch down in LA. They had decided that when she did, she would contact him one last time, on the burner from Inga's stash, then destroy the phone. The perspective of hearing Maya's voice once more felt nice. He didn't expect it to and overcorrected by recoiling all the way to guilt: it was as if this somehow diminished the memory of Inga.

The woods parted, revealing a harshly lit clearing. The train slowed down and rolled to a halt in the glare of tower-mounted floodlights. A car attendant walked the corridor, sliding every compartment's door open.

First in were the Latvians—a man and an older woman with a German shepherd straining against the leash. The two seemed concerned mostly with whatever the dog was trained to sniff out, and they were in and out of the compartment in a matter of seconds. The man held a little mechanical device for counting passengers, glanced at Falk, and clicked it once; a somewhat discomfiting *Ugunskrusts* tattoo covered the back of his palm.

The Russian officer came in next. She was a blonde barely above Maya's age, with gunmetal eyes and a thin mouth, wearing the green shoulder boards of the FSB border service. Falk said hello and handed in his too-crisp blue passport.

"Thomas Richard, yes?" she said.

"Richards," corrected Falk.

"Yes-yes." She began leafing through the book in search of a Russian visa. Luckily, it came preloaded with one, courtesy of the almost certainly nonexistent Tyumen Oblast External Trade Council. The organization wasn't even a CIA front. The Russian Ministry of Foreign Affairs had long outsourced visa processing to private companies for kickbacks: ironically, they were the ones inventing phantom councils and conferences, to make their own jobs easier.

The officer took out her stamp, then paused, set it aside, and frowned. "This is your first trip to the Russian Federation, right?"

"It is."

She ran her thumb over the pages, as if trying to see if they would rotoscope into a cartoon if flipped fast enough. "And in the last, uh, *three days*, you visited the United Kingdom . . . Morocco . . . and Latvia."

"I've had a pretty hectic workweek," said Falk.

"I can see that," the woman replied, no expression on her face. "But how did you get *to* the United Kingdom? There's only the exit stamp, no entry."

Great, he heard Maya's sarcastic lilt in his head. *We got ourselves a competent one.*

"The stamp is in my old passport." Falk decided it was time to start sounding a little incensed. He was, after all, a wealthy businessman traveling in style. "Which I lost. Which is why this one is new. Is there a problem?"

"Hmm." It was hard to tell whether she bought it. "I see. Please wait. I need to check on something."

She walked out, taking the documents with her. Falk frantically tried to compute the next steps. His cover was as flimsy as they came. The passport was part of a go bag, meant to be used once in an emergency; he was now crossing his third border with it. If it tripped any internal alarms at the Agency, so be it—he'd deal with it later—but if the Russians had kept Falk's face on file from his earlier visits, he was more or less toast. No one had gone to the trouble of building a proper legend for Mr. Richards. Any real scrutiny would immediately reveal a Falk-shaped void larger than a thirteen-story nesting doll.

Even dying in a hail of bullets on Demin's doorstep now seemed less stupid than the very real perspective of getting nabbed at the border. Harlow might get him out in some tawdry spy swap, but his life would be over; every insane thing he'd done over the last week would stay forever in vain.

Falk involuntarily glanced at one of the two armchairs. Jammed deep between its cushions was his subcompact handgun. He sat down. Not that he was in any way prepared to shoot his way out of a passenger train, but—

The officer came back, her face unreadable. "Everything's in order," she said, handing him the stamped passport. "Enjoy the rest of your trip."

For a few minutes after she left, Falk sat very still. Then the train began to move again, wheels playing their accelerating two-note *Jaws* riff as they passed over rail joints. The darkness outside the window was now Russia.

■ ■ ■

MUNICH
AUGUST 25, 2021

Maya thought she'd be a nervous wreck but she slept through the entire flight from Riga to Munich, passing out at takeoff with no pharmaceutical help. These were the best two hours of sleep Maya had gotten all week. She was almost upset that the journey's first leg was so short.

The Munich airport had a gleaming new terminal with fancy retail; just moving through it made Maya feel like parts of her basic old self were flying in from all directions and attaching to her like Iron Man's armor. She walked into a Hermès and bought a conservative scarf for Mom and a fun one for Baba Polina. She went to Duty Free and slathered about six different toners, serums, and moisturizers on her face and neck. An Australian backpacker in the line to the register hit on her, as if they were ever going to be on the same continent again. She sat in a green lounge with environmental facts on the walls, ate a Bretzel, and watched two kids fight over an iPad charger.

The only thing that kept Maya tethered to the last days' terrors was the phone Falk had given her. It came with one number in Contacts— that of Falk's own identical burner, which only had hers. Maya could feel it in her bag, exerting a certain dark pull. She alternated between the temptations to call him for a chat (he'd hate that!) and to throw the phone out and sever the last connection between them.

Who was this guy to her, anyway? A volunteer bodyguard, an unusually intense two-night stand, a dangerous pet? When they last embraced at Departures in Riga, Falk kept looking everywhere but at her. Perhaps he was checking the corners for Demin's men. Or perhaps it was something else.

She imagined him alone on the night train to Moscow. ("Whoa, expensive taste, buddy," she said when Falk specifically asked for a first-class compartment. "*I'm* flying economy.") If she were in that compartment with him, they'd most likely be having sex right now. Over the last two days and nights they'd fucked too many times to count, mostly as a mutually agreed-upon coping technique. Only the last time felt different. They were at the Airbnb, after the noontime organ concert, before heading to the bank. Taking her to a cathedral to listen to Bach was an out-of-character, weirdly boyfriend-y move, and it puzzled her until she realized how *sad* Falk was that morning. For him, Riga was a city of the dead. He wanted a glimpse of normal life, if only for an hour before it all went to hell. And that's what the sex that day was like, too. Not two people using each other for a shortcut to oblivion. Just . . . two people.

"Passengers traveling to Los Angeles, the flight is about to start preboarding," the PA announced. The business-class crowd, heavily Slavic from the looks of it, began massing at the gate.

You know what? She *was* going to text him. Just one line, to let him know she had safely made it to Munich. Maya took the phone out of the bag and turned it on.

It rang at once, so loudly and so immediately that she almost dropped it.

"Ha ha, fucking busted," Maya said in a singsongy voice, putting the phone to her ear. "You looove me. Can't live withooout me."

"I'm sorry, I don't understand English," an older man said in Russian after a pause. "But I would very much like to speak to Maya Chou Obrandt."

Maya felt the walls of the airport contract around her, until the whole world became a windowless phone booth. She recognized the voice.

"My name is Gennady Vladimirovich Demin. I am the head of the

172

bank you visited earlier today," the man continued, as if this was a routine customer service follow-up.

"How— How did you get this—"

"You called the bank from it when you made the appointment," said Demin patiently.

Right. I did, didn't I.

"Okay. But why are you—"

"Maya . . ." said Demin. "May I call you Maya? I am inviting you to come to Moscow tonight, as my guest."

"You're a fucking murderer." Russian cursing wasn't exactly Maya's forte—neither Dad nor old Soviet cartoons taught her that side of the language, obviously, and she had no Russian friends as a teen—but she was pretty sure that *ty yobanyi ubiyca* did the job.

"That I am," Demin agreed, with a wistful cast to his voice. "And however you've come to know this, I'm glad that you do. Let there be no secrets between us. But I haven't hurt you before, when I very easily could have. I hope this will help you trust my solemn promise that I won't hurt you now, either."

"Great. Thank you for not killing me. Superkind of you. So why would I want to go to Moscow, again?"

"Because it's the only way you can save your father's life," Demin said and hung up.

As she stared at the phone, figuring out whether and how to tell Falk about this, a shadow fell across the screen. Maya lifted her head. Right in front of her, though at a respectable social distance, stood a sandy-haired man in a checked brown suit, with the bearing of a sommelier. Behind him she could see a line of passengers already boarding the LA flight.

"So. No one is forcing you," said the sandy-haired man in English with a strong Southern German accent. Demin must have scrambled some local help. "If you do decide to come, which he hopes you will, please take this."

He held out his right hand, showing an Aeroflot boarding pass in Maya's name. "The flight leaves in an hour. You can be in California by this time tomorrow, with your papa." The *Papa* made her shudder.

"Now seating Groups Two and Three," the gate agent announced over the PA.

"Well," said Maya, getting up, "that's my cue. Please move aside. We're in a public place and you will not like what's going to happen in about three seconds if you don't."

"As you wish." The man stepped to his right and back, as if practicing a waltz. Maya walked past him, half expecting a stealth toxin injection as she did.

He had prepared something worse. "Just one last thing," she heard behind her back, polite and quiet. "We already know you couldn't live with him dead. So please tell me, how will you live knowing *you* killed him?"

■ ■ ■

MOSCOW
AUGUST 26, 2021

If anyone could get Falk inside KhromBank, it would be the man named Vasily Balashov. Moscow was a megalopolis of twelve million that operated like a medieval castle town. A set of concentric circles, the smallest of which was the Kremlin wall and the largest the sixty-seven-mile Ring Road, it radiated all its power from within the innermost two; perhaps a total of five hundred people ensconced there, most of them in the same few neighborhoods, steered the entire course of Russia's political (five to ten men, though some would argue just one), financial (30 to 50), cultural (200 to 300), and even gastronomic life. To move within these circles, literal and otherwise, you didn't need to know everyone. You needed to know one person who knew everyone else. There were a few of these human switchboards walking around; Balashov was Falk's.

The former FSB officer had asked to meet at White Rabbit, a hideously expensive restaurant on Smolenskaya, claiming it was the safest place in Moscow for a *treff*. Seeing how it stood kitty-corner from the Ministry of Foreign Affairs and did double duty as a diplomat canteen, Falk conceded that he might have a point. What better place to lunch with a spy than in a room full of them.

More perplexing than the location was the restaurant's decor, built around motifs from *Alice in Wonderland*. Why a place serving elevated Russian cuisine would need paintings of Victorian clocks and top-hatted rabbits was anyone's guess. As Harlow once quipped to Falk on his first tour, *Every restaurant in Moscow is a theme restaurant. The theme is that you're not in Moscow.* Falk handed his Carhartt jacket to a wardrobe attendant clearly more used to handling Gucci and followed a hostess to the table.

Balashov had scored the best spot in the room—a booth directly in front of the giant rose window looking out onto the ministry's spire. He had already ordered a slew of seafood appetizers and was close to finishing all of them. He had a shisha pipe going, too, which seemed like a terrible combination. Seeing Falk, he jumped to his feet and vigorously waved him in, like someone helping a student driver parallel-park.

"Great to see you," Falk said, sitting down, and only then actually looked. Balashov was thirty-five, but belonged to the male Russian phenotype that looked fifty years old from college through retirement. He had also managed to double his weight since Falk saw him last. The booth was meant for four, but Balashov took up his side almost entirely.

"*Fantastic* to see you," the man boomed in response. "Hope you're here to make some Kremlin fuckers cry blood."

Falk instinctively looked around. He wasn't yet used to Balashov's status as an out-and-proud opposition star. Back in 2012 to 2014, when Harlow turned him and Falk ran him, he was a midlevel FSB agent with writerly ambitions—always a red flag—and a cocaine habit so massive that he soon stopped being useful to either side. In 2020, however, something changed in Balashov. He had used his time in quarantine to clean up, find God, and write a series of tell-all essays about government corruption that actually had prompted some small reforms. The Russian intelligentsia and Western press alike embraced him as a rare late convert willing to talk, and he seemed to have just enough unused dirt on his superiors to wangle himself some kind of immunity.

"Look how you flinched just now." Balashov's laugh shook the table. "Relax! This is a watering hole, Ari. All kinds of animals drink side by side here."

"Vasily," said Falk. "I'm going to be very quick. I need—"

He stopped, because at this point, with precise comedic timing, a waiter thrust a menu at him. It was printed on vellum and copied from the chef's own hand. Falk returned it without reading, pointed at a half-eaten shrimp plate on the table, and asked to get the same.

"Sakhalin sweet prawns with guacamole and raspberries. Great choice," said the waiter and switched his attention to Balashov. "Anything else for you, sir?"

"Absolutely! I'll have the Kamchatka crab knuckles in caviar sauce, and let's get my friend here some sea urchin." Balashov turned to Falk. "Have you tried Murmansk sea urchin? It wipes the floor with the Japanese stuff."

"Great choice," repeated the waiter. He then leaned in closer to Balashov's ear, as if to tell him about a secret special dish. "Thank you for all you do, Vasily Olegovich. Don't let the bastards get you."

"What was that?" asked Falk when the waiter left.

"Oh, nothing," said Balashov, clearly pleased. "I gave a little speech the other day that's making the rounds."

"I like this version of you, Vasily," said Falk. "You've really found yourself."

"Road to Damascus, my friend, road to Damascus. Have you had yours yet?"

"My what?"

"Revelation. The only one worth having. The one where you realize it's all bullshit and people are the same everywhere."

"I might be in the process of one," Falk answered.

"Fuck yeah, brother. Now, how can I help you?"

Falk leaned in. "I need someone disgruntled at KhromBank. Preferably at their Skolkovo HQ."

"Oh ho ho," said Balashov. "Tough ask. They run a tight ship there."

"I'm sure they do. And I'm sure you know every rat on it."

"Yeah, yeah. Got it." Balashov nodded and fell silent, tapped his index finger against his lip. The waiter brought the prawns and the sea urchin and apologetically told them that the crab would take a few more minutes. "They're killing it right now," he added.

". . . It's doable," Balashov finally said. "But you gotta give me something, too."

Falk spooned some grayish-yellow urchin into his mouth. It tasted like Jell-O made of iodine. "Anything you need," he said. "You know we're sympathetic to the cause."

Balashov stared somewhere past the food, through the plate and into the table. "No, not that. Something I can take back you-know-where to justify this meeting. And it has to be good."

Falk felt like an idiot. "I see. So what you're telling me is, you're still on the clock."

"Don't be a child, Ari," Balashov said, trying to condescend while still avoiding eye contact.

A whole tableful of puzzle pieces clicked together. Balashov's spectacular Saul-to-Paul conversion was a psyop, the revelations in his essays preapproved, and the corrupt officials he was blasting had likely just fallen out of favor with his bosses. His new brief was to cosplay as an opposition firebrand while shuffling favors back and forth between interested parties.

For a second, Falk acutely missed Anton and his kamikaze integrity. So many good people dead while these bottom-feeders thrive. *And always will, because we let them, because we need them.*

The memory also bolstered his resolve. "Fine," he said. "I got something. It's good. Too good for you, to be honest."

"Restroom, five minutes." Balashov got up, slapped breadcrumbs off his sweater, and left. Falk listlessly poked at a translucent prawn, ordered an Americano, gulped it down, and followed his own white rabbit toward the toilets.

The wallpaper in the men's room brought the restaurant's theme to a maddening apex: it teemed with hundreds of lapine silhouettes big and small, so many and so close together that Falk felt seasick looking at them. They all seemed to be hopping over one another.

"I'm here!" said Balashov from inside a stall. "You can talk."

"The name is Philip Broward," said Falk through the nausea. "It doesn't matter if you know who that is, so long as your boss does. Tell him he's got a day, maybe two, before the Brits move on him."

"All right." Falk heard tapping, then the sound of an outgoing Signal message and an incoming reply. Balashov flushed and emerged from the stall, buttoning up his pants.

"You got yourself a deal," he announced.

"Is this tradecraft or did you actually take a shit in there?" asked Falk. "Don't answer that."

Balashov put his palms under a faucet for a few seconds. "Be careful what you wish for," he said in English. "Um, dinner's on you, right?"

"Yes, yes. Go eat your crab. I've taken care of the check. Sorry, no handshake, for at least two reasons."

"Fair enough." Balashov gave him a wave and left the restroom whistling the theme to *The Fixies*, a popular kids' cartoon. Falk waited for the tune to fade out of earshot, spat into the sink, and washed his hands like he hadn't since the first spring of Covid.

■ ■ ■

She spent the Munich-Moscow flight calculating her odds of surviving the night, and landed on 30 to 70. Then they put her up at the Ritz.

The entire experience was an unnerving mix of luxury travel and prisoner transfer. The German escorted Maya to the gate but took her burner in exchange for the boarding pass. At Sheremetyevo, Maya was led past all controls via a back passage reserved for diplomats and celebrities and met on the other side by a yawning consulate staffer who issued her an entry visa on the spot. When she emerged in the arrivals zone, with no luggage to pick up, the first thing she saw was a black-suited driver holding a tablet that read MAYA OBRANDT. His S-Class stood parked right outside, in violation of every imaginable airport rule; if he could get it through the revolving doors, he'd have probably driven it into the hall. "I get it, I get it," she murmured to herself, getting in. The message was loud and clear. She was in the care, and thus at the whim, of the people who ran the whole fucking place.

The hotel, a gaudy folly with a glass portico meant to evoke Fabergé, looked empty. Russia had long dispensed with the masks and quarantines but kept the travel restrictions in place; there were barely any Westerners getting in or Russians getting out—which, Maya suspected, was the way people like Demin liked it. Her small steps echoed in the marble-clad lobby as she approached the reception desk. Sure enough, they already had her key.

The coddling had recalibrated her brain so much that she caught herself getting slightly miffed to find the room a regular size, not some kind of czarina suite. *If only we got used to terrible things with the same speed*, Maya thought. She hopped onto the bed in her shoes, kicked off the annoying extra pillows and tasseled runner, and closed her eyes.

It was morning already—she had lost an additional two hours flying east—and sleep, unsurprisingly, wouldn't come. The sun was going toe to toe with the blackout curtains and winning. Maya tossed around for a while, got up, watched some Russian TV, took a long hot shower, ordered a room-service BLT, and ate the L and the T out of it.

The hotel stood half a block from the Kremlin, on an avenue that dead-ended into Red Square. Maya had never seen either. It seemed weird to do touristy things under the circumstances, but she had no further instructions or even messages from Demin or his minions. She looked at the room clock. Almost noon.

"Oh, why the fuck not," she said out loud, putting her shoes back on.

The air outside was a full ten degrees colder than in Riga, the chill slipping its fingers under her light jacket. Maya didn't know what she expected to see or feel. The Obrandt family lore depicted Moscow as a place of hunger and misery, the Old Country, as abstract as the shtetl was for Baba Polina's generation. More recent clichés suggested a Babylon teeming with oligarchs and sexy assassins. In the kinds of movies for which she sometimes auditioned, the city's image was reduced to a stock-footage shot or two before cutting to Prague or Budapest where the rest of the film would actually be shot.

The real thing, it turned out, was also a bit of a put-on. There was something ineffably false about it all, the Italianate facades, the flown-in street furniture, the too-vast spaces. The avenue in front of the hotel was an eight-lane highway, fringed by buildings the length of a block each.

Towering LED billboards advertised IKEA and car insurance. This could be Berlin *or* Beijing.

She tried to cross toward Red Square, but the only way to do it was through an underground passage that doubled as a Metro station. For the sole gateway to the empire's crown jewel, it was surprisingly dingy. There was life in it, though: commuters stampeding through the Metro turnstiles, kiosks selling patriotic tees and anti-Western iPhone covers. For a moment, Maya fixated on the number of Central and East Asian faces in the crowd. Despite her roots, she never got to play one of those sexy assassins herself—in the minds of Hollywood casting directors, no Russian woman looked like her. They were, clearly, wrong.

She emerged from the underground and walked around the great square for a bit. The convex expanse seemed designed to make you small. To her, it was a familiar feeling. Maya tried to remember some of the crazy shit that went down here. The parades with tanks and nuclear rocket launchers, dictator du jour waving from atop Lenin's tomb. The eight dissidents who dared to come out against the invasion of Czechoslovakia. The performance artist who nailed his testicles to the pavement a few years back. That was all she could recall.

She felt no awe or fear, just emptiness, inside and out. Imagine traveling half the world and ending up with the same maddening questions. *Who am I? Why am I here? Is my father alive?*

"Excuse me, miss," said someone behind her. Maya almost expected to see the German creep again. This time, however, it was a beautiful, low-voiced woman in a fitted charcoal pantsuit and kitten heels. "Are you ready? Mr. Demin is expecting you. I am Katya, his executive secretary." Her English was excellent.

"Nice to meet you," Maya automatically responded, setting aside the question of how, exactly, Katya had tracked her down from the hotel.

"Follow me." The secretary turned around and led the way, heels metronomic on cobblestone. At the mouth of the square, by a brick double gate, Maya could see the same car and driver who had picked her up at the airport.

"It's about twenty minutes to Skolkovo this time of day," said Katya from the front seat, once they circled the Kremlin and spun out onto New Arbat. Modernist towers rose on both sides, angled against the road to form a giant herringbone. "Maybe a bit more."

"Maybe a bit less," the driver said grinning. He lowered his window, reached under the seat with his left hand, and, like a movie cop, slapped a blue magnetic beacon on the car roof. The S-Class veered left into the turning lane and stayed there, going ninety miles an hour flush against a wall of oncoming traffic.

"What happens when there's a more important guy driving the other way?" Maya acidly asked.

"The president usually takes a helicopter," responded Katya with a smile.

They made it to Skolkovo in ten. The vast park looked like a dilapidated movie set of a progressive Scandinavian suburb: wide alleys, glassy buildings, all thoroughly empty of life and most left not quite finished. *What the hell is this place?* Maya thought. Her befuddlement hung in the air so palpably that Katya felt compelled to turn and explain.

"It was meant to be our Silicon Valley," she said. "Tech start-ups, innovation hubs, that sort of thing. Then"—a touch of sarcasm crept into her voice—"plans changed." Maya smirked, letting Katya know she got the reference to the invasion of Ukraine. Outside, immaculate shells continued crowding the view. The Russia that could have been.

The car approached a striking black edifice in the shape of a truncated pyramid, set away from the rest. "We're here," said Katya. "Have you seen the Matryoshka before?"

"Can't say that I have." The vibe Maya caught from KhromBank's ominous headquarters was half nuclear plant and half necropolis. A slanted plaza led up to the entrance, making the mere act of getting to the doors feel like kissing the ring. You didn't walk into the Matryoshka as much as rose to its level.

The driver followed Maya and Katya inside, which suggested that his job description switched to something else; odds were, he was a driver in the same sense Vitya was a bartender. The glass elevator that took the three of them to the top floor moved not straight but diagonally, gliding along the outer pyramid wall. When it began to move, Maya, who didn't expect inertia to yank her sideways, grabbed the railing.

"It's an acquired taste," Katya allowed. This was likely the closest she ever came to saying anything negative about her place of work.

As floor after floor whooshed past, Maya coolly noted her own total lack of expectations. Once the machine reached the top and the doors opened, awaiting her on the other side could be, with a roughly equal probability, her smiling father, an aproned torturer with his tools laid out on a steel tray, a stilted formal dinner with KhromBank's CEO, or a firing squad. Or, for that matter, Ari Falk. It suddenly occurred to her that the Matryoshka must be pretty high on his list of places to visit, too.

If only they hadn't taken her burner away in Munich.

"Heyyy, I don't suppose I could borrow this thing to send one message, could I?" Maya asked Katya, nodding to the mobile in her hands and trying to infuse the doomed request with as much sisterly solidarity as her acting talents allowed.

"Ugh, so sorry," said Katya, hiding the phone. She'd been furiously texting someone, with multiple folded-hands emojis. "It's the bank's security policy. We can't." Of the two of them, she might be the better actress.

The elevator stopped. At this height, the pyramid's footprint shrank in half compared to the ground-floor lobby; the doors opened onto a square empty space with one office door on each side. The driver exited first, gesturing for Maya to follow him to the door on the left. Katya, her job evidently done, said "Bye, sorry again," and rode back down.

Maya expected a villain's lair. She saw a coworking space. The office was large but bare, with a reclaimed-wood desk, an ergonomic chair, and sparsely hung photos on the two walls that weren't glass. Off to the side lay a guest area with a coffee table, a couch, and two Wassily chairs, the same ones Karikh had in his Riga office. He must have gotten them to be more like the boss. In one of the chairs, reading the Russian edition of *Esquire*, sat Gennady Demin.

"There you are," he said, getting up. Maya was bad with men's ages past a certain number but would place his at a sporty sixty-five. His head had either been totally bald for many years or shaved very close and very often. She had to admit that he looked more or less like every other vaguely sketchy white man whose funds her father managed. Or, as it happened, stole.

"Please take a seat anywhere." She opted for the couch. "Lyosha, do you have something for me?"

"Yes, sir." The driver took out a padded envelope and handed it to Demin.

"Attaboy. Dismissed." The driver nodded and left. Demin walked over to the desk and sat down in the ergonomic chair. "Coffee for you?"

"No, thank you."

"Again," said Demin absently, looking for something inside the desk as he talked, "if we intended to harm you for any reason, we'd have done so in Riga or Munich. Our coffee is safe and, in my opinion, delicious. Aha!" The item in question was a brass penknife in the shape of a quill. Demin set the envelope in front of him, carefully cut it open on one end, then picked the other end up. A mobile phone slid onto the desk.

Demin looked at his watch. "Perfect timing," he said. "Now let's y
and I make a call."

For a second longer, Maya still hoped they'd be calling her
ther. Then she recognized the phone. It was her burner, confiscated
Demin's agent at the gate last night.

"Mother*fucker.*" Maya got up and walked directly toward the d
speaking through a crooked, clenched-teeth grin. "You have no i
where my father is, or how to contact him. I sorta suspected that g
in. I thought maybe you'd ask me to record some kind of hostage vi
to press him into resurfacing. Which is honestly not that bad of a p
I might have even gotten on board with it voluntarily. But you c
have done *that* anywhere." She put her palms on the desk and lea
in, staring him in the eyes and fearing nothing. "No. It's so much n
pathetic, isn't it? You learned that a certain man is on his way here,
you brought me in as a human shield. That's all."

Demin regarded her with a look of amused respect—eyebrows
lower lip jutting out—that seemed to be halfway to a Robert de Nir
personation. Without breaking eye contact, he slowly reached for the s
letter opener lying between them, and just as slowly put it back in a dr

"As the saying goes, 'away from the sin,'" he said.

"Glad you find this funny," Maya replied. "Now, for the bad n
That man on his way here? He doesn't give a shit about me. At leas
compared to the people in his life that you took from him. So go ah
call him, show him you have me at gunpoint, whatever. He's still g
to fucking merk you and your Lyosha and however many goons it t
to get to you."

"May I just say something?" Demin interjected. "You were bo
the US, right? Your Russian is *very* good." Then he picked up M
phone, held it up to her face to unlock it, and tapped on the first
only number in its address book.

■ ■ ■

The admittedly repulsive deal with Balashov gave Falk access to Khrom-Bank's top personnel dossiers, with copious internal and external (meaning, FSB's) observation notes. The most promising file was that of Yekaterina Lisichenko, Demin's thirty-seven-year-old executive secretary. Lisichenko was an ultracompetent superachiever with degrees in economics from both Moscow State and NYU. She was also a Ukrainian in a country that annexed a piece of hers, and a lesbian in a country that legislated away her basic rights. She loved her career but had grown to hate Russia, and her file included plenty of blunt WhatsApp and Telegram texts to prove that. Interestingly, Demin was made aware of this twice, by his own human resources department, and dismissed it both times. One response from him, included in the dossier, simply read "If we only worked with patriots, we wouldn't have anyone smart to work with."

Falk had no time to develop a careful approach to Lisichenko. He went for a crude catfish, texting her in the guise of an old NYU fling in town for one day only. She responded at once, suggesting they meet at a craft beer hall inside a trendy market off Kutuzovsky Avenue—halfway between Skolkovo and the city center.

They set the date at one. At 12:15, Lisichenko texted: Ugh, sorry might be late, boss is making me do private errands again.

What is it? Falk responded, adding a gif of Tina Fey in *30 Rock* doing an eye roll.

Picking up some girl at the Ritz.

Sounds hot.

Done!!!!!!! she wrote at one fifteen, after he had ensconced himself at the market. So sorry. ETA 10 min.

No worries, wrote Falk and waved at a server. Can't wait to see you, he added. She responded with a row of folded-hands emojis.

For a few minutes, Falk sat drinking a surprisingly good beer and watching the midday shoppers. With each year, Muscovites were becoming harder to tell from their counterparts all over the West; Uniqlo and Instagram were doing what generations of politicians and philosophers couldn't. Something dark kept percolating, however, under the increasingly glossy surface—more arrests at home, more assassinations abroad. A full-scale crackdown in exchange for craft IPAs and iPhones. Even the stalls of the market around him, brimming with tropical fruit and international bric-a-brac, were hiding a much harsher reality: by law, only Russian citizens were allowed to peddle produce. Back at Camp Peary, they used to teach future officers that creature comforts and liberty went hand in hand, that "no two countries with McDonald's have ever gone to war." That phrase wasn't even true on the day it was first uttered. It was a complete joke now. Could things have ever gone another way?

Maybe if someone else had won in 1996, he thought. Installing the hated Yeltsin for the second term may have saved Russia from a Communist comeback, but it created a nation of cynics. The only lesson anyone learned that year was that *democracy* was just a fancy word for submitting to the US. Everything that followed stemmed from that.

The phone buzzed again. Falk picked it up, anticipating a new excuse. Perhaps Lisichenko was onto him. His work that day was, admittedly, pretty slapdash.

It was a voice call from Maya's burner number. She was supposed to be landing at LAX in under an hour—the plane must have caught some tailwind. A profound sense of relief came over Falk, with a bit of instant nostalgia swirled in. Here was their last conversation, and he'd have to keep it short and scan the crowd as he talked.

"Hey," he said, grinning. "Miss me yet?"

"You know," said Demin on the other end, "you two answer your phones the same way. It's quite touching."

A minute later, Lisichenko entered the Dorogomilovsky Market, furtively fixing her hair and jacket as she did. She walked past the butchers' rows and into the beer hall, scanned the lunchtime crowd at the wooden trestle tables, and did not see her friend anywhere. Near one of the tables, a plastic Wet Floor sign had just been set up; behind it knelt a Tajik woman in a blue apron, mopping up a large beer spill and retrieving the last shards of broken glass.

■ ■ ■

Something odd was happening with time and space. Maya watched Demin call Falk on her phone, and a second later Falk was in the room. Okay, in reality it must have taken him about fifteen minutes to get there, which in the grand scheme of things still felt almost instant: Moscow was a city of a thousand square miles, after all. Even Demin, she thought, looked surprised.

Falk walked rather calmly for a man at gunpoint, which was his status at the moment; Lyosha the driver shuffled behind him with a pistol pointed at his nape. Nearly invisible in Lyosha's other hand was a much smaller second gun, and she recognized that one. He held it by the barrel and was in the process of stuffing it in his jacket pocket as they walked. Falk must have ceded it voluntarily. Both of them had a shared look of two professionals who understood each other and the ritual in which they were engaged. It was almost amicable.

As soon as Maya and Falk locked eyes, he gave her a quick embarrassed smile—something along the lines of *well, this is stupid*, as if they were two people who had said goodbye at the end of a date and kept walking in the same direction. He then turned and addressed Demin, the decision-maker in the room.

"Permission to inspect Ms. Obrandt," he said in Russian.

"Of course," said Demin. Falk walked over to the couch where Maya sat, gently took her by the chin, and turned her head left and right, checking for bruises.

"No harm has come to her," said Demin. "And none will. In fact . . . Lyosha, are we good?" Lyosha nodded. "You may leave."

"Are you sure, Gennady Vladimirovich?"

"Yes. Off you go." Having dismissed his goon, Demin sat down in one of the Wassilys and gestured for Falk to take the other. Once he did, the three of them formed a weirdly casual-looking group around the coffee table, as if they were about to discuss the plans for the KhromBank office Christmas party.

"Well," said Falk. "I think I see now why I had no trouble at the border."

"First things first," said Demin. "I do apologize for dragging the two of you here like this. But it was the only way you'd come, and I really needed to talk to you. As absurd as it sounds, Mr. Falk, you and I have the same problem."

"If that problem is 'too many colleagues still alive,'" said Falk, "you've solved it for me and seem to be solving it for yourself, too."

Demin sighed. "There we go. Okay, let's start with the banner headline. Mr. Falk, I didn't kill your coworkers. I'm trying to find out who did."

"Hey," said Maya. "It worked for O.J." She was trying to match Falk's flippancy, but Demin just gave her a confused glance and kept talking.

"As you know," he continued, "I am looking for someone who owes me a great deal of money. That someone is your father, Ms. Obrandt, which you also already know. And yes, I am sorry to say that, but I am very angry at him. The problem—the common problem I've mentioned earlier—is that *someone* is one step ahead of me, killing everyone who may have seen Mr. Obrandt alive."

For a few seconds, Falk and Demin just stared at each other. "Is this a joke?" Falk finally said.

"Far from it. But please think about it for more than a second. If I'm desperately looking for a man, why would I kill the people who might know where he is? I would *question* them, sure. I might even be forced—sorry, but we're all adults here—to liquidate them *after* I questioned them. But Mr. Falk, those brutes who attacked your office, did they look like they were interested in talking to you?"

Maya glanced over at Falk. She knew him well enough by this point to see how furious he was. When he spoke up, he spoke with the eerie calm of someone just about done talking.

"I have video of the two assassins walking into your 'bank' "—Falk put audible quotes around the word—"retrieving weapons, and heading directly to my office."

"That's right," said Demin. "And I assume you also have video of me executing GRU Major Nikolai Karikh for letting them in."

"What?!"

"Mr. Falk, those two were mercenaries I had never seen before. Someone used our vault for a weapons cache and gave them a GRU unit's call sign. Someone wanted it to look like us—and succeeded. When I knew it was Karikh who let this happen, I took appropriate measures immediately."

A stunned silence settled upon the room. Maya had never seen anyone take the most incriminating evidence in the world and turn it into an alibi.

"Hey," Demin added, making his own ghoulish attempt at levity, "didn't you almost kill him in that airport bathroom yourself? I can't blame you. Karikh was one annoying character."

"Okay," said Falk, wincing hard. "Okay. Okay! Let's assume you're telling the truth. What would you have us do?"

"The very thing you're doing," said Demin. "Find Obrandt. Just tell *me* when you do."

"You mean, when we find the money," interjected Maya.

"Alas, no." Demin leaned forward, extending his hand toward Maya's over the coffee table. She jerked hers away. "This will be hard for you to hear, and I'm sorry. How close are you with your dad?"

"Close enough," she snapped.

"As Comrade Stalin said, the son—in this case, the daughter—does not answer for the father. You have nothing to fear from me. But there is only one person in the world who benefits from the deaths of everyone who's seen Paul Obrandt after August 14. That person is Paul Obrandt."

"No." She felt angry enough to strike this man in the face right there and then; it was the kind of rage that accompanies, or rather masks, the realization that the other side might be partially right. "What are you saying? No no no. Hell no."

"I'm not sure Obrandt's the type," said Falk softly. He was talking to Demin, but it sounded meant for her.

"Oh, I'm sure he's not," replied the old man. He stood up with a soft grunt, walked toward the windows, and looked outside at the architectural sprawl of Skolkovo and the thin yellowing forests beyond. "I know him pretty well. We were friends once. He may not even know the details of what's being done in his name. But five billion dollars buys a lot of firepower, Mr. Falk. Like, say, the entirety of ChVK Orlok."

Demin pointed to one of the framed photos on the wall. "Come look," he said. "I still have this. We were all young once, you know. Full of hopes."

Falk got up, gesturing for Maya to stay put, and walked over; she disregarded the gesture and joined him. The photo, an enlarged snapshot with a burned-in date stamp—5-4-1995—showed three people at a restaurant table. Their body language didn't scream best friends, but they seemed comfortable enough around one another. Maya recognized her father at once: younger, thinner, with jet-black hair, but still very much the Paul Obrandt she knew. In the center sat Demin, already well into middle age, sporting a mustache. The man on the far right was older than both of them, with sunken eyes and a haunted look undercut by a comically awful sweater.

"Who's that?" asked Maya.

"Sergei Konovalov. I doubt you know who that is. No one does these days."

"The scientist," said Falk.

Demin raised his eyebrows. "Very good. Did your paths ever cross?"

"Sadly, no. He died before my time."

"Yes," said Demin. "In fact, this may be one of his last photographs." He stared at Falk, then Maya, as if inviting them to draw some kind of lesson from this.

The name Konovalov actually rang a bell—or, rather, two bells at once. Maya could recall someone in her family mentioning it with admiration, most likely Baba Polina. (It certainly wasn't her father. Paul Obrandt hadn't said a single positive thing about any Russian as long as she was alive.) But there was something darkly comical attached to it, too; something you wouldn't want to discuss in front of a child. Suddenly, she remembered.

"Oh yeah," she said to Falk in English. "Didn't this guy crash his car with a hooker in the front seat?" Konovalov's death was one of the foundational myths of Russia's onetime image as the Wild East, a vortex of excess and lurid possibility, a place where even a sixtysomething Nobel laureate can die in a Lamborghini while getting a blow job. It was the kind of trope that still showed up in Hollywood movies twenty-five years later.

Demin's face hardened. Despite claiming not to speak English, he clearly understood every word. "You shouldn't judge anyone's life by the way it ends," he finally said.

"Especially when you're the one ending it," Maya spat out. The general gave Falk a side scowl that read *control your woman*, which only made her madder. Demin's implication—that her father was not just a thief but a blasé, methodical murderer like himself—had pushed everything happening to and around her into a realm of unreality. She felt as if she were watching herself on a surveillance monitor. The real Maya was hovering nearby in some incorporeal form, whispering *hmm, interesting strategy, let's see where she's going with this.*

"Are we . . . free to leave?" asked Falk.

"Provided you don't go after my company or myself ever again, you are," said Demin, still looking at the photo. "KhromBank has not exceeded the accepted scope of its foreign activities."

"He means," whispered Maya loudly, "that they're only killing other Russian citizens."

Falk took her hand. "Let's go."

"Not so fast." She refused his touch the same way she did Demin's. "I have questions, too."

"Is that so?" Demin turned around, cocking his head to the side. Falk automatically stepped in between them.

"Why don't you tell us how my father and you met to begin with?"

"Ah, well," said Demin. "That's a reasonable request. Twenty-five years ago, I had something he needed and he had something I needed. So we formed a company together."

"Yeah," said Falk. "GallTeleCom. I've looked it up. The whole thing was built on the Soviet Army's unused 800MHz frequency band, which alone would be worth hundreds of millions on the open market. Let me guess, you two bought it off your army buddies for peanuts."

"A moot point," Demin replied, a bit defensively, she thought. "The government took it over as soon as it saw profits. That's *the* thing about this country, isn't it? The tsar giveth and the tsar taketh away, whichever flag flies above the palace. Nothing's ever truly yours, so you may as well steal whatever's not bolted down."

Falk raised his eyebrows a bit. The general's words seemed to have surprised him, and not unpleasantly.

"But it wasn't Paul's fault," Demin continued. "He was—is?—a financial genius. So he went back to America, and I kept investing with him. He's made many fortunes. Until the day he decided to make his own."

"Was he ever a Russian agent?"

Demin chuckled. "That depends on your definition of the word. Do you mean, did he advance the interests of the Russian Federation? Let me put it this way, this building wouldn't stand here if not for the money he made us. And hey, why not? We are both capitalist countries with fully compatible financial systems, aren't we? At least on paper. But if you mean shield-and-sword, then no, your dad never did any of that stuff." *Shield-and-sword*, Maya assumed, was Russian for *cloak-and-dagger*.

"What was supposed to happen in Riga?"

"Repayment of old debts." Demin sighed. "Okay, Ms. Obrandt, last question. I admire your grit, but this isn't a press conference."

"I've got one," Falk cut in, showing Demin his phone. On the screen was a blown-up photo of Olga Ostashevskaya—not the old composite but a screen grab from an Istanbul airport camera, white scar clearly visible. "Do you know who this is? He was traveling with her."

Demin studied the picture for several seconds. His face betrayed no twinge of recognition. "Sorry," he said, "not a clue. She's not one of ours. Interesting woman, though, good for him."

The audience over, he sat down at his desk and pressed a button that turned out to summon Lyosha. The speed of the driver's appearance suggested he'd been guarding the door the whole time. "Give Mr. Falk his tiny gun back, please," said Demin dryly, leaning back in his ergonomic chair. "Oh, and one last bit of advice from an old man. You two should stick together. You make a nice couple."

Is he right? Is my father a murderer? Maya thought, as Falk walked her out of the building in a protective half hug. The slanted plaza in front of the Matryoshka accelerated their already brisk pace. Did it even take a special kind of man to kill another, or was that just a fib to help us avoid seeing ourselves for who we all were? Take Falk, with his teenager's wardrobe and bad tendon and love for, who was it, Fiona Apple?—he'd killed someone in front of her not three days ago and didn't seem particularly haunted by it.

Having rotated in Maya's head several times, the thought suddenly spun onto another, even more terrifying plane. If Paul Obrandt had indeed ordered, or even accidentally facilitated, the deaths of Falk's friends, would Falk kill *him* if he ever found him? Were their two adjacent quests one and the same, after all? Did she, in her mad determination to find her father alive, actually—no, no, this was far too awful to consider.

Falk called a Yandex Taxi, a homegrown Uber partner, to take them to the airport. The inside of the cab reeked of artificial pine sap and authentic body odor. Maya sat silently spiraling in the back seat as the car sped toward the Ring Road. A mile or so before the interchange, traffic slowed to a crawl; the driver, bored, turned on the stereo. Russian rap, the flow too fast for a nonnative speaker to parse.

"What is this?" asked Falk, grinning. "Crank it up, man!" The driver obligingly boosted the volume until the bass frequencies made the car's flimsy speakers rattle.

"*You're* in a chipper mood," said Maya.

"Hardly. Just don't want him to overhear us," said Falk into her ear.

"Look, for what it's worth, I don't think your father did anything other than run away. Demin was fucking with you to see how you'd react. He seems to do that a lot. When you came back at him with the questions, he was clearly pleased."

"So you still think it's GRU?"

"No. The proof Demin furnished was pretty ironclad."

"Wait, what was his proof? Did I miss it?"

Falk looked at Maya and laughed a small, sad laugh. "He let us walk out alive, that's what."

She turned and stared out the window. The paranoia that had been flooding her brain abated a bit. The taxi rolled past a rough-looking *Plattenbau* neighborhood, some houses bearing signs of a recent spruce-up.

"You know," Maya said, "Dad barely ever talked about this place. I mean, when I was a kid, he liked to mention how little they had, all the usual stuff about long lines and bad toilet paper. Universities that wouldn't let Jews in. That sort of thing. I could never tell if these were his real memories or just teachable moments for my benefit. But he never mentioned coming back here after the Soviet Union fell. Those few words Demin just said about their old company were more than I'd ever heard from him."

"Demin is a character," said Falk, clearly thinking about something else. "An absolute monster, of course, but not a cynic. And not a functionary. He's playing a game of his own, and I'm not sure that game aligns all that neatly with the Kremlin's." He sighed. "Ah, what's the fucking difference. It's all moot. We have no threads left to pull. Ostashevskaya's a ghost. Karikh is dead. It's a graveyard of leads. Let's just get you home."

"Hey, chief," the driver said suddenly, lowering the music. His worried eyes in the rearview mirror focused not on Falk or Maya but on something or someone farther behind, and it made her turn her head. "These friends of yours?"

■ ■ ■

Falk had first clocked the black G-Wagen on the Minsk Highway, almost as soon as they left Skolkovo. His first thought was that Demin had sent one of his many Lyoshas to tail them to the airport, which frankly seemed reasonable. Whoever was behind the wheel was skillful enough to stay five or so cars behind and avoid changing lanes too much. Still, he could feel the hulking SUV's presence like a cold stare in the back of his head. It made him miss parts of what Maya was saying. For the driver to notice the tail, however, it must have done something much more conspicuous.

Falk turned around. The G-Wagen was now one car behind and two lanes to the left, and nosing in to get even closer. This wasn't a tailing position.

"Hey," said Falk to the driver, trying to keep his voice casual. "Don't turn on Ring Road. Take Kutuzovsky to the center."

"What's happening?" Maya asked. "Are we not going to the airport?"

Behind them, the G-Wagen swung right, muscling into a gap between two small sedans. Had it looked any less intimidating, the car it cut off would have surely laid into its horn. But if the post-Soviet years taught the Russians anything, it was the tacit understanding that you don't question the actions of a black Mercedes.

"Oh shit," said the driver, nervously looking over his shoulder. "AMR plates. Looks like you've pissed off the wrong people."

The AMR license plate series was a federal perk. It could have been any number of entities—FSB, police, presidential staff—none of them good news. The G-Wagen was now directly on their left and pulling up. It was almost twice as tall as Yandex Taxi's Prius.

"Gun. Gun, gun, gun," yelled Maya, pointing. She was seated on the driver's side, with a better view of whatever was happening on the left.

Falk leaned over her, simultaneously pressing her down toward the seats just in case. The G-Wagen's windows were tinted but he could make out two people inside, both in the front. From the position of the passenger's shoulders, Falk deduced he was holding something with both arms, right below the edge of the window.

He reached for his CZ in return. Whoever their pursuers were, they weren't Demin's, he fleetingly thought—otherwise, why give him back the gun? Then again, it wasn't exactly an adequate weapon for a situation like the one brewing in front of his eyes. Maybe it was like handing a gladiator a mace against a live tiger. Not enough to win, just enough to keep things interesting for a minute.

"What is this shit?!" The driver saw the pistol in Falk's hand. Yanking the wheel to the right, he screeched into the rightmost lane, which fed the Ring Road on-ramp. "I don't want any part of this."

"I said don't take the exit," said Falk.

"Oh, I'm not," the driver said. The Prius turned onto the highway's gravel shoulder and stopped. To their right, a copse of anemic aspens, raised on exhaust fumes, separated the road from a strip of auto body shops. In front of them, the raised Ring Road interchange spanned the horizon.

The G-Wagen reacted fast. It swooped right into the breach created by the Prius's sudden departure, then rolled onto the shoulder, too, coming to a stop a hundred feet ahead of them.

The driver unbuckled and began to grab around for his phone and wallet, preparing to abandon ship. "I don't need this," he mumbled. "I've seen enough of this fucking bullshit in the nineties."

"Drive," said Falk. He was half lying on top of Maya in the back seat, covering her body with his. "Drive into the trees, you idiot. Don't get out. It's a terrible idea."

"Fuck you," the driver said, slammed the door, and took off running.

He managed one and a half steps. Two shots rang out almost simultaneously. With his face down, Falk could only hear and feel the body graze the side of the Prius and hit the gravel behind the car. Below him, Maya breathed very fast.

Falk lifted his head and stole a quick look ahead, between the seats. The doors of the G-Wagen had opened, releasing two gunmen in bulletproof vests. Moving in unison, guns at the ready, they were inching toward the taxi.

"Okay," whispered Falk into Maya's ear. "There's one way this works. I shoot and you drive. Can you?"

"Maybe," she answered. "Yes. Yes."

"They will shoot back. They will miss if you stay low. So stay low. On three. One, two—" Falk rolled off Maya, giving her room, lowered the right passenger-side window, stuck out his gun hand, and fired twice without really aiming. At the same time, Maya lunged feetfirst toward the driver's seat.

Return fire followed immediately. Two or three bullets smashed into the hood, two hit the windshield. Maya screamed but didn't stop scrambling. Falk shot a few more times, buying her the time to reach the pedals. Through the cobweb of cracks in the glass, he could see the gunmen continue to advance.

"Fuck, fuck, fuck!" Maya threw the car in reverse. Two more shots hit the engine block.

"It's going to—" said Falk, then fell silent as the taxi, with a sickening yaw, rolled over something the size of a large speed bump.

"Now what?!" Maya steered furiously, flying backward down the shoulder. In front of them the attackers, having lost the drop on the Prius, had turned around and were running back to the G-Wagen.

"Into the traffic."

"Oh god, oh shit, here we go." She hit the brakes, switched into drive, and barged onto the road, immediately pushing into the middle lane so they wouldn't have to pass right by the gunmen. A Lada behind her braked hard to avoid collision, and got rear-ended by a Gazelle. Both stopped to yell at each other. This was the best thing that could possibly happen: the right lane came to a standstill, cutting the G-Wagen off from the road.

A combination of flashing lights and continuously blasting horn got them past the interchange. As soon as they cleared it, the traffic thinned out; this time of day, most people weren't heading into the city.

"Amazing job," said Falk. "Now we have about thirty seconds on them. Doesn't sound like a lot but it is. You gotta drive fast, though."

"Southern California, baby," Maya answered, flooring the gas pedal. The adrenaline must have kicked in. "Where to?"

"Just straight," said Falk. "Believe it or not, this road eventually hits the US Embassy."

They flew down Mozhaysky Highway, then Kutuzovsky Avenue, weaving in and out of traffic and making ample use of the turning lane. Brick facades flashed by, sprouting more ornate stucco detail as the car neared the center. In the back seat, Falk alternated between monitoring their six for the G-Wagen and looking at the back of Maya's head with a feeling he had a hard time placing. It wasn't love as he understood it. It was more of an incredibly intense fear that anything bad should happen to this human being. Then again, maybe that's all love was.

It took him an extra second to process the sound of the sirens behind them.

"Great, the pigs," said Maya. "What now?" A white Ford with the telltale blue stripe had emerged from a side street, gaining fast.

"Don't slow down. Let me think." They had just passed the Kuk-lachev Cat Theater, one of Moscow's weirdest attractions, which meant the embassy was just over a mile away. That was the good news. The bad news was that, like every other US embassy in the world, it was guarded both by the US Marines and a local police detail. If Falk and Maya tore onto the grounds in a bullet-riddled stolen cab, with more cops and unidentified gunmen in hot pursuit, the only question was which side would shoot them first.

"Ari! What do I do!!" The Ford was on their tail, issuing distorted instructions in Russian through a loudspeaker.

"Just keep driving."

The idea that came to him was a little on the insane side, but who cared anymore. Falk picked up his phone and dialed a British number from memory.

"Keegan, it's me."

"What's going on?" It was about noon in London, but Alan Keegan sounded sleepy.

"It's Falk. I need help."

"Are you *calling a friend* back there?!" Maya screamed from behind the wheel.

"Look, mate, we have to have a talk about boundaries," said Keegan. "I am not the friendly hacker who gets you into places. I have an organization to run."

"I don't need a hacker. I need your organization. I'm in a Yandex Taxi, heading to the corner of Konyushkovskaya and Novy Arbat."

"In Moscow?!"

"No, Alan, in Singapore," said Falk. "Yes, in Moscow. And I need a bunch more Yandex Taxis going to that same address. Tell your volunteers it's a prank. Which it sort of is."

"Jesus Christ, Ari. FleaCollar is a research network. We don't do ops."

"Well, maybe you should!" Falk yelled. "Tell me this: You ever save anyone?"

"What?"

"You expose. You bring to light. Commendable. Have you ever *saved* anyone?"

A silence met him.

"So fucking save me now. Konyushkovskaya and Novy Arbat." Falk hung up and turned to Maya, trying to steady his breath. "Okay, now I have to ask you to do something extremely counterintuitive. You need to drive normal. Like a regular cab."

"I don't think I can," Maya said, glancing back. Sweat covered her face, plastering strands of hair to her forehead and nose. The cop car hung on to them, barking garbled commands. A second one was speeding down a service road on the right, preparing to join the party. "I'm kinda locked in sicko mode here."

"Sure you can. Just breathe."

Maya bit her lip, changed lanes, and began to slow down. Almost at once, Falk could see the black G-Wagen reemerge behind them, catching up. It had its own police car on the tail, though following at a far more respectful distance: the AMR plates must have worked their magic.

If Keegan doesn't come through, we're done, Falk thought. The situation had gotten completely out of hand. He rolled down the window and, with one final pang of regret, tossed Inga's CZ. Whatever was waiting for them next was best faced with no weapons on one's person.

The deranged caravan reached the bridge over the Moskva River. Falk could see the ribbed white slab of the Parliament building on the left; the US Embassy complex stood right behind. "Turn right," he said, touching, then grabbing, Maya's shoulder. "Get on the embankment. Now!"

The Prius barely made the exit. Two of the three police cars and the G-Wagen did, too. They dove under the bridge they had just crossed, losing all sight of the road ahead as they rounded the curve of the embankment. The pursuers had lost the visual on them, too, though just for a few seconds.

"Well," Falk said, "here goes nothing." The curve straightened out. The cab emerged into a side street and came to an almost immediate stop.

"Oh my god," whispered Maya.

"Son of a bitch," said Falk, a huge grin spreading over his face.

The street was paved with yellow taxis from the riverside to the Parliament. At least three hundred cabs had descended onto one block; from far enough above, it would look like the world's largest omelet. The squall of horns had to be audible from the prime minister's office. Some of the drivers were already outside their cars, arguing, laughing, and calling tech support.

Acting in sync without a single word spoken, Falk and Maya jumped out of the Prius—the bullet damage to the front was far more extensive than he had thought—and ran toward the embassy. By the time the police arrived at the traffic jam's delta, five or so seconds later, another dozen Yandex Taxis had already wedged between them and the abandoned Prius. Behind the cop cars, the black G-Wagen pulled up, observed the scene, and rolled away unpursued.

They zigzagged through the snarl, swerving and ducking from rearview mirrors and open car doors, past the antiterrorist cement bollards, to the metal gate in the distance. The US Marines, unnerved by the commotion and now treated to the sight of two disheveled people sprinting toward them, exchanged quick glances and raised their M27s in unison. Still running, Maya managed to grab a hold of her US passport and waved it over her head. Falk followed suit.

"Ma'am! Sir! Slow down! Slow the *hell* down!"

They did. In any other circumstances, Falk would find this learned tough-guy twang annoying, but right now it was the sweetest sound in the world. Carefully walking into the soldiers' earshot, Falk rattled off his rank and his department ID number and code. The marine closest to him nodded and snapped off a quick salute. "And the lady?"

"Civilian. I'm bringing her in."

"Yes, sir. Follow me." The marine gestured for his partner to keep manning the entrance. A side gate creaked open. Exhausted, smiling, dizzy, Falk and Maya stepped onto US territory.

■ ■ ■

"So, tell me something," Maya said. They had gone through an airport-style security check and were now being ushered across a stone courtyard, past a flagpole with the drooping Stars and Stripes, to the giant glass cube-shaped building at the center of the complex. "You're completely, irreversibly fucked, right? Seeing how you're supposed to be in London right now."

"Yup," said Falk. "But it's just as well."

"I'm sorry."

"Don't be. There's a lot of Russian literature I haven't read yet. Aldanov, Gippius, all the minor Silver Age folks."

The marine left them in a small waiting room with a row of uncomfortable chairs, a watercooler, and portraits of the president and secretary of state. A few minutes later, a young man in a sack suit and rep tie came in, looking about as federal-issue as the rest of the room. Falk had five years on him max but felt a whole generation older, such a prep-school aura the guy radiated.

"Mr. Falk?" he said. "Jim Otterbeck, State. May we speak privately for a minute?"

"Woooo, spy shit," said Maya, evidently still riding the adrenaline wave. The young man slowly blinked several times. "Should we be concerned about—?"

"No, no, she's fine. She's just been through a lot," said Falk hastily. "Let's go."

They went out into the hallway ("See ya, *Otterbeck*," Maya yelled through the closing door) and took a narrow staircase several floors up. When they came to a cramped lobby with an additional metal detector and a turnstile, Otterbeck fished two cards out of his jacket pocket—a biometric ID and its generic day-pass cousin—and silently handed the latter to Falk. Two swipes, a buzz of a remotely opened door, and, finally, Narnia.

Falk hadn't set foot in Moscow Station in seven years, ever since the creation of his Riga unit. To his eye, nothing had changed. It was the same warren of carpeted rooms and hallways, decorated with dorky photos depicting arguable triumphs of democracy: Hasselhoff atop the Berlin Wall, Muscovites toppling the Dzerzhinsky statue, an Afghan woman voting (*they might want to move that one down to storage*, thought Falk). Perhaps the computers had gotten a little sleeker. The people certainly hadn't.

"Normally," said Otterbeck with a touch of displeasure, "we would debrief and proceed from there. But I have been instructed that your case is . . . special. DD/CA will debrief stateside." DD/CA was Harlow, Deputy Director for Covert Activities. "I am to arrange logistics and check if anything needs to be handled urgently."

"Actually, yes," said Falk. "I need a line to Stuart Akinyemi at the SIS."

"Of *course* you do." Otterbeck couldn't help himself. "Well, in my estimation, between six and eight people from here to London will need to sign off on that, so if you've got a week—"

"Fine," Falk growled, spooking the young man and a staffer crossing the hallway twenty feet behind him. "You want this on you, be my guest. Grab a pad and take down the message. 'Move in on Broward now. You've got twenty-four hours.' Happy? Now it's urgent *and* you're responsible."

"Broward, as in Philip Broward?" Otterbeck knit his preppy brow.

MICHAEL IDOV

"Yes. Why?"

"Oh. So you haven't heard."

"I've been a little busy, Jim," said Falk, trying to sound ornery to mask the oncoming wave of guilt. It had barely been four hours since the White Rabbit bathroom. Surely Balashov's bosses hadn't had the time to exfil—

"Broward died in London an hour ago," said Otterbeck. "A hit-and-run on a block with no CCTV. Is there something we should know?"

Of course. How could I forget. The Russians don't exfiltrate. No asset is worth the trouble. In a way, this freed Falk of direct responsibility—with Broward dead, he didn't fuck over the Cousins by helping a GRU agent escape from under their noses—but that thought was too squalid to dwell on. It did, however, lead him to another.

"Forget it," Falk said. "Hey, one more thing. Moscow Station handled an asset exfil request from me about two weeks ago. Can I, uh, look at it?"

For a few seconds, Otterbeck appeared to think very hard of a reason to say no. "Well," he finally said, "it's your case, and they haven't stripped you of your clearance yet. So I don't see why not. Just log in as yourself."

He walked Falk to his workstation, logged out, and stepped away in a show of discretion. Otterbeck's cubicle was festooned with Russian rock memorabilia; he was apparently a big fan of the band Mumiy Troll. Falk smiled—for all the puffed-up airs, the guy could be him a few years back. He caught himself making a mental note to tell Maya about it. She'd laugh.

He logged into the system and pulled up his own letter demanding immediate extraction from Istanbul for agent Emblem, aka Anton Basmanny. Though only two weeks old, it appeared to originate in some long-forgotten alternate reality. Falk reread his own lines—proud, impatient, passive-aggressive—and sighed. *In light of Emblem's uniquely resonant contributions, one would expect a modicum of consideration,* etc.

206

The mail client the Agency used, an in-house version of Outlook, logged every reader and every action taken. Or, in this case, not taken: Falk's request languished at Moscow Station from August 10, the day Anton first noticed someone watching his safe house, through August 13. That squared pretty well with the station's general attitude toward the Soft Unit and its little dramas.

At 8:30 a.m. Moscow time, August 14, someone finally punted it to Langley, where it was marked as read at 10:41 a.m.—dead of night in the US—by a familiar abbreviation: DD/CA. Deputy director. Rex Harlow.

By 10:43, Harlow had approved it, setting what must have been a world record for speedy paperwork, flagged it "priority," and routed it back to Moscow with a note attached. The note was so short—nine characters and two spaces—that, at first, Falk dismissed it as some sort of auto-generated security code string.

PUT_ON_TQ77

His eye snagged on a familiar combination of letters and numbers. He reread it.

Put on TQ77.

Put Anton Basmanny on Flight 77, Antalya Airlines, international code TQ.

Falk checked the sender metadata again. The instruction came directly from Harlow.

Otterbeck loitered by the door, all but tapping his Timex. Falk logged off. "Thank you," he said, getting up from the desk. "Is DD in Langley right now?"

"No. He'll debrief in New York. Anything else you need to check?"

"No."

"Good. We found a seat for you on a diplomatic flight out of Vnukovo."

Once they were in the courtyard, Otterbeck handed Falk off to two marines with two matching duffel bags each. "They'll take it from here," he said with manifest relief, awkwardly shook Falk's hand, and hightailed it back into the building. Falk almost sympathized. It must have been unpleasant for a young ambitious officer to stand next to this loser, about to have his epaulets ripped off and his saber broken over his head. Failure was contagious. Otterbeck would probably spend the rest of the day disinfecting his workstation.

"Sir," said one of the marines. "Ready to go?" Hands busy, he moved his jaw in the direction of a Jeep Cherokee idling nearby.

Falk looked around. "And Ms. Obrandt?"

"She has no clearance, sir. They already took her to Sherme—Shemere—the airport. She'll be boarding the six p.m. to LA."

"Just to check," said Falk, "did she, uh, leave any message for me?"

The face of the marine betrayed no outward sign of amusement, and Falk felt grateful for that.

The gates opened, letting them out into Bolshoy Deviatinsky Lane. A couple of news vans were parked across the street, reporting on the Yandex Taxi prank. As the Jeep turned toward the bridge, a grand view of the city opened up on all sides, the Moskva rippling in the August sun as it snaked toward the Kremlin; a chance to bid farewell to a place so central to Falk's life and one he would likely never see again. He did not look up once.

CHAPTER SIX

Service Elevator Out of Service, read the message taped to the door. The old man appreciated the elegance of the phrasing. The second sentence was not as pithy: *Please Take Back Stairs When Throwing Out Trash!!!!!*

"Oh, like hell I will," said the man aloud to the sign. His studio apartment was perched on the top, ninth floor of a prewar co-op with double-height ceilings, and the seventy-three-year-old was not about to stagger down eighteen flights of stairs with armfuls of garbage. He pressed the button, calling up the oak-paneled and carpeted guest elevator, and hoped for a solo ride all the way down.

He was almost home free when, with cruelly comic timing, the contraption stopped on two—who takes the elevator one floor down?—and let in a perfectly healthy-looking woman he didn't know. He didn't know anyone in the building. In any given year, he'd spend less than two weeks here. First it was all the overseas postings; now most of his life revolved around McLean, Virginia, and the maddening city across the Potomac from it. Ostensibly, he had bought the apartment to be closer to his two

209

sons when they attended Columbia, in reality to be farther from his ex-wife. Neither was a factor any longer.

The woman leveled a look at the two black trash bags on the floor, took in the man's worn plaid lounge pants, glanced up at his face, and sighed performatively.

"Sorry," he said.

The doors opened; he limped, laden, across the marble lobby and out into the stifling August night. Brick and asphalt radiated the day's dead heat back into the air. The alley behind the building overflowed with rotting garbage, all manner of refuse somehow forming a single sickly sweet smell.

The man was about to heave his bags atop the pile when his field instincts kicked in. Someone was here, in the dark, behind him. And that someone was here for him.

A trained part of his mind quickly catalogued the contents of the trash for makeshift weapons. Another gauged the distance between himself and the potential attacker.

He breathed in and out, letting these flashes of intent subside. There would be no hand-to-hand combat by the bins tonight. If they found him, they found him.

They, incidentally, could refer to any number of *them*. You didn't live to see your seventies in his trade without amassing an extremely wide assortment of *them*. But he had an idea.

The only thing still at stake was dignity. The deputy director of the Covert Activities department let the trash bags drop, cleared his throat, and stood up a little straighter.

"Whoever's there," he said, turning around and squinting into the dark. "Get it over with."

"Oh, dear Rex, 'it' is never over." The years had whittled Cormorant's voice down to a whisper, but the smile accompanying these words was clearly audible. "Why don't we step inside for a minute. You can make me that terrible tea you like."

■ ■ ■

OVER THE ATLANTIC
AUGUST 26, 2021

Falk was used to diplomatic flights being half-empty, but the 737 out of Vnukovo had barely a seat without a wool-trousered ass in it. Most of the passengers were embassy staffers going home, with no prospect of coming back; with the US-Russia relations back to the Cold War temperature, both countries were busy gutting their own and one another's missions in a tedious tit for tat of personnel cuts and spy expulsions. Ironically, since spies were more valuable than regular staff, they were the last to leave. Looking around, Falk didn't see a single Moscow Station face—although he wouldn't know anyone brought on after 2014.

By some sick irony of fate he got placed in 12A, Anton's seat from the fateful Antalya Airlines flight. A splitting headache began at takeoff and got only worse eight hours in. The adrenaline comedown after the highway chase, the political podcast filtering from the Bose cans on the next-seat neighbor's head, and the mild but unceasing North Atlantic turbulence made for a brutal combination. Most of all, though, it was the chain of discoveries Falk had made over the last twenty-four hours, all of which felt semirelated but refused to connect. Ghostly facts massed on the margins, like floaters in the mind's eye, combining and recombining and forming nothing; each time he'd focus on one, the whole set would scatter. Falk felt the atavistic need to fix them to a physical spot by putting them on paper.

"Excuse me," he said to his seatmate. "Do you have a pen?"

The man in 12B was large and ruddy, with a mop of straw-blond hair and wearing a lilac linen oxford rendered violet by sweat. An American from an anti-American cartoon. *They always send those guys,* Falk thought, the same way the Russians always send us short bruisers with colorless eyes. Each country weaponizing its own caricature. The man didn't hear him through the podcast, so Falk waved at him.

"What's up?" He peeled away one headphone, revealing a beet-red ear. "Ah. Sure." The pen, produced from his breast pocket, felt warm.

Falk took the sanitary bag, tore off a small piece of it, and laid it out on the rickety tray table. Writing anything down was the dumbest thing a spy could do, but it felt like the only way to still the howling headache. He promised himself he'd eat the paper later.

"Rx," Falk wrote in the smallest possible letters on rough paper. Rex Harlow.

"Dm/G," he added next to it, the chords forming the basis of the R.E.M. song "Drive," but also Gennady Demin.

"Op." Paul Obrandt.

"Bs." Anton Basmanny.

These were the known players, minus Olga Ostashevskaya, whose real identity was still a mystery. The simple act of listing them made the pain ebb a bit. Encouraged, Falk drew a tiny circle around Op and connected it to Dm/G.

In 1995, Paul Obrandt and Gennady Demin—a brash twenty-five-year-old Jewish immigrant with a US passport, and an already seasoned GRU operative with a grudge against the system that raised him—went into business together, purchasing an unused frequency band from the Russian army. The company they started, GallTeleCom—the "Gall" part must have been a nod to Demin's time as a diplomat in France—inventively combined a mobile phone carrier with a television and radio network. It failed, or rather got repossessed by the Kremlin, a year later; the fallout created a lifelong rift between the partners, which

Obrandt was on his way to fix before ghosting Demin and vanishing with the money.

Next, Falk drew a line between Bs and Op. *A bullshit op, indeed.* Obrandt escaped during an operation whose ostensible goal was to intimidate blogger Anton Basmanny. This wasn't luck, either. Harlow, his own boss, personally saw to it that Anton ended up on Obrandt's flight. His "put_on_TQ77" memo created the pretext for Obrandt to slip away undetected.

A fast, angry slash of the pen linked up Rx and Op. Paul Obrandt was a spook after all. Moreover, he was Harlow's spook. The only way Harlow would sacrifice a pawn like Anton would be to save a knight. How had the old man put it in Berlin? *Native assets are fair game, but they came way too close to killing a case officer of mine.*

Falk recalled that Harlow came on as the head of Moscow Station in 1995, the same year Obrandt showed up in Russia. Obrandt must have been a protegé, a Falk before Falk. The only way he'd be able to waltz in at the ripe old age of twenty-five and start up a massive company is if GallTeleCom was, at least in its American-owned part, an Agency front.

Which also explained its swift takeover and nationalization a year later. The Kremlin must have found out.

It made absolute sense that Demin would be left with nothing—a rather mild punishment, by the Russian standards, for letting the fox into the henhouse—and blame Obrandt for it. *That* was the "old debt" he spoke of; the debt Obrandt had been working off since then.

The headache abated, but slight nausea rose in its place. If Harlow helped his officer abscond with five billion dollars, or even a fraction of it, was it not conceivable that he would help him with the rest, too—like murdering a few witnesses? This was quite a thought, considering Falk was flying to New York to be personally debriefed by Harlow. *Where's a MiG when you need it,* he thought, and even involuntarily glanced out the window. Blind, moonless murk met his gaze. The rudimentary map on the seatback screen put the plane above Newfoundland.

Something about the tiny schematic he'd drawn still bothered him. Something still wasn't right. The whole adventure, whose roots reached back a quarter of a century and whose shape was now beginning to emerge in Falk's mind, lacked something fundamental: a purpose.

Why would the Agency bother establishing a Russian media network in 1995, smack in the middle of the two countries' post–Cold War honeymoon period? To shore up the free marketeers' chances against the Communists in the 1996 election? But back then that kind of thing was done openly and proudly. A team of US advisers had not just helped keep a deeply unpopular drunk in office for the second term but went bragging about it to *TIME* magazine. The IMF threw in a 10.2-billion-dollar sweetheart loan. (On later reflection, perhaps rubbing it in the Russians' faces that their president was being managed from Washington was not such a brilliant idea.)

And why would Demin go along with it? The army frequencies were a gold mine. He could have gotten the seed money elsewhere.

It all had to be for *something*. For *someone*.

Falk picked up the pen and added one more cryptic sign to his graph: "kV."

Kilovolt, but also Sergei Konovalov. Before 1995, a brilliant scientist, a national icon, a paragon of integrity. After 1995, a dirty joke, seared into the popular unconscious alongside an image of a burning supercar. Even Maya, born stateside three years later, had heard about The Guy Who Died Getting Blown in a Lambo.

But not to Demin, no. The GRU general, who seemingly did nothing without a clear objective, not only kept a photo of the disgraced and forgotten Konovalov on his office wall, but made sure to point it out to Falk.

Jesus Christ, I'm an idiot, Falk almost said out loud. *He basically told me.*

In three quick strokes, he connected Harlow, Obrandt, and Demin to the little kilovolt icon, crumpled the paper into a pill-size clump, and asked the passing flight attendant for a glass of water.

■ ■ ■

PALM SPRINGS
AUGUST 26, 2021

Maya made a promise to herself that she wouldn't cry in front of Mom or Baba Polina. She said nothing about crying the moment she saw the *house*, a squat midcentury ranch Obrandt had bought his mother with his first million. Like every other place visited mostly in childhood, it looked smaller than it once was, as if the years and the desert air had shrunk the house in half. Or maybe it was her who kept growing. On her way from the car to the entrance, she fleetingly worried about fitting in through the door.

The mother-daughter hug lasted a full second, which may have been a record. "How was the flight?" Emily asked. She looked better than she had four days ago, something Maya couldn't say about herself. "Did you sleep? I can never sleep on planes."

"I slept in the Lyft a little."

"You didn't drive?"

"You told me to come here straight from LAX."

"That's like, what, four hundred dollars? Maya Chou!" Emily shook her head. "We're a middle-class family now, you know."

Maya left this without response. They walked into the low-ceilinged living room, depressingly neat and done up in a mix of Desert Modernism and International Grandma. A lighted trophy case held sparse mementos of the old country: porcelain worker-and-peasant figurines, a red tea set Baba Polina had never put out, and, incongruously, an Italian souvenir plate that said *Amo Ladispoli*. A small pile of Obrandt family photos lay on the dining table. Emily must have been organizing them.

"Where's all your luggage?" her mother asked, looking her over.

"Left it in Portugal. At the house."

"Ah yes," said Emily. "The house. Of course. What's it look like?"

"Can I see Baba?"

Emily sighed. "She's in the back bedroom. Why don't you take a quick shower first, though, dear."

It was a fair point. Maya was still wearing the sweat of the Moscow car chase. The westward flight across eleven time zones had stretched the day to the point of absurdity: her version of August 26 was now entering its thirty-third hour.

The bathroom, filled with contraptions for geriatric self-care, made her cry again. Maya closed her eyes, lifted her face toward the lime-caked showerhead, and made the water as hot as she could handle, as if trying to scald her tear ducts into compliance.

"There, that's so much better," said Emily when Maya got out, red and smelling like rose soap. "You want to go in together or by yourself?"

"By myself for now, if that's okay."

The bedroom looked to be in the process of mutating into a hospital suite. A five-function ICU bed had replaced Baba Polina's spartan twin. Electronic monitors crowded the credenza. Someone—likely Emily—had piled up a mess of throws and quilts at the foot of the bed, less for warmth than as a pushback against the room's creeping institutionalization. In the center of it all lay Baba Polina herself, tiny and dark, asleep. One bandaged wrist rested on the cover of a Russian paperback she must have dozed off reading; she'd stuck her glasses in as a bookmark.

Maya softly lowered herself into an armchair next to the bed, not sure whether to speak up or to let her grandmother rest. As soon as she sat down, however, Baba Polina's sunken, red-rimmed eyes fluttered open.

"Hi, Grandma," said Maya in Russian. "I'm really happy to see you." She hesitated, unsure what to say next. "It's been a tough few days for all of us. I'm glad we're together now."

Baba Polina turned her head toward the sound, slowly and carefully, as if operating a piece of delicate machinery. Her gaze found Maya. "Anna?" she said. "*Anechka, eto ty?*"

Maya bit her lip. "This is Maya, Grandma. I don't know who Anna is."

"Anna, you came."

Maya put her hand on Baba Polina's hot dry wrist. "Maya. Maya Chou Obrandt. Your granddaughter. It's okay. How about I get you some water, huh?" She got up, trying to wince the tears back into her eyes.

"Hey, your Russian sounds better," said Emily from the doorway, startling Maya. She had been watching, for who knows how long. "Have you been doing Duolingo?"

"Yeah, kind of," said Maya on her way to the kitchen. "Who's Anna?"

Emily followed her. "No idea. Sometimes she just calls women Anna. Young and not so young. Nurses. There's no pattern. I think it helps if they have dark hair."

"She ever call *you* Anna?" Maya found a pitcher of filtered water on the countertop, rinsed a dusty glass, and filled it halfway.

"I don't think so." Emily looked around the kitchen. "Hungry? I can make—" She opened the fridge. "Well. Eggs, I guess."

By the time Maya came back, Baba Polina had used the bed's controls to pull herself up into a soft recline and put her glasses back on. Maya held the glass in front of her lips, and she took a polite sip before gesturing *enough*.

"Good book?" asked Maya, pointing at the paperback cover. "What's it about?"

"An affair!" the old woman said, and let out a soft giggle.

"Oh my. You're naughty, Baba! Good for you."

217

"Maya?" She suddenly perked up, as if a new person walked into the room. "*Maechka?*"

"Yes!" Maya kissed her waxy forehead. "That's me. Hi!"

"Your father is dead," Baba Polina said casually, as if by rote. "It's very sad."

"Yes, it is. Hey, Baba," said Maya, to change the subject, "want to look at some family photos? I found a whole bunch in the living room."

Baba Polina yawned. Maya decided to take it as a yes, ran to the dining table, and scooped up some pictures, hurrying back while her grandmother still recognized her as her.

"Here we go," she said, perching on the edge of the bed. "Let's see what we've got!" The first photo was a black-and-white shot of teenage Paul Obrandt, the same one used in the funeral slideshow. She shuffled it toward the back of the deck, ostensibly not to upset Baba. "Look, it's Mom in Taipei. Ooh, our first Swiss ski trip, I remember that. And this is you and me at the San Diego Zoo. I'm, like, four."

"Five," said Baba, finally engaging. In the photo, Polina held a pig-tailed Maya up above the crowd for a better look at the panda. *A father's job*, Maya thought, *not a grandmother's*. Perhaps Paul was the one who snapped the picture? *Right, who am I kidding. He was off somewhere, like always, probably plotting his escape from us already.*

The next few shots were from Paul and Emily's 1997 wedding. As soon as she saw the first one, Baba Polina shook her head no and kept shaking harder with each new photo until Maya got the message. "Okay, okay, Baba," she said. "Jeez." She flipped through the remainder, to see if there was anything there more like the San Diego Zoo one. No luck. The rest were all Paul Obrandt's career highlights. Paul making a speech. Paul getting some bullshit award. Paul ringing the bell at the New York Stock Exchange. Paul in a restaurant with—

Maya's breath caught in her throat. The room felt several degrees colder. The photo in her suddenly unsteady hand was a four-by-six print of the one on the wall of Demin's Moscow office: young Paul, mustached Demin, the gaunt scientist in a bad sweater. Same poses, same looks, same burned-in date stamp—5-4-1995. Except this photo showed four people at the table, not three.

Before framing his print, Demin had cut off the rightmost figure: a gorgeous, raven-haired woman in black. She was very young—younger than Maya now, inappropriately young for her sweatered companion. She had no scar on her cheek yet. But there was no mistaking those eyes and that elegantly elongated face.

Her father's mystery travel companion.

Olga Ostashevskaya.

"Baba," asked Maya in a slightly strangulated voice, "do you know who this is?"

Baba Polina squinted and beamed. "Of course," she said. "It's Anna. It's my Pavlik's Anechka."

"Baba . . ." She stole a nervous look at the doorway. Emily was in the kitchen, making eggs; Maya could hear the skillet sizzle. "How do you know her?"

A gnarled finger caressed the side of Ostashevskaya's face.

"I'm not stupid, Maya. I know my son's wife."

"Baba,"—she felt like her heart was going to break through her ribs when she whispered the next question—*"when was the last time you talked to him?"*

■ ■ ■

The address Falk overheard his companion tell the driver was on Amsterdam Avenue, which seemed a bit posh for a CIA facility. Agency offices in Manhattan tended to cling to the city's grimier edges, with a special preference for the ungentrifiably noisy blocks abutting FDR Drive. Only having pulled up to the building did Falk realize that the debrief would take place at Harlow's own apartment. In any other circumstances, he'd see it as a sign of respect.

The officer who picked Falk up at the airport was an even frostier version of Jim Otterbeck. He didn't say a word during the whole ride. The only bonding moment between the two of them occurred in the form of a simultaneous side glance once they stepped into the building's marble-clad lobby: Harlow's pied-à-terre was the kind of place only the oldest living generation of officers could have once afforded. CIA salaries didn't exactly keep pace with the New York housing market.

They took the elevator to the top floor, Falk thinking of Inga, as he would likely do in every elevator for the rest of his life. Otterbeck Two stepped out first. Falk was gratified to note that he took a second to locate the right apartment number. If he hadn't set foot here before, he was a little less likely to be one of Harlow's own off-the-books henchmen.

The deputy director opened the door wearing, despite the August heat, an Aran cardigan and what looked like flannel pajama bottoms. In the nine days that passed since their meeting in Berlin, he seemed to have aged another decade.

"Ari," Harlow said, putting a weightless hand on Falk's shoulder. "Good. Good to see you." He turned to Otterbeck Two and gave a shallow nod. "Hello, Jim." *You gotta be kidding me*, Falk thought. "Come in, gentlemen, come in."

The inside of the apartment looked like Harlow had it furnished around 1990 and changed nothing since. On the way down the corridor, Falk even espied a desk with a Macintosh SE and a fax machine, both yellowed like bad teeth, both on. Perhaps this was the way the deputy director kept his private comms secure—by keeping them obsolete. An ancient AC unit vibrated in the living-room window, blasting arctic air and white noise.

Harlow took him to a messy kitchen in the back, gesturing at his companion to fall behind. The younger man nodded and took up an uncertain residence next to the fax. Courtesy or egress prevention, it was too early to say.

"All right, son," Harlow said, lowering himself onto a flimsy chair. Falk did the same. A cassette recorder, about as old as everything else in the apartment, lay on the table between them, among empty take-out containers. "First things first. I've seen a lot over the years. Sometimes I even think my capacity for surprise is gone, so thank you for proving that wrong. Because, usually, when I send someone to London, they don't pop up in a high-speed chase in Moscow days later."

Falk steeled himself. He knew what he had to say. He had rehearsed it through the last two hours of the flight, the bumpy La Guardia landing, the silent car ride over. Yet, in the moment, his vestigial respect for the chain of command still gummed up the works.

"Sir," he finally said, "for your own sake, I suggest you keep the recorder off and have Officer Jim back there take a nice midnight walk in Riverside Park."

Harlow chuckled. "There will be a time for a heart-to-heart," he said. "At least I hope there will be, depending on how this shakes out. But don't let the setting fool you, kid." He started the tape, leaned in, showing Falk a polished bald spot encircled by tufts of cottonlike white hair, and spoke into the machine's honeycomb grate. "Initiating recording, August twenty-sixth, twenty–twenty-one, eleven thirty-two p.m., DD/CA Harlow conducting debrief of case officer Ari Falk, ID number—"

Falk mirrored his pose. "A quick correction, sir," he said into the recorder.

Harlow raised his head and glowered at him. "Did I mess up your ID?"

"No. But I'm afraid it's case officer Falk conducting debrief of DD/
CA Rex Harlow."

"All right now, enough of this." Harlow sounded more tired than
angry. "If you insist on being uncooperative, we are talking elsewhere."

"Rex," said Falk. He had never called Harlow Rex before. "On August fourteenth, you put a man named Anton Basmanny on a flight from
Istanbul to Riga. This part is an easily verifiable fact. You then tipped
off the Russians, specifically the Defense Ministry that Anton had so
recently and spectacularly humiliated, that they could force the flight
down over Belarus and come get him. This part is an educated guess.
Either way, it gave you the opening you needed to take an old asset of
yours, Paul Obrandt, and vanish him off the same flight while everyone
looked the other way."

"What is this nonsense," said Harlow with a touch of uncertainty.
"Can we get back to—"

"And, hey, I understand," Falk continued over him. "You needed to
save your guy, so you used mine. You took a brave, bright young man
and discarded him like a fucking Kleenex, but that's what we do in this
trade, don't we? It's what I myself have done for years."

"You understand nothing," Harlow growled. Then he reached out
and, in an admission all the more embarrassing for being wordless, turned
the tape off.

"Good move," said Falk. "Because I also know *why* you went to such
lengths to protect Obrandt. You see, twenty-five years ago, you and your
Russian counterpart, GRU general Gennady Demin, got the admirably
insane idea that you could run a third-party candidate against Boris and
the Commies. Who knows where you got the money, but Obrandt was
your bagman. Yes?"

Falk fell silent, waiting for a reaction. Harlow leveled a heavy stare at
him and said nothing.

"Just in case your next words are a signal and Jim comes through the door," Falk added, "I have Demin on tape. And I have Obrandt's daughter fully read in." This was a semibluff, but, folded in with the rest, he could tell it worked.

"A fascinating hypothetical," said Harlow at last. "So, in your imagination, what happened next?"

"Next, the FSB found out, I assume. Or Demin's own rivals in military intelligence. A CIA-funded candidate under their noses? With his own pet TV network?" Falk gave a low whistle. "You may have ended Russia's brief romance with democracy right there and then. At any rate, someone torched your candidate, literally."

"Konovalov was a great man," Harlow muttered, as if in spite of himself. "Don't be glib."

"Sorry. When this happened, both of your heads should have rolled. But there was no real blowback for you, or for that matter for Demin. Why? Well, my guess is, thanks to Obrandt. He was more valuable as an actual businessman than as a pretend one. So you sold him to the Russians as their pet banker—and bank for them he did, brilliantly, for decades, with the Agency looking the other way. This is just conjecture, of course, stop me whenever."

"And then?" Harlow seemed genuinely intrigued.

"I don't know what happened next. You tell me. Maybe Demin got greedy in his old age. Maybe *you* did. Maybe the sanctions got to Demin's bank, and Obrandt's fund was the nearest source of cash. I don't really care what you two cooked up, Rex. I just need people to stop dying."

In response, Harlow got up and walked to the door, limping more than usual. "Hey, Jim," he said into the hallway. Otterbeck Two popped out of the living room. "Take a walk. See you at Teterboro in the morning."

"Are you sure, sir?" the officer asked, cocking his head to get a better look into the kitchen.

"Yes. We're good here. Thanks." Harlow slowly came back to the table, then had an evident change of heart, shuffled toward the stove, and put on a kettle. At the far end of the hallway, the front door opened and closed.

"The first time I met Paul Obrandt," Harlow said, opening a cupboard and taking out a canister of Assam, "his mother served me this tea."

"His *mother*?"

"He was fifteen. Ladispoli." The old spy sounded lost in thought, and it didn't feel like a stalling tactic. He hummed, smiled, shook his head. When he sat down and spoke again, his voice was different, defeated but wistful. There was no anger there. It was a "we had a good run" type of voice, and it scared Falk more than anything that came before.

"It's funny, Ari," Harlow said, measuring out his words. "You're not wrong, per se. In fact, you've done impressive work—I hope someday you'll share how you got so much intel in so little time. And yet, you are as catastrophically lost and mistaken as a man can be. Because all you're seeing is the money motive."

"And what motive should I be seeing?"

"Love," said Harlow simply. "I was there the moment he fell in love with her, did you know that? Even *she* wasn't there." He grinned at some faraway reverie. "Just her picture in a newspaper clipping. He saw it, and that was it. Boom. Love. I kid you not."

"I'm sorry, I don't follow," said Falk. "Who fell in love with whom?"

The kettle on the stove began to whistle. Falk got up, turned it off, and sat back down.

Harlow sighed. "Paul Obrandt. My biggest mistake. Oh, he was brilliant, Ari, you're right about that. Twenty-five, sharp as a tack, a millionaire already. Filled with just the right resentments. A world to prove and a world to conquer. I could have sent him to Moscow with ten bucks to his name and he would have made a fortune before landing. To be brutally honest, I picked you for my team in '06 because you reminded me of him a little."

Even engrossed in Harlow's speech, Falk briefly wondered if Maya shared that assessment, and what it would mean if she did.

"Doesn't sound like a mistake so far," he said, to say something.

"Not yet. But I should have pulled him the moment he got the hots for her."

Finally, Falk got it. "Olga Ostashevskaya."

Harlow nodded. "More impressive work. Her real name is Anna Geluani."

"Italian?"

"Georgian—well, Svanetian, to be precise. Unbelievably smart. Achingly beautiful."

"Anna Geluani," repeated Falk. It felt strange to put an all-new name to the face he'd obsessively studied for the last ten days, but it somehow fit her.

"Anna was Konovalov's secretary, and a natural choice to run his campaign. She was already running his life sunrise to sunset. But, remarkably, not vice versa. The man had integrity." Harlow sighed, and Falk got an inkling that he himself was not immune to Anna's charms at the time. "To say that Obrandt fell hard is to say nothing. So did she. The devil of it was, they couldn't make it public, even though both were single."

"Right," Falk said. "Because it would connect Obrandt to Konovalov and give up your game."

"So, for a few months, they snuck around like a couple of ninth graders. GallTeleCom's media holdings, meanwhile, did their job. Konovalov hadn't even declared, and he was leading in some polls already. An actual, honest-to-goodness unity candidate. Oh, we were *giddy*, Ari. Best time of everyone's life."

"Sure. Until the FSB murdered him."

"*And her,*" said Harlow. "Anna was the hooker in the car. At least that was the story they fed to the press. Fuckers even picked the model. Lamborghini Diablo, subtle, isn't—"

"Stop." The pieces in Falk's head, so close to forming a whole, resumed the same chaotic dance that preceded his revelation on the plane. "Stop. Bullshit. I saw Anna with my own two eyes. Istanbul, eleven days ago. She's in her forties. He's on the run with her as we speak."

Harlow smirked. "And now, my son," he said triumphantly, "you know what the deal was, who made it, and what the money is for."

For a second, the world went dark with swirling shards of the story.

And then the shards snapped together so violently he wished they hadn't.

"Jesus Christ," said Falk, jumping to his feet. "Obrandt switched sides to save her. His soul for Anna's life. Yes? Demin had her vanished from the crash and shipped away as Ostashevskaya. She'd never know what he'd done for her. That's . . . Faustian."

"You can say that again," replied Harlow. "As I said: the only motive was love."

"And in return?"

Harlow let out a mirthless cackle. "Demin valued his half of the telecom at five billion. So that's the price he quoted Obrandt. 'Five billion and you're off the hook, you get to see her again.' Can you imagine?! Any other man would read this as the sadistic life sentence it was. My Pavlik? He went ahead and made the money. Took him twenty-five years, but still!"

"You sound admiring, Rex. It was twenty-five years of working for the Russians."

"And the Chinese," said Harlow breezily. "You didn't even hear the real Faustian part."

Just a few seconds ago, Falk thought the worst was over. Now he braced himself for the ton of bricks he knew was coming with the old man's next sentence. He even considered delaying it somehow. Changing the subject. Taking the teakettle and bludgeoning Harlow to death so he wouldn't have to hear it.

"The Chinese?"

"An old project of Demin's, I guess. Once stateside, Obrandt was to marry and legitimize an MSS sleeper agent with a Taiwanese cover."

■ ■ ■

"The omelet's ready!" yelled Emily from the kitchen. "Well, 'omelet' might be an overstatement. It's a frittata at best."

Maya kissed her sleeping grandmother on the forehead and walked over to the table, calculating every step. Her mind was in such frantic overdrive that her body wanted to compensate by slowing everything else down. The photo of Obrandt and Anna, nestled in the Ziploc between the farewell letter and its translation, burned her pocket.

"Thanks, Mom." She poked the food with the fork. "I'm actually not superhungry right now. My internal clock's all out of whack."

"I bet. It must be the middle of the night in Portugal," said Emily from across the table. She didn't make any eggs for herself, but sat down for company, half hidden behind an iPad Pro the size of a cafeteria tray.

Should she tell Falk? But how? Maya no longer had any ways of contacting him. They'd taken away their burner phones at the embassy. She doubted she'd find the guy on the socials.

"Mom," she said, "how much trouble did Dad put us in, exactly?"

"Not 'us.' Me. He had the sick sense to make me the fund's chairwoman. But, to answer your question, more than a bit. Some of the investors on the Asian side of the fund are quite . . . insistent. But we'll survive, I promise. I'm already working on some things."

Should she tell *her*?

"Do you ever think," Maya said carefully, "that Dad just wanted a different kind of life?"

Emily sighed. "Who doesn't, baby. Sadly"—she swiped across the tablet screen with two fingers, from spreadsheet to spreadsheet—"most of us don't get to choose."

Maya made herself eat another piece of egg. "May I be excused?" she blurted out, so earnestly that her mother laughed.

"Of course, dear. You're a grown-up, you don't have to ask." Still laughing, she reached over and touched Maya's hair with her palm. "I'm just glad you're here and you're okay."

For the first time in who knows how long, Maya felt tender, almost protective, toward her mother. Did she know about Anna when she and Obrandt met, less than a year after the date on that photo? Was he heart-broken, numb? On the rebound? If he loved that woman enough to reunite with her twenty-five years later, what did that make his entire life with them in the interim—a plan B, a distraction, a detour, an alibi?

"Mom," she said, "how well did you know Dad?"

Emily put down the tablet and turned off the screen. "What exactly are you trying to say?"

"Nothing. I'm not saying, I'm asking."

"Yes, but asking what? If I could predict that he'd do something like this? No. Believe me, if I could have stopped him, I would have."

"No, no." Maya paused on the precipice, then dove in. "Did you two love each other at any point? Were we ever a real family?"

For a few moments, her mother seemed to weigh the feasibility of pretending she didn't hear any of it. "Baby," she finally said, "whatever choices your dad made, he loved you very much. And so do I."

"And what about you? Did he love *you*?"

"Maya Chou, what is this?"

Some frenetic force brought Maya to her feet before she knew it. "What if I told you," she yelled, pacing the kitchen, "that he was madly in love with someone else when you two got married? That he *stayed* in love? That that's where he went now—to be with *her*?"

Emily sat, staring into the black lock screen of the iPad in front of her. She didn't even move her eyes to follow Maya around the room.

"I know that here in the West," she said quietly, "we are all raised on this idea of romantic love as the highest form of emotion. And it is certainly a powerful feeling. Powerful enough to make you move heaven and earth. But also powerful enough to make a complete fool out of you. And that's the difference. Where I come from, we believe in love too. But we also believe that throwing your life away for it is not honorable, it's selfish."

"Mom? I just told you Dad's alive. You don't seem very shocked."

At last, Emily lifted her head and made eye contact. She seemed close to crying—closer than she was on the day they heard the news. "It's not that. It's that I would have *vastly* preferred not to know."

"I'm sorry, I guess," said Maya. "Do you want me to tell you how I found out? It's a pretty insane story."

Emily gave an indifferent shrug. "I assume he contacted you."

Something stopped her from mentioning Baba Polina. "Yes. He left me a note. At the house, in Portugal." Maya could feel her mother study her face as she said this; Emily's unerring lie-detection powers had been the downfall of every teenage scheme Maya had ever tried to pull over on her. Luckily, what she just said was technically true.

"Did he tell you where they went? Did he invite you to join them?" Having spat out these questions, Emily winced, hard, even baring her bottom teeth for a split second. "Actually, don't tell me. Don't tell me any of it." Her hands formed two small white fists against the dark wood of the table. "It's best that you leave."

"Mom. What the fuck."

"*Language*. Go back to LA, now. I'll see you at home in a few days."

"What about Baba Polina?"

"I'll have her moved. Either there or to Cedars-Sinai. I'll let you know if, uh, if anything changes."

"Mom! What's going on?! You're scaring me."

Emily got up, impulsively half hugged her—which felt more terrifying than anything that came before—and sat back down. "It's going to be okay. I promise. Take Grandma's car."

After several minutes of spooked, silent rummaging through Baba Polina's tchotchkes, Maya found a key fob with the Chrysler logo. The dusty Pacifica stood in the garage, antenna bent against the low-slung ceiling.

Emily did not come outside to say goodbye. As the car rolled out into the desert dusk, Maya thought she heard the landline phone ring in the living room, but it was hard to tell over the sputter of the engine.

■ ■ ■

Falk stood up and walked over to the window, to avoid staring at the old man across the table. The Hudson lay like a band of pure darkness beyond the trees; New Jersey twinkled on the far shore. Above the line of lights, his own haggard reflection stared back.

He strained to process the enormity of Obrandt's sacrifice. Twenty-five years of dull, treasonous servitude. Twenty-five years of monomaniacal moneymaking. Twenty-five years in a sham marriage. All for a phantom chance of reuniting with a woman he knew for six months in 1995.

It was a hell of his own design, but the banker wasn't alone in it. Falk's thoughts turned to the unwanted daughter roaming the halls of that giant loveless mansion. Intuiting the void at the center of it all, thinking she's somehow at fault. Thinking she shouldn't exist. And then he wasn't feeling sorry for Obrandt, or Harlow, anymore.

"Thank you for telling me. But enough ancient history." He turned away from the window and peered into the deputy director's eyes. "Who's covering for them now? Who murdered Anton and my colleagues? Who chased me and Maya in Moscow?"

In response, Harlow got up, limped to the fridge and took out a half-full bottle of Polish vodka. "I'm sorry, son. I'll need some reinforcements to get through the next part."

"Sit down. Let me." Falk picked two cleanish glasses from the back of a shelf and poured a double into each. 70 percent courtesy, 30 percent precaution. Perhaps 60-40.

Harlow downed his vodka like water and gestured for more. Falk just gave him his own untouched glass and watched the old man's unshaven Adam's apple move up and down as he drank.

"I'm going to tell you," Harlow said slowly, already slurring a bit. "And only when I'm done telling you will you understand *why* I told you. Deal?"

"Sure."

"You're a smart kid. Smart enough to have sussed out most of this. Ever think how we got a hundred and fifty million to start a telecom in Russia? Five years after the official end of the Cold War?"

Little hairs stood up on Falk's arms and nape. He felt gutted and liberated at once, healed and sickened. "It wasn't a real Agency op, was it. You had outside funding."

"Bingo." Harlow grabbed the bottle, sloppily splashed more vodka into his glass, and drank up.

"Who?"

"Obrandt and I used to call him Cormorant. An inside joke of sorts. I'm going to keep calling him that, if you don't mind."

"Private capital? A politician?"

Harlow made a vague hand gesture that could mean *both* or *neither*. "Why?"

"It was a chance to do *good*, Ari. How often do these come along? So, yes, when I came in to head Moscow Station, I had two briefs, one a little more secret than the other. So what? Can you imagine the turn history would have taken, had we succeeded?" Harlow clambered to his feet as he spoke. A small tear formed in his left eye and slid down a craggy cheek. "A Russia that's gone through a proper truth-and-reconciliation process, reflected on its sins, and moved forward? No poisoned journalists. No back-to-USSR nonsense. No Weimar *ressentiment*. A normal country, led by grown-ups."

"Yeah. That's what Anton was fighting for," said Falk bitterly, getting up too. "And you and your Cormorant got him killed."

"They promised they'd scare him straight and send him back!" the old man bellowed. "Which they did! That was it! How could I know Cormorant would start cleaning house like that?"

"How did he find out?"

"My own damn overcaution," spat Harlow. "I asked Istanbul Station to strike Paul's and Anna's aliases from the flight manifest. The problem is, to *erase* someone's name, you first have to *write* someone's name. The bastards logged it in the system. Next thing I know, an ex-SADAT mercenary in Istanbul buys a ticket for the same flight, and Moscow flags two Orlok contractors en route to Riga. That's a lot of unaccountable private firepower on the move. I had to get Paul and Anna out of there, and in a way that wouldn't alarm the guy tailing them." Harlow looked at Falk, blinking. "I'm so sorry, son."

"But why?!" Falk yelled in his face. "Why kill every witness? Why send an assassin for a damn *boat captain*? Why is it so fucking important that Obrandt stay dead in the eyes of the world?!"

Harlow sighed. "And you've been doing so well. I was really hoping you'd figure this part out yourself."

"Say it."

"Why, it's about Anna, of course," the old man said. "Cormorant had no idea she was alive! He was okay with Obrandt out and about, as long as Demin controlled him and the Chinese had an eye on him, but Anna?! Imagine someone recognizing her. And she knows everything. Can name every name, his, mine. She was *in the car*, for fuck's sake. Still got scars and burns to show for it. So, yes, Ari, you've been staring right at it this whole time. He is going after Anna and everyone who's seen her."

Falk felt the blood drain from his face. "Where does that leave Maya?"

Harlow transferred himself onto a ruined leather ottoman in the living room, and lay supine as if for a therapy session. Tufts of white batting stuck out of the cracks in the cushion, looking like a parody of his own hair.

"Oh," he said looking into the ceiling, "she'll be dead by tomorrow. He came by not two hours ago to get her whereabouts. Sat where you sat. Drank the tea. Promised to leave you alone, though, if you play ball."

A long silence fell, broken up only by the rattle of the AC. "Aw, come on, son," said Harlow and crossed his legs. "No pouting, now. I warned you. Why do you think I'd tell you all this? You're not *that* great of an interrogator."

"I am a soldier. Let him come after me. Leave the girl alone."

"And here it is again." The old man tossed until he got comfortable, hugged a cushion, and closed his eyes. "The love motive."

"Rex. Please. Focus. All the other killings were abroad. He's been using Russian and Turkish mercs. Would he really go after Maya on US soil?"

"I think you know the answer to that," Harlow murmured, falling asleep. "She won't be safe for as long as she's alive."

"Th-then let's resurrect Obrandt," Falk stammered. "Let me go public. Keep you out of it, hang it on Cormorant. Where are they? Where did you hide the two of them?"

The sound Falk heard next was so familiar to him that he found it almost reassuring for a second: the percussive syncope of a nine-millimeter round being chambered. He looked down and met the eye of a Gen5 Glock.

"Kinda hoped it wouldn't come to this," said Harlow, wide awake and fully lucid. "But knew it would."

The old man held the gun at thigh level, jammed between his body and a cushion. He must have fished it out of the couch as he tossed about, masterfully keeping Falk's attention elsewhere.

"Rex. *Sir*. Come on."

"Uh-uh. Hands up."

Falk put his hands in the air. "Look," he said, trying to sound calm. "You're the only one in the world who knows where Obrandt is. Let me go to him, talk to him. I'm sure he'll understand we're just trying to save his daughter. And please, for god's sake, put that thing down."

Harlow's jowls tightened as he took better aim. "You see," he said from the couch, "at some point tonight you will realize there's no point begging me. Once you do, you will decide to torture me or bring me in instead. What I can't quite figure out yet is which one I prefer."

"I'm not going to torture you," said Falk. "Come on. It doesn't have to be like this."

"Still in the begging phase, then."

"No, listen. Someone put it like this to me recently: institutions can't be moral. Only people can. Right? You knew this when you worked with Demin to elect your guy. So please recognize it now, too. You keep covering for this Cormorant, and you help no one. We take him down, we save Maya, and, well, it's all been worth something."

"Sorry, son." Harlow shook his head no. "My duty is to you and Obrandt, not to her. What's that *Little Prince* line the Russians love so much? 'You become responsible for what you have tamed.'"

"What?"

"We both did our best for our agents," said Harlow. Then, in a single, almost gracious move, he turned the barrel of the Glock upward, stuck it under his unshaven chin, and pulled the trigger.

For a minute or so, Falk stood over the body, breathing little ragged breaths and listening to the building. No alarmed steps down the hallway, no raised voices. No lights switching on in the apartments across the courtyard. The loudest sound, apart from the subsiding whine in Falk's ears—the private echo of a gun going off three feet away—was the clatter of the AC unit.

The shot had opened up the top of the old man's head, launching bits of matter over the arm of the couch; the cracked cushions were fast filling up with blood. Falk made himself look. The body had fallen back into the supine position from which Harlow aimed the Glock at him just minutes ago, but this time it lay diagonally, feet on the floor, on the verge of sliding down or flopping over. Against every instinct, Falk knelt and lifted the old man's legs back onto the couch, stabilizing him.

Then, via some kind of extremely minute teleportation, he found himself in front of Harlow's work desk, staring at the fax machine. A late-90s model, it was connected to the landline and, in a pinch, could function as a phone.

Autopilot overtook him. Back in Tangier, when Falk first googled "Paul Obrandt," only one listed US number had come up, for a Polina Obrandt in Palm Springs, CA. Before he knew what he was doing, he found it in his notes and punched it into the machine's keypad.

"Hello." The calm female voice on the other end was at once like and unlike Maya's.

"Hi," Falk said over the crackle of static. "I'd like to speak to Maya Obrandt."

"She's not here. Who's asking?"

"I know who and what you are, Emily," said Falk. "And I can help you get back what you lost. Is this a safe line?"

When the woman spoke again, her tone betrayed a hint of weariness. "As you are well aware, there's no such thing."

"Good," Falk barked. "I *want* the MSS to listen in. I am calling to make a deal."

"What kind?"

"You get your husband's money when we find it. In return, you and your organization swear complete, ongoing, institutional commitment to your daughter's safety, starting now."

"Why do you care about my daughter?"

"Inconveniently enough," said Falk, "same reason you do."

■ ■ ■

LONDON

AUGUST 28, 2021

Forty-eight hours later, Alan Keegan got off the Tube in an unusually foul disposition. As a rule, he didn't allow the news of the day to affect his mood. The keystone of his philosophy was a firm belief that the world had always been an ocean of shit, and an ocean of shit it would remain, with tiny islands of grace and decency dotting the map here and there. All one could do, really, was to lay down one's route from isle to isle, and pray for clement seas.

That said, on some days the headlines all but conspired to make even this worldview seem too optimistic. Russia ordered more troops to the Ukrainian border. Yet another incompetent PM was in the process of becoming an incompetent former PM. Across the pond, the world's largest economy and grandest democracy continued to teeter a few votes away from falling into the hands of people who believed their opponents drank children's blood. The Polish politico, whose neo-Nazi past FleaCollar had exposed with such pluck and rigor and even received an award for doing so, confidently sailed to reelection.

The story that upset him the most that day, however, had little global significance. In fact, it was so local it barely made the news at all and caught his eye only because he had an alert set to the name. *Maya Chou Obrandt, 23, dead,* in a freak auto accident on I-10 between Palm Springs and Los Angeles. The car she drove, a 2004 Chrysler Pacifica rust bucket registered to her grandmother, flew off an empty stretch of the desert highway in the middle of the night, tumbling to rest a full hundred feet from the road; it was found well after sunrise, burned to the chassis.

The only thing that made this private tragedy at all newsworthy was the fact that the victim's father, well-known investment banker Paul Obrandt, had died by his own hand exactly two weeks earlier. Some of the coverage stopped just short of implying that Maya, who had a history of dependency, was affected enough by that death to get behind the wheel on drugs. The rest focused on her modest portfolio as a character actress, with one of the portals going so far as to file the news under *Entertainment.*

The three minutes' walk from Clapham Common to the bedsit was the perfect length for one song. Keegan popped in the AirPods and scrolled for something fast and angry, to drown out the melancholy, but his taste ran to milder stuff; the loudest band he had in his library was Ladytron. Ladytron, then, it would have to be.

He was almost through "International Dateline" when he saw Falk sitting on the steps of the house. It could only be him, but it still took

Keegan a few extra seconds to make sure. The rogue ex-officer looked gaunt, bent, shrunken somehow inside his oversize jacket. A living illustration of the phrase *half the man I used to be.*

"Tea?" asked Keegan in lieu of a greeting. Falk shook his head no. As he did, light from a lamp across the street hit one side of his face, catching a large, fresh bruise.

"Thanks, but I just came to drop something off. I owe you for Moscow, remember." He reached into a pocket and handed Keegan a portable drive.

"Oh good, a dodgy USB stick. Will it fry my system?"

"It will fry *a* system," Falk said.

"May I at least ask what it is?"

Falk winced. "It's a story, Alan."

"What about?"

"Mostly murder."

"Aren't they all. What kind?"

"Oh, the usual," said Falk. "A mystery US individual ordering hits on American citizens around the world, using Russian and Turkish mercenary outfits."

"Good Lord. Is that what happened to the girl?" blurted out Keegan.

"*And,*" Falk continued, pointedly refusing to hear the question, "there's a bonus for history buffs, too. Involves the Agency helping the Russians hide the murder of the only good presidential candidate they ever had."

"Source?"

"A deathbed confession."

"Jesus fuck." Keegan felt the need to sit down. Falk saw it and moved, freeing up some space on the step. For a while they just sat there side by side, watching insects dance in the halo of the lamp.

"What am I to do with all of it?" Keegan finally asked.

"Put it on FleaCollar, obviously."

"Are you sure? If this pans out, your entire organization is in for it."

"Fine by me. Burn it to the ground. Let them start again."

Keegan slowly inhaled through his teeth, thinking. "You know, you asked me once if FleaCollar ever saved anyone, and it stuck with me in an extremely unpleasant way."

"Sorry."

"So whom would we be saving now?"

"Whoever's the next target," said Falk.

"What about you? Do you need time to get gone? I can hold off on this for as long as necessary."

"I don't care. Run it today if you want."

"I just want to, uh, make sure," said Keegan, "that you're not doing this as a kind of destroy-the-world thing just because, you know. Because she's dead."

Falk gave him a blank look. "Who cares why I'm doing it?"

He clamped his hands onto his kneecaps and stood up with a wince. As the spy walked away, Keegan noticed a limp that wasn't there before.

"Wait," he called out. Falk slowed his uneven steps. "Come on, man. A cup of tea won't kill you."

"That's what they said to Litvinenko," deadpanned Falk, turning around. Keegan laughed, less because it was funny and more because he was happy to catch a glimpse of the guy he knew. "I set you up for that one, didn't I."

■ ■ ■

Falk sat at Keegan's white table, staring at the lichen-covered angel out in the garden. In his hand was a chipped mug of Darjeeling. He brought it to his lips and put it down; it was still too hot. Across the table, Keegan hunched over his laptop, typing furiously. FleaCollar volunteers all over the globe were already hard at work compiling and fact-checking bits and pieces of the Cormorant story.

"It's going to take a while to ID the son of a bitch," said Keegan. "But we will. That's a promise."

"Thank you."

"Do you want me to keep looking for Obrandt and what's-her-name, too?"

"No. My last lead was Harlow. The trail went cold when he did. And, honestly, I wouldn't want to know now. I'd be too tempted to end Obrandt myself, for causing all this."

"Well," said Keegan, reading a new message that popped up on his screen. "Even so, you might be interested to know where his billions went."

Falk blew on the surface of the tea. "I might."

Keegan opened an attached PDF, read some of it, mouthed *wow*, and turned to Falk. "A few hours ago, there was a series of wire transfers from Switzerland to China so massive they affected the franc-renminbi exchange rate. And guess what? The Chinese bank they went to happens to be a major investor in Obrandt's fund. Now that's what I call an ROI." Keegan smirked, then stopped himself. "I'm sorry. I don't know what's wrong with me."

"It's okay," said Falk. "Look, you don't have to walk on eggshells around me. We weren't a couple. I only knew her for a week." The tea finally reached drinkable temperature. He took a symbolic sip and got up. "I better get going. Thanks for everything."

"Do take care of yourself," said Keegan earnestly. It was, Falk surmised, the British equivalent of a bear hug.

The street smelled of rotting leaves. As Falk ambled toward Wandsworth Road, his gait changed, as if a weight had been lifted; he walked faster and faster, eventually breaking into a hobbling jog despite the sharp pain in his ankle and a darker, duller ache between his ribs. Wet chill hung in the air. He pulled up the hood as he ran.

Falk slowed down only thirty minutes later, by the illuminated Chelsea Bridge. In front of him stood, listing to one side as he did, a much-pissed-upon phone booth, repainted black and refurbished into a public Wi-Fi spot. He took out his mobile, found the signal, logged on, opened an obscure Chinese messenger app that never made it out of beta, and typed "It's done." Then he threw the phone into the Thames and walked on, trying and failing to stifle a smile.

2021:
THE PRICE OF RESURRECTION

In the windless night, the water looked viscous. Ripples moved like muscles under silk. Paul Obrandt took off his shoes and left them on the deck. Then he climbed over the gunwale and threw himself into the Gulf of Cadiz.

The plan was mostly Harlow's, and he trusted the old man's professional expertise even more than he did his late-blooming desire for redemption. For weeks, they had gone over it again and again—finding and quashing what-ifs, reinforcing weak spots, finessing the timeline, stress-testing their own logic; it felt more like civil engineering than spycraft. They'd considered every angle, prepared for every contingency. He had even taken up swimming again, doing laps in the mansion's pool under Emily's slightly puzzled gaze.

There was only one thing, it turned out, for which Harlow hadn't prepped him: how much this would feel like an actual suicide.

The water was colder than Paul expected. Even in these tropical climes, the Atlantic never got quite warm enough. The bespoke cashmere suit felt like a mass of icy seaweed hanging off his limbs. He was wearing a life vest he'd smuggled aboard and inflated with his own ragged breath minutes ago: taking one from the yacht's supply would give away the game. On the contrary, Harlow had instructed him to toss overboard a heavy object, so the investigators would think he'd used it to drown faster. He had found some anchor line, still coiled on the thimble, and rolled it off the side of the boat just before jumping.

The *A Mar* was now two hundred or so feet away, glowing like a Christmas bauble on the water—the warm orange light of the flybridge, the portholes pulsing blue as the party continued without him. At this distance, Paul could still hear the thump of the Balearic beat and the drunken yelps of Portuguese executives inside. As he bobbed on the water, gently pushing away, both slowly faded.

A plastic pouch flapped against his thigh, containing a Czech passport, a cheap Xiaomi phone with the battery taken out, and a small cubic device with what looked like a camera lens on one side. It was an iris-scan-activated code generator, tied to a Swiss account whose number changed with each scan; even the account's owner didn't know it. Once in Riga, he would use the device to transfer his fortune to Demin. The seeds of a new life, and the literal sum total of the old one, all in one bag.

Would he miss anything about the last twenty-five years? It was hard to say. The way Paul had structured his time after his return to the US as Demin's serf left very little distinction between forced routine and voluntary habit. He did what he did. He got up, made money, stole some of it, made more, and went to bed. Everything else—family, charity, leisure—was subservient to these two clashing objectives: grow the fortune he thought of as his bail bond, and do it slowly enough to get away with it. Sometimes he saw himself as the prisoner in *The Shawshank Redemption*, one of the very few movies he liked, extending an escape tunnel by one fistful of gravel a day. The hardest part was not the digging. It was never trying *two* fistfuls.

He'd miss his mother, Polina, but found a sort of solace in the fact that she wouldn't miss him. Her Alzheimer's had progressed enough that she would barely recognize him in the room. Granted, Paul hadn't been in the room all that often: ever since coming back from Moscow, he pushed his parents away as hard as he could. Only now, on his last few trips to Palm Springs, did he sometimes whisper the truth, knowing she'd forget as soon as he left.

He would, in all honesty, miss Emily. The first year of their marriage was just as hard on her as it was on him, and from that side-by-side suffering, ironically enough, something like affection began to grow. Three years in, when she gave birth to Maya, they were almost a normal family. Almost a happy one, even. He'd seen far worse relationships within the West Coast billionaire set that presumably *didn't* start as cover stories—though who knows. After the crash of 2008, however, once Paul's secret math began suggesting he was now on track to hit his goal by the age of fifty, not forty-three as he'd hoped, things took a turn for the worse. The rages returned, more explosive for having been stifled all these years. He would never let himself start drinking—that would be far too Russian—but began to cope in other ways. There was the cocaine; the high-priced escorts (though he was so terrified of walking into a honey trap that he mostly ended up embarrassing himself); a yearlong affair that made him feel, absurdly, like he was cheating on Anna. Emily grew as distant as she'd ever been. The mere sight of Maya, then ten, caused Paul physical pain.

Oh, how he'd miss Maya. Brilliant, willful, self-hating Maya, always a mess, always a challenge. The third victim of Demin's cruel arrangement, she knew this without knowing it. Two suicide attempts, two rehab stints, all by twenty-three. She had gone sober six weeks before his scheduled disappearance, and this time, miraculously, it seemed to stick; it was the only thing that almost stopped Paul from going through with the plan.

He couldn't bear the idea that his actions would push her off the wagon, or worse.

So he did the only thing he could think of. He gave her a way out and a sliver of hope. The house in Portugal he bought sight unseen—it wasn't much more expensive than the suit on his back—setting foot in it for the first time on the same day he boarded the yacht. The money, 250,000 euro, was just enough to start an independent life if she wanted to, not enough to coast through it. As for the letter, it was a manic, reckless improvisation; had Harlow known about it, the old spymaster would be understandably furious. But the only real hint he had placed there— the mention of the year 1995—was a pointer to his past, not to his future.

The girl was better off without him. The world was better off without him. (In this belief, Obrandt wasn't too far off from someone actually suicidal.) Still, wouldn't it be great if, one day, she could see him just one more time? See her father finally free of the curse that had turned him into a monster? Meet Anna?

Obscene, naive, egotistical dream.

A distant flashlight clicked on and off three times just above the water, reflections turning the dot into an *i*. The other boat was here. Paul broke off his waterlogged reveries and began to paddle toward it.

The captain and the only crew member of the *Selena* was a squat Portuguese man with massive eyebrows, wearing a faded Tweety Bird T-shirt. His countenance, for some reason, inspired immediate trust. "Jose Alves," he said, tossing him a towel. "Welcome aboard."

"How long until Tangier?" Paul asked.

"Five hours if we hurry."

"Please do." Five hours until he'd see Anna. Twenty-five years down. Five hours to go. The unimaginable was becoming real.

He went into the musty stateroom and changed into the outfit laid out there: sagging track pants and a rugby shirt that must have come from the same thrift-store pile as the captain's Tweety. A bottle of cheap tequila stood next to the bed. The clothes were a part of the plan, the tequila wasn't.

"That's for you, sir," yelled Alves from the deck. "Warm up."

"Thank you." Paul unscrewed the bottle cap and took a few pulls. All this already felt like the beginning of a new, exciting life—with only Anna, the point of it all, missing.

He glanced at himself in the small wall-mounted mirror, and the excitement faded. Staring back was a fifty-year-old with gray hair and bluish Nixonian stubble. Blurry, too: the astigmatism was getting worse. Asthma, hernia, ulcer, high blood sugar. *What a fucking catch*, he thought. *Better throw me back in the sea.*

Does Anna know? Has she seen his photos over the years? Is she prepared to greet this ludicrous ruin, or is she still picturing a lithe twenty-five-year-old with burning eyes?

There *were* no photos of Anna. Unlike Obrandt in his golden Californian cage, her existence had to be hidden from the world entirely: she'd already died once. Per terms of their deal, not even Harlow knew where she lived. Until last week, that information stayed with Demin and Demin only. Over the years, Paul imagined her aging in myriad ways—lean, zaftig, hippyish, elegant, Botoxed, sunburned, frostbitten—but all these images were just fanciful filters applied to the same twenty-three-year-old face. Ultimately, he didn't care what she'd look like. As long as she was Anna Geluani, he loved her.

The cashmere suit lay in a sopping pile on the stateroom floor, a puddle spreading around it. Paul opened the door and tossed it up the stairs to the deck, where it landed with a double wet splat.

"Get rid of this, please," he called to the captain.

"Are you sure, sir? Looks like a really nice suit."

"Sink it." Paul took another swig of the tequila and lowered himself onto the bed. Who was he kidding, it was impossible to even think about sleeping at a moment like this—

Hey, sonya-zasonya.

Wake up, sleepyhead.

Paul opened his eyes. The inside of his mouth tasted like copper. He must have been out for at least an hour. The port side of the boat was bumping gently against something solid.

"He's down there, miss," he heard Captain Alves say somewhere above. Paul bolted upright just as the door flew open. With zero ceremony or hesitation, Anna Geluani burst into the room and hopped onto the bed next to him; the space was small enough that these two actions were technically one.

She screamed. He sobbed. They embraced so fast and so hard they didn't see each other's faces until disengaging a minute later.

The years had done their thing, but so what? She was *herself*—in the way she fidgeted, smiled, threw her head back. He reached out and touched a deep demilune scar on her left cheek; it hadn't been there before.

"The price of resurrection," said Anna. "And that's all I'll say about it."

"It's beautiful."

"Oh, please." She scrunched up her nose in mock affront. "You cornball."

"Your English is . . . better."

"You should hear my Arabic," she said, taking him by the hand and dragging him outside. Paul more or less realized that the *Selena* had docked while he slept, but he still didn't expect to step out into the middle of a busy city. Tangier hummed around the marina, oblivious to his arrival. Even in the dead of night, cars blew their horns and motorbikes rattled up and down the port road.

He thanked Captain Alves and reminded him to lie low in Tangier for two full weeks. This was one of Harlow's contingencies, in the unlikely case some overzealous Portuguese detective would decide to question every sailor in Algarve where they were that night.

"I've been staying at this terrible Airbnb down the road," said Anna, still squeezing his hand. "Want to come in for a minute?"

"I think we need to head to the airport," Paul replied. She looked at him quizzically, and he finally realized. "Yes. Yes."

The sex was awkward at first, a cautious mutual rediscovery. After a few tentative moments, however, their bodies remembered each other and themselves and switched to full, glorious autopilot. Afterward, dizzy and happy, Paul stared up at the cracked ceiling, listening to the sound of the shower. His Rolex Submariner on the nightstand was closing in on three a.m., the time they were supposed to check in with Harlow.

"See?" Anna said, nude but for a towel turban on her head, leaning down to kiss him. "It's like fucking a bike." They both cracked up midkiss, knocking their front teeth together, which only made them giggle harder.

"You know," Paul said through the laughter, pulling her toward him, "I have to tell you something. I wouldn't *terribly* mind dying right here and now. I'm kind of all set."

"Don't say that." She was, all of a sudden, serious. "Never say that."

"Sorry."

"You're forgiven." She stretched and gave a contented yawn. More scars ran down her torso, whiter than the rest of her skin, almost phosphorescent in the dark: two vertical stripes along the spine, an irregular star across the lower back. Paul reached over and traced one of the star's rays.

"I want to know about the accident."

Anna sighed. "You can't help yourself, can you. Is this going to be a barrier between us?"

249

"I need to know if he did everything to protect you. If he kept the promise."

"Who, Demin? What difference does it make? What are you going to do, *not* give him the money?"

"Please."

"Fine." Anna put on underwear, opened the closet, and pulled out a dark, angular jumpsuit. "I mean, I only know what they told me afterward. Demin drugged both of us, Konovalov and me, at a restaurant the previous night. I dimly remember doing shots with him. I woke up in the hospital with half a dashboard clock in my face." She turned her back to Paul. "Zip." He did.

"I guess his plan was that, once we passed out, they'd take us to the countryside, put us into the Lamborghini, and burn it," she continued. "The FSB were involved at every step, so it had to look real for *them*, too. They started the fire and drove off. Demin's men pulled me out thirty seconds later. The only problem"—Anna touched the scar on her cheek—"was that hundred-liter fuel tank. It blew up almost immediately."

"Jesus Christ."

She sighed and sat down on the bed again. "This isn't the full story. I'm not sure you want to hear the rest of it."

"I do."

"The truth is," Anna said, with difficulty, "I came to in the car. Five seconds before the fire. Maybe ten, I don't know. Long enough to realize exactly what was going on. Sergei was conscious, too. I still remember his— No. Enough." She fell silent. They sat holding each other until the clock struck three.

He reached for the phone, installed the battery, and turned it on. It buzzed at once.

"Paul," barked Harlow on the other end. "Stay calm. You're being setup. Don't know by whom yet, but I can't have you two land in Riga."

Paul glanced at Anna. "Got it. We'll lie low right here, or in Istanbul." She stared at him, mouthing *What?*

"Negative. If you don't board, they'll know we know."

"Let me get this straight. We have to get *on* that flight but we can't get *off* it."

"In so many words, yes. I have a play I'm working on. Proceed like nothing's changed. I will exfil you when they least expect it."

"You mean when *we* least expect it."

"That, too. Good luck. Kill the phone." Harlow hung up. Shell-shocked, Paul mechanically took apart the Xiaomi.

"Please tell me what's going on," said Anna.

"Nothing. Harlow being overcareful."

"*Pavlik.*" She switched to Russian. "This is our new life together. Let's not start lying to each other quite yet."

Paul nodded. "You're right. Okay . . . we might or might not get attacked on our way to the bank."

"Ah." She shrugged. "I assumed as much."

■ ■ ■

The first leg of the flight was torture. Every airport passerby, every fellow passenger could be their killer or their savior. This was, ironically, the first time Paul had ever traveled anywhere with Anna; they made for a distinguished couple with the body language of teenagers in love, and people liked to look at them.

They made it to Istanbul unscathed, and, little by little, he began to relax. Anna dragged him into the airport's only clothing store that was open at eight a.m. and picked out an outfit to replace Alves's rags—cheap chinos and a half-zip pullover. This was another first. No woman other than Polina Obrandt had ever shopped for him.

Once they boarded the flight to Riga, Paul briefly fixated on a hard-looking Turkish man who sat down across from them in business class, but he pulled his baseball cap down over his face and went to sleep before the plane even began to taxi. Perhaps Harlow *was* being too cautious. Perhaps everything was going to be all right.

Next thing he knew, they were being buzzed by a Belarusian MiG.

"Is this it?" asked Anna. Her hand on his trembled a bit, but she sounded calm.

"Hard to say." He felt compelled to match her tone. "It may be the Russians. It may be Harlow, somehow. It may even be unrelated, as funny as that sounds. Whatever it is, I love you."

"I love you too."

As the plane banked toward Minsk, coming in for a forced landing, the cabin filled with frightened multilingual chatter. If anything, Paul and Anna, who had been steeling themselves for something just like this, looked more collected than most.

Once they were on the tarmac, a blond, gawky young man got up and began making a heartfelt speech in Russian-accented English. He was either a journalist or a comedian and appeared to be under the impression that the plane had been diverted because of him. "Don't turn around," Anna whispered. "Everyone's filming him. Just keep looking ahead." Sometimes her grasp of tradecraft seemed stronger than his. Not for the first—or the thousandth—time Paul wondered how, exactly, she had spent these twenty-five lost years.

The next time they saw the same kid was in Belarusian custody. They'd been kept waiting for two or so hours in a featureless Soviet office, under a fluorescent lamp that kept going on and off; no one had yet come to greet, interrogate, or threaten them. Suddenly, the door flew open and two soldiers shoved the kid inside. He sat down with his back turned to them and stayed motionless for a good long while.

"That was a nice speech," said Anna in Russian when he finally glanced at them.

"Thanks," the kid mumbled. On second look, he wasn't that much of a kid—perhaps in his late twenties. "I don't even remember what I said. I think I blacked out."

"What are you doing?!" whispered Paul into her ear. "He might be one of them, working us."

"I'm sorry."

"So, uh, where are you from?" asked the emboldened journalist or comedian, looking at Paul.

"Places." Perhaps a little outright rudeness would end the conversation.

"I'm sorry," repeated Anna, this time addressing the kid. "My husband has been a little on edge." She smiled and put her hand on Paul's shoulder.

My husband. Hearing these words, he finally realized why she was doing this. Were their story to end here and now, in this tawdry office, at least one stranger would have known them for what they were. Husband and wife.

Paul's eyes burned. He turned away as fast as he could.

He sat staring at the wall, concentrating on his breath, until the sound of the turning lock made him look back. Two soldiers or guards came in, ones he hadn't seen before and wearing different uniforms from those who had led them off the plane.

"Come with us," said one of them in brusque Russian. Paul got up, unsteadily. So did Anna. Looking only at each other, they walked out into a dark dank hallway.

"Sorry about all that," the same soldier continued in clipped British English as soon as the door closed behind them. "You two must be nervous *wrecks.*"

Wrecks.

Rex.

Harlow.

The rush of relief Paul felt was so violent it almost knocked him off his feet. He stopped, grabbed Anna's shoulders, and started laughing like a maniac. The soldiers stood and patiently waited for his fit to pass. This, too, was an excellent sign.

"Wait," said Anna. "That poor kid in there. He's a loose end now." She turned to the Brit, pointing at his bullpup rifle. "You got live rounds in that thing?"

"Jesus, Anna!"

The soldier understood what she meant before Paul did. He and she exchanged a glance of instant rapport, roughly translatable as "get a load of that idiot." Then he raised his rifle, aiming at the hallway wall, and set it to single rounds. "Two enough?"

"I should think so. Hang on." She touched the crumbling concrete, making sure it was soft enough to absorb a shot. "Do it."

He nodded and put two bullets into the wall, an inch and a second apart. The noise was deafening.

"Kid's gonna shit his pants," said the other soldier, in singsong.

"Nah, he's pretty tough," said Anna. "Hope he's not in trouble on our account."

The soldiers pushed open a heavy sliding door. Sunlight flooded the hallway, catching whirls of concrete dust kicked up by the gunshots. Paul stepped outside; they'd been kept in an abandoned-looking industrial building on the edge of the airfield itself, facing the apron. A 747 with unrecognizable airline livery had just touched down and was taxiing their way.

"Looks like your ride's here," said the second soldier.

"A ride to where?" Anna asked, straining to be heard over the approaching jet engines. The soldier grinned and shrugged.

Hand in hand, they ran toward the roar.

■ ■ ■

Two weeks and a day later, a young woman with close-cropped hair stepped off the Seatran ferry from Surat Thani, ensconced inside a crowd of mostly white mostly tourists. *Unglaublich, ich habe schon einen Sonnenbrand*, moaned a man in an aloha shirt in front of her, touching the back of his neck; it was, indeed, already red as raw brisket. The gangplanks shifted and sang. Beyond lay the docks of Nathon Pier, with *Welcome to Koh Samui* in English and Thai script over peeling blue paint.

The young woman did not have a name. Or, rather, the name she had was so new and assigned so randomly that not only did it hold no personal meaning for her, it seemed to throw the very concept of "names" into question. It was just two characters in a brand-new People's Republic of China passport, handed to her by the same man who then had taken her grandmother's car and drove off to flip it into roadside bushes. The eVisa she had gotten online herself; it allowed Chinese nationals a fifteen-day stay in Thailand. Beyond that, she'd have to contact the consulate. But in those two weeks, she'd probably have to find yet another name anyway.

At the airport, she had spoken to the border guards in Mandarin. Unlike her Russian, it was good enough to fool a nonnative speaker. Affecting broken English was, frankly, harder: in the previous life (or was it two lives ago?), if a casting director had asked her to do this sort of thing at an audition, she'd have taken offense. Perhaps she could phase in her normal pronunciation at a later time, having first enjoyed a year or so as the brightest student in some ESL course. She hadn't really thought this through yet.

In the young woman's hand was a piece of paper with an address, scribbled in longhand. She didn't need it—she'd memorized it ten times over—but, she reasoned, a taxi driver might. If she were to be fully honest with herself, however, she'd have to admit she was keeping it as a souvenir. Apart from the Chinese passport, it was the only material memento she had of the man who gave it to her. The man would no longer have a name, either. Nor would he ever contact her again, or she him.

"How the fuck did you get this?" she had asked him last night, when they stopped kissing. They had met up in a faceless parking lot in Inglewood, a stone's throw from LAX; she had driven in from Palm Springs earlier that day, and he flew in from New York. At least two planes roared overhead while they embraced.

"Funny story." He grinned like an idiot, not even trying to mask his excitement. "After you told me what you told me, we checked all incoming calls to your grandma's house for the last two weeks. Nothing unusual. But then your mom got the idea to look into Flavia's phone." Flavia was Baba Polina's nurse. Two days after Paul Obrandt's supposed suicide, while she was giving Polina her daily bath, someone called her mobile for seven minutes from a number in Cape Town. The app that *generated* the number, however, did so over the Wi-Fi signal of a café in Nathon, Koh Samui, Thailand. The rest was a matter for Chinese spy satellites.

"It's still so weird to me that you're working with Mom," she couldn't help saying.

"Yeah, well," he parried, getting into the Pacifica. "Imagine how weird it is for *me*. You look good, by the way."

He meant her new buzz cut. In response, she had silently taken out the baggie with freshly shorn hair and handed it to him through the driver's-side window. Then she leaned inside and kissed him again. "Please stay safe."

"No promises. This thing needs to look totaled when they find it." He had turned the key in the ignition. The engine screeched and coughed. "Though it's pretty close as it is. Get in."

She had walked around the car and sat in the passenger seat, forgetting for a second what this part was about. She remembered only when she saw the hangdog look on his face.

"Right. How much blood do you need, again?"

He cleared his throat. "A couple, uh, a couple of pints. It's in the upper range for onetime donation but it's safe. You will feel lightheaded for a while."

"You don't say." She began to roll up her left sleeve.

She couldn't remember now if they said anything else of consequence before he drove into the night. Memories ran together like lines in a jammed printout, some moments legible, some smudged or folded in on themselves. LA was Olhão was Tangier was Riga was Moscow. Nothing mattered but where she was now, and where she was finally going.

The young woman decided not to risk a taxi ride after all. A packed *songthaew* bus dropped her off at the edge of town. It was pitch-dark when she got to the address on the paper, and the ubiquitous tokay geckos had already started the two-syllable chant that gave them their name. One stared straight at her from beneath the carved wooden gate of the villa, cocked its diamond-shaped head, said "tokay," and darted in. She interpreted this as an invitation.

The house glowed at the end of a flagstone pathway. A swimming pool threw caustic shapes onto a side wall, light rippling like lace. The young woman rehearsed, one last time, what she'd say and when. What she'd answer when he inevitably asked how she found him. The number of the account in the Chinese bank. What she'd say her mother would do if he refused to transfer the money there.

The dark-haired older woman who opened the door looked as familiar as a stranger could possibly look; it felt like meeting a celebrity. For a split second, her large, close-set eyes studied the visitor. Then, without saying a thing, she turned around and ran in yelling in Russian, one name making up most of the sounds issuing from her throat: *Pavlik, Pavlik, ona tut, Pavlik, Pavlik, Pavlik.*

"Hi Dad," said Maya, stepping inside.

ACKNOWLEDGMENTS

Thanks, first and foremost and always, to Lily.

This book wouldn't exist if not for Amanda "Binky" Urban and Matt Leipzig, who encouraged me to take the plunge if not pushed me into the water outright. Enormous gratitude to the first readers of the very first draft—Ari Gandsman, Elena Smolina, Anne Vithayathil, and Roman Volobuev. An enthusiastic wave across the ocean to Anna and Joerg Winger. Vielen dank to Anna Kraft for finding the time to check my abysmal German.

I owe a debt of direct and indirect inspiration to Christo Grozev and everyone at Bellingcat, the teams at RFE/RL and Votvot, as well as every reporter, investigator, blogger, comic, filmmaker, and musician broadcasting truth from within an oppressive regime.

While most of *The Collaborators'* settings correspond to my own past addresses, the details of Paul Obrandt's year in Ladispoli come from interviews with Max Adelman and Vadim Finkelstein, essays by Svetlana Boym and Maxim D. Shrayer, and Karen Wolman's contemporaneous reporting in the *Christian Science Monitor*. The book's version of the GRU org chart is based on a 2018 *Meduza* article by investigative journalist Daniil Turovsky.

Slava Ukraini, Žyvie Bielaruś, Rossiya budet svobodnoi.

ABOUT THE AUTHOR

Michael Idov is a novelist, director, and screenwriter. A Latvian-born American raised in Riga under Soviet occupation, he moved to New York after graduating from the University of Michigan. Michael's writing career began at *New York* magazine, where his features won three National Magazine Awards, and he has also been the editor-in-chief of *GQ Russia*. He is also the author of *Ground Up* and *Dressed Up for a Riot*. Michael has worked on numerous film and TV projects, including *Londongrad*, *Deutschland 83*, *Leto*, and *The Humorist*. He and his wife and screenwriting partner, Lily, divide their time between Los Angeles, Berlin, and Portugal.